LOST

ALSO BY RICHARD BARRE

The Wil Hardesty Series
The Innocents
Bearing Secrets
The Ghosts of Morning
Blackheart Highway
Burning Moon

Short Story Collection
Christmas Stories: In the Tradition of Rod Serling

Echo Bay
Lost

LOST

RICHARD BARRE

Down & Out Books
3959 Van Dyke Rd, Ste. 265
Lutz, FL 33558
www.DownAndOutBooks.com

Cover art and design by JT Lindroos

ISBN: 1937-4957-8-7

ISBN-13: 978-1-937495-78-7

For Frank Goad and Audrey Moore:
Friends...Confidants...Treasures

Puntarenas, Costa Rica
Four Months Earlier

The woman's jacket catches on the door handle, and she curses before it releases her, mitigating the din inside the crowded bar. As she steps off the stoop and away from the slanting light, her heels click on the worn paving. Unsteadily at first, then with greater resolve.

For at least a block her ears ring with the noise she's left, lips burning from Ramiro's roughness at the back table where they'd sought refuge. Ramiro, drunk and showing off—bold from their afternoon together and the hundred-proof guaro.

A wiser-now Ramiro.

Nobody called her that.

Two blocks, her senses gradually adjusting to the waterfront: soft creaks, muffled laughter from dimly-lit doorways, the kiss of tide against lapstrake and aluminum. Breaths to chase the cigarette smoke and body odors: night air laced with hints of diesel, fish smell from wood grids and railings, cooking grease, backed-up gutters, alley rot.

A cat darting between buildings with a rat in its mouth.

Three blocks, and the shadows have begun to harbor eyes, footsteps to echo her own. Not that matching Ramiro shot for shot has tempered her ability to filter real from abstract. Actually the guaro is her ally. Like the hot and swarming impersonality of the bar, it helps her deal with what she is doing.

More accurately, the one she is doing it to.

Not that she doesn't deserve her fun, God knows—try raising two children with a husband who's always gone. Bodies were to enjoy, and hers isn't getting any younger. Besides, what woman had a husband whose idea of a wild night was listening to Bizet or reading Garcia-Lorca? None of her friends, that was *sure, most giving her a wide berth once they hear who she married.*

They have no idea what it's like. And what it isn't.

Hell with it, she thinks, almost losing a heel in a grate. He wouldn't harm her. He wouldn't dare. But it's hollow, and with each step her imagination flays her nerves. What if someone is following her? What if he has found out? What if they have been seen together, the rum fueling her defiance also drowning her caution?

So empty her bravado seems in the deserted streets.

Finally, there is the bus stop, a pool of light against the darkness, her island of safety. And after standing in its shelter a moment, headlamps. Better than a bus, she thinks, elated now at her good fortune—a taxi responding to her wave and pulling over. Someone in the back seat willing to share the ride. The front, too, it appears...getting out to open the door, let her in back so she can thank her benefactor. Maybe even get him to stop at a liquor store, the night still relatively young.

Until the door shuts and the taxi speeds from the curb.

Until the front passenger hands her a bottle and, with eyes like struck flints, tells her, "Drink up, Serena. Tonight's on us."

Until she becomes aware that the man propped up beside her is Ramiro through all the blood.

PART ONE

Ben

PART ONE

1
Newport Beach, March 10

Ben Metcalf walked right into it.

Just outside The Score, his favorite sports bar, his kind of people—Loren the bartender, for openers. Two guys just materializing as he was chirping off the locks in his year-old Grand Cherokee, the red one Shay liked to be picked up in, not Kate's Lexus. The one guy, he recognized: Walter. Thick black dude he occasionally saw bench-pressing about half the gym, telling him now, "Nothing personal, Mr. Metcalf. You understand. Just something to jog the memory."

"Till next time," the thin one Ben didn't recognize chortled as Walter's first blow landed, a kidney punch that spun him off the Cherokee's door and into the uppercuts that left him on his knees, airless and slack-jawed. At which time the thin one joined in, stereo rib kicks, Ben thinking his thirty-seventh birthday was a hell of a day to get shown the exit.

At least they gave him a second while Thin said, "Your wallet, if I might?"

Through the shallowest of breaths, Ben nodded and felt his left rear pocket lighten. "Well?" he heard Walter ask.

"Forty bucks, living in a house like that." Thin shaking his head for emphasis. "Fucking pathetic."

Ben smelled the damp asphalt inches from his nose. Letting it play out, not aware of anything broken.

That would come later.

There was a moment's pause, the sound of a paper being torn from a notebook to land in front of his eyes. Thin saying, "Your lordship's receipt for the forty. Nod if you're clear the next one gets delivered closer to home."

"Clear," Ben managed.

Hearing Thin observe, "Walt must like you, Mr. Metcalf. Usually they don't talk for a week."

"Mr. Metcalf's okay, he's gonna make this right. Aren't you, Mr. Metcalf?"

"Yeah." Barely recognizing his own sound; more squeak than voice.

Thin next: "And is there a date we might pass along to Mr. Devore?"

"April," Ben wheezed—holding up an index finger to signify the first. Commission date on the Carver Aft Cabin the actor had been drooling over. Johnny What's-his-name, Ben all too familiar with the look: dreamy eyes, faraway expression, half short of breath this close to his dream. Hours spent explaining every feature to the guy as he mooned into the chrome.

Commission date provided Johnny's financial history found a star-struck loan officer, Ben half-wondering how it would play if he referred Johnny directly to Little Al Devore. Out of one pocket and in the other.

One big circle jerk.

"April Fool, Mr. Metcalf," Thin was saying now. "I don't know, Walt—maybe we should start on that pretty daughter of—"

Ben heard something thud against the Cherokee, then Walter.

"We don't do that, Tommy. *I* don't do that."

"Fuck, Walt, it's a figure of speech," Thin Tommy came back about two registers higher. "Don't you go to the movies?"

Using the distraction to expand his air intake, Ben heard a familiar voice: "Ben...you all right? You need help out there?" He felt a hand grasp the back of his jacket—then Walter hoisting him to his feet. Bent against the pain and laying odds on how much ice and Ibuprofen before this one was under control.

"Well, hotshot?" Tommy said, smoothing the suede. "Tell the lady how it feels to act responsible for a change. That glow that comes with paying down your debt." Chortling again as he and Walt eased their way across the street and down the block.

"Okay, Loren, thanks," Ben tried after they'd turned the corner, letting a wave compensate for his voice as he pocketed the receipt and brushed grit from his hands and pants. Deciding as she came toward him that a little more Loren and another birthday beer wasn't such a bad idea in light of things.

Heading home looking like shit for one.

"Just business," he thought to add.

Ben checked his wrist: nearly seven already.

Time—there was another one.

"Just what a girl likes to see," Loren said. "The guy she's with looking at his watch."

He put a hand on hers, stroked her wavy blonde hair, ran a finger down her perfect profile. "Sorry, I'm just distracted."

"*Tell me about it...*"

"Probably the birthday. I'll be better next week."

She was silent, gazing out at the waves thumping in on The Wedge, where he'd bodysurfed as a kid. Corona across the channel, Balboa aglitter behind them, the pier just visible from there, his own house up the rise behind PCH one of the pinpoints. And Jeb's, of course—Jeb who owned the boat dealership he worked for, not to mention a fair part of Newport Beach—somewhere back there on Lido.

Jeb Hallenbeck.

Kate's father.

Ben watched a Sea Ray heading in, one of the big sedan bridges, likely from Catalina. Followed by a Hatteras rigged for fishing and a vintage Bertram—three portside red lights nose to tail. And what might be a Hunter 43 tacking toward the west jetty; pretty thing out for a sunset sail, champagne by moonlight. He caught himself imagining it: that feeling of weightlessness.

"Ben...?"

"Sorry, Loren, what were you saying?"

She sighed and shook her head, tried it again. "The film guy I met, the one who agreed to read my treatment? He was in earlier and said it had potential."

"That's terrific."

"Meaning don't hold my breath."

"Meaning congratulations. Way to go."

"At least *say* it like you mean it."

"Of course I mean it."

"Probably seems trivial to you," she said, her face set. "The money you have."

That edge—not so much subject as phrasing—the unspoken *married into*. Or maybe it was just him: still ticked that he'd let himself get into this position. Not to mention a kidney that likely would pass blood later.

"Things aren't always as they seem, Loren."

No shit...

"Tending bar is a means, Ben, not an end. I've said it before."

They sat watching a Hampton, that distinctive profile, sliding out toward the channel's mouth: San Diego, maybe Ensenada.

"Some fine night," he said. "Will you look at that moon?"

She leaned forward, stared down at her hands. "I really have to get back. Besides, I'm getting chilled."

"Yeah. Me, too," he said, thinking pizza with Shay and a video—the high times of Ben Metcalf. He got up gingerly, surprised he didn't feel his stomach more: tomorrow, and especially the next day. He put an arm around her as they walked up the breakwater to the turnaround. Pausing at the Cherokee to feel his trial kiss come back with something like passion.

"Happy birthday," she said as they broke.

"I just wish we could spend some time together," he said, nuzzling her hair. "Hit a B&B or something."

She regarded him. "And have your daughter spot us again."

"I told you how I handled that. You were interested in a boat. End of story."

"And she believed it..."

"Why not? You are, aren't you?"

"Drinks at the Pelican, my hand on yours..."

He let her in the Cherokee and started it, levered into gear. Quiet on the way back through Balboa's now calm streets. At one point, eyes straight ahead, she asked him if he was sore from his slip back there—how he'd put it when she'd pressed for details.

"Some. Not as bad as I thought."

8

She took in a breath, seemed to decide on something. "Ben, I don't like to harp, but nobody's getting any younger here."

All of twenty-six. Or was it seven?

He smiled at her: white shorts, *The Score* polo shirt, suede coat unbuttoned over it, those legs extending down to ankle socks and white-on-white Avias. Miss All-American sports bartender. What all the guys wanted to chase their drinks with. He'd stumbled into deep conversation with her one wet Sunday during a Niners-Packers debacle—missing the point spread and feeling particularly alone, Kate out of town on a presentation, Shay weekending at a friend's. He'd been impressed, the more they'd talked, with Loren's outlook and drive. Maybe even a little envious.

"I'm not, anyway," he said.

Nothing.

"Getting any younger, that is."

"Forgive me if my timing's bad," she said, "or if it's a lot to ask on your birthday, but I really need to know where we're headed."

As they waited out the light at Main Street, Ben felt a draft despite the heater's being on. Half a green cycled while an older couple ambled across.

"Take a number," he said quietly.

2

It was almost eight, the moon well clear of Balboa's masts and lights, the Friday night crawl on Pacific Coast Highway, the sweep of coastline. Ben topped the bluff and swung into his drive, leaving the Cherokee out in case it came down to pizza.

Cracking the window, he ran a hand over sand-colored hair he'd worn sport-short forever and according to Shay was coming back. Deep breaths until Walter and Tommy faded and were replaced by what was in front of him: primarily how he'd wound up there. Set in "The Headlands," a development overlooking the harbor, the house was part of a deal in which one of Jeb's clients needed cash. Jeb had jumped on it, offering to let Ben and Kate assume the payments while he put up the equity—Jeb's to appreciate, which, of course, it had. Near triple what he'd paid for it.

That was in '95, before Ben decided he owed it to his father-in-law to accept a job offer he otherwise wouldn't have thought twice about turning down. Four years into marriage with Kate—now a VP at TeleDigm—two since the papers Ben had filed to adopt Shay had been approved. Father and ex-husband Henri Dufresne still chasing down the pro skiing career that had gone south before he and Kate divorced in mid-'90.

He remembered meeting Dufresne once, at a hearing Kate asked him to attend just before she and Ben married in '91. Dufresne wanting to meet before they finalized the settlement and he went back to Europe. Satisfying himself that Shay would be all right with the Ben part.

Ben found him not unlike many French he'd met, some of which he wrote off to the pro-athlete mentality. But there'd been something he hadn't anticipated—a certain *tristesse* detected over their fast drink together.

"Face it, she's more than either of us deserves," he'd told Ben as they bottomed-up, then went outside into bright sun. Down the steps to where a black Porsche was waiting, a model type at the wheel. "But that old man..." Letting his headshake say it.

Prior to that, Ben had barely exchanged ten words with Jarrod Hartzell Hallenbeck. Decorated fighter pilot, America's Cup skipper, boating magnate. Widower, father, grandfather.

Presence—even when not around.

"Just do as I did not," Dufresne had said—leaving Ben to wonder about the specifics if not the intent. Dufresne, the man who would give up all rights to Shay two years down the road, the papers coming back notarized from someplace in Italy where he was competing. Five months later, dead in a horrendous eighty-mile-an-hour wipeout replayed endlessly by the networks and sports channels.

Ben retrieved his briefcase, started toward the two-story neo-Mediterranean. By design and despite the plantings, walkways, and lap pool he'd added himself, the house would always be more imperious than welcoming. A venue for entertaining clients and superiors, largely Kate's. He wondered sometimes what she really felt about it—a thought he sometimes applied to *them*.

It occurred to him that every light seemed on, a Kate trademark, though she wasn't due back until tomorrow. Indeed, as he turned the key and opened the door, he heard: "*Today is Ben's birthday—happy, happy birthday. Happy birthday to you, happy birthday to you, happy birthday, dear Ben, happy birthday to you.*"

"Surprise, surprise," he said. Smiling as she relieved him of the briefcase and stepped into his arms as he tried not to wince.

"Ben, you okay?"

"Tweaked something at the gym," he said, brushing her lips with his before she could ask him if he'd taken anything for it. "Let me look at you." Holding her out at arm's length.

Trim and still sporting an innately Newportish charm, that effortless sexuality—thirty months older than he was and still looking as if she'd stepped out of *Self* magazine. Wildflower-honey hair with sun streaks and highlights, the skirt half of a navy business suit under a loosened cream blouse. Shoes kicked off and coming close to Julia Ormond in *Sabrina*. Maybe even to Audrey Hepburn in the original they'd rented after seeing the remake.

"Better now that I'm home," Kate said. "And somebody's been celebrating already."

For a moment Ben thought she meant Loren, and froze, realized as she sniffed him, asked how many he'd had, that she meant his breath. He let his smile re-form. "I didn't think anybody'd be here." Kissing her again, this time tasting gin. "How come?"

"Your birthday or a seven-million-dollar deal," she said. "Tough choice."

"You nailed it early?"

"All but the ink. So...*hasta luego*. I got Shay at Jennifer's—she's upstairs." Backing toward the kitchen. *"Going Gourmet*, all right? They were just here."

"What—not pizza?"

She smiled back, cocked her head at the stairwell. "One of us is adjusting as we speak. Want a Beefeaters?"

"Beer, if there's some left." Noting as she left the room the chocolate monster on the dining table, *Happy Birthday Ben* inside the candles and a wrapped package next to the half-dozen cards between his knife and fork. Silver and crystal he thought they'd hocked, chandelier lights down, music on the stereo.

Kate emerged from the kitchen holding a frosted mug she set down to plant one on him, Ben trying to recall the last time the three of them had dinner together in the dining room. Food smells and the rest of it fueling in no small measure his unease.

They'd come to the part where Shay and Kate would take out the cake, light the candles, and parade it into the room. *Happy Birthday* into the glow. Dinner had been fine, the exception being Shay's relative detachment. Still they'd followed Kate's lead and kept it even-keeled, the greeting cards mostly from old friends still working as lifeguards up and down the coast. One was from a high school teammate who detailed boats and still called him "Clutch" despite what happened later. Another, from Darnell Light, he intended to follow up with a call. The final one was from his mother, who'd phoned that morning from the Costa Mesa tract where she still lived, regardless of his entreaties.

"Not much to report," he told Kate, who'd been stuck in Veracruz since last Sunday and wanted to hear all about Evelyn's call. "Beyond her doctor shining her on and another friend dying off." Pausing to hear his mother's voice again, the cigarette rasp that still dogged it five years into cold turkey.

"She asked if I'd forgotten the anniversary of Thurman's getting shot."

"What did you tell her?"

"No luck yet." Ben cleared his throat to signal a change of subject. "What else...thanks but no thanks to the mall-walking you proposed. Too far or too inconvenient or something."

Kate had a sip of wine and studied him. "Fifteen years last week."

"Thurman? Something like that."

"How come you always call your father Thurman?" Shay put in without looking up.

"That was his name."

"Sounds disrespectful the way you say it."

"You'd have to have known him, Shay."

Deputy Thurman Metcalf, the man nobody but Ben and Evelyn Metcalf really knew. A privilege best suited to the shrinks and therapists who would have charged double—one for each side of him—had his wife and son prevailed on him to go.

"Anyway, it's what he told me to call him. You've heard me say that."

This time, Kate read him and steered the talk. "Ben, malls are like toadstools around here. One of us could even take her."

"Ours not to reason why," he said, putting away the last of his Caesar.

"*Theirs but to do and die,*" Shay murmured. "*All in the valley of death.*"

"And a happy birthday to you too, Shay." Half-trying to raise a smile, her standard "*Daaaad*" to go with it.

"You're the one quoted it. I just finished it."

"So you did," he said.

13

"Besides, it's *your* birthday."

"Who says families don't talk anymore?"

"We're a family? Thanks for telling me."

"Maybe it's time to ask what you're doing to help make us one."

Said the kettle to the pot.

"All right, kids," Kate said. "Timeout."

"Sorry." Ben thinking now that if Shannon Kay Metcalf were *trying* to contrast with her mother—Kate in her office clothes, another Beefeaters and a sauvignon blanc giving her a nice flush—she didn't have far to go. Faded jeans, rips at both knees, sweatshirt she'd helped build the pool in last year, brown hair pulled back.

Pretty if she'd let herself be.

Like the moods, part of being fourteen, he hoped. A private-school fourteen—his and Kate's ongoing debate: sheltered-from-it versus equipped-to-deal. He watched Shay work a bite of lasagna and set down her fork.

"Mom, can we cut the cake soon? I'm really tired."

Kate reached over to palm her forehead. "You feeling okay?"

"Told you, just tired." Watching Ben and Kate exchange looks before getting up to follow her mother into the kitchen.

Ben was still reflecting when they reentered with the cake, Kate carrying, Shay bringing up the rear and handing Ben the knife after he'd made his wish and blown out the candles. He cut them each a slice, then himself one. Knowing where Kate had ordered it: a place they used to go for coffee and a bear claw Saturdays after they'd made love.

Past tense.

At least the cake was as he remembered—chocolate with a rum-laced filling. They'd about finished, Ben thanking them both for the surprise, when Kate said, "Well...?"

"What...this?" Picking up the package and shaking it.

"Never in a million years," Kate said.

"Kleenex? Surf wax? Neckties?"

"Since when do you wear neckties?"

"Codpiece? Edible briefs?"

"Daaaad."

He looked at Shay. "Your turn."

"How should I know? Open it, will you?"

"Yeah, Dad," Kate said.

At that, Ben had to smile. What little he knew about being one he'd learned from books and the seat of his pants—Fighting Thurman Metcalf and Darnell Light not exactly poster children for the being-a-dad category. More like Dennis Rodman in a bridal gown. One thing sure, though: Like roundball, it came best when you weren't forcing it.

He had the paper off now, only to discover another wrapped box and yet another, his anticipation starting to go beyond a silent prayer. Fearing the worst as the packages got smaller and her grin bigger—expensive the corollary to small—he opened a last wrapping, tore the tissue from what was inside.

*Oh, God...*Three first-class airline tickets...photographs of a boat under sail and power...guidebook and travel brochure for Costa Rica, glorious in living aquas, greens, sunset reds, and lavenders.

Seventy-five hundred at least. More probably.

In the mirror behind her, Ben's smile looked stricken even to himself.

Frosting-smeared dishes, Shay announcing that no way could she take two weeks off from school, leave her friends, yadda-yadda, before marching upstairs. Ten by the brass chronometer, thin dings to mark it—Ben having settled into a Rob Roy over ice, Kate another glass of wine. Saying after a sip, "So much for thinking I'd have to stop you from doing backflips."

"It's just totally impractical right now," he said, feeling like a shit. Each time he shifted in the chair his hurts reminding him why.

"Jeb said he could spare you, if that's what's on your mind."

"Permission granted, huh?"

"Unworthy, Ben."

"What's on my mind is money, Kate. The thousand-pound eight-ball we're behind."

Only too aware of how it sounded. As if she'd been the one twisting his arm to lay it off with a weasel like Al Devore.

15

Regular games, playoffs, Super Bowl: black Sundays. The meanest season in all the years of trying to win Evelyn Metcalf some breathing room after Deputy Thurman left her with gutted insurance and a ransacked IRA. SOB DOA at Fountain Valley Regional, the gang banger who'd fired first already dead from the old man's service nine—a matte-finish S&W he'd let Ben hold, run a rag through, shoot sometimes on Anza-Borrego escapes from the main events he had with Evelyn. Deep-sixed the night of Thurman's funeral.

Twenty, Ben had been. Five months before the point-shaving mess that bought probation and swift closure to any NBA aspirations he might have had coming out of college. Bye-bye college, period: Cal State Irvine's most promising shooting-guard prospect shot down. And he'd been the one loading the bullets.

"I didn't use *our* money," Kate was saying.

"Come again?"

"Savings bonds. Mine since I was a kid. "

Explain it to Walter and Tommy, Ben thought.

"And the boat is Craig and Nancy's. You know how they've been pestering us to use it. Supplies and fuel, that's it. Why I splurged on the tickets."

"So cash out."

Double shit. Triple, quadruple shit.

"Nonrefundable. And not the airline's idea, Ben—mine. I figured it was something I could do to make up for being gone so much. I thought it would please you. But I can't say I didn't expect this."

Ben tipped the Rob, felt its heat as she picked up steam.

"It's so typical of us lately. One goddamn trip."

"Which I appreciate, Kate. I really do. It's just that—"

"What..."

"Have you thought about Shay?"

Quintuple shit: We have a winner!

"What about her? She's fourteen, she'll come around." Pausing to drive it home with shining eyes, breaking off to glance up the stairs before coming back to him.

"All right—who is she?"

He felt a shriveling. "What are you talking about?"

"The one Shay saw you with, the one she's all conflicted over. Don't tell me you haven't noticed."

Hoping it passed for exasperation, Ben blew a breath. "That's what's bothering her? Some fling I'm supposed to be having?"

"Tell me this isn't you not wanting to leave her—whoever-she-is I smelled on you before dinner. The perfect wife and mother I may not be, but I am not *stupid*."

"Then please don't act like it."

A door slammed upstairs, momentarily snapping them in that direction, then into silence.

"Wonderful," Kate said finally. "Happy birthday."

"My fault, as usual."

"Not altogether. I'm inadequate for being ambitious, or not making more out of it, or less of what she thinks I should be making of it, or something."

"As you say, she's fourteen."

"*I* deserve better. *Me*."

"You're being melodramatic, Kate. Not to mention reckless."

Please welcome to the Hall of Fame: Total Shit, Benjamin Dean Metcalf.

"Am I? Prove it. What's really stopping you from going?"

Loren, the debts and Little Al, Walter and Tommy: Redemption starts here. All you have to do is tell her.

"Nothing's stopping me," he said.

Dried frosting on an empty plate—Kate staring at him.

"Nothing," he added, as though closing a deal with himself. Tossing off his drink and sliding back his chair.

"Not a goddamn thing."

3
Southeast of Puntarenas, Present

Wind rattling the fronds sent the tractor's dust off to the southwest, threw a shifting mosaic of afternoon sun and shadow down the overhung row and across the driver's face.

A green tunnel beneath a shallow green ocean, he thought. And the rattle...as if the trees were talking to him of past harvests. Day after day of fat green bunches, *racimos* that only the strongest of the men could tote to the wagons, the railroad cars, the ships. Of the auctions that made growers wealthy one year and *masa*-poor the next, but United Fruit's *norteamericano* investors fat and happy regardless. Of fiesta-like harvests and tourist-board posters, bananas in every cereal bowl north of the equator. Conversely, of blight and insects, strikes and weather; of the candles lit to stave them off.

The driver, a coiled man with dark hair, sunglasses, and a Virgin of Barrancanitas tattoo revealed by his sleeveless shirt—plus a more amateurish one of a hummingbird on his forearm—thumbed back his raffia hat and gulped water. On a whim, he killed the ancient four-banger to let the trees talk to him unimpeded—the way the sea called him. Let the wind attempt to banish something that, like blood, would never truly fade, even if soaked in salt water. Clang of bars, bang of tin mess plates, the unremitting din of a hell to which he would never return.

Not in this life, *alabanza al Dios*.

He was squinting at the dying fronds interspersed with green when his eye caught movement, heart doing a little fandango as he saw her. Five inches shy of four feet, skipping down the row he was aerating. Paper or a sheet-sized envelope clutched in her hand.

"Papa, look what I have." With an assist, clambering to settle on his lap, feather his cheek with *besitos,* her little kisses. "It's for you."

He turned the envelope in his hands, unbent only because of what was inside. Unmarked with a return address, no stamps or postmark. Just *Enrique Matos.* Not a name many people sent things to.

"I thought Abuelita made it clear you weren't to play by the gate."

"I wasn't, Papa. I was in the swing when he saw me."

"*Who saw you?*"

"The man with this." Little chirp at the end, as if Papa wasn't getting it. "He called me his *frijolita.* He put it through the gate."

"Anna—this is important. What man? What did he look like?"

"A *man*. Like you," she said after running it through her six-years-old-and-gaining-on-him software. Reaching up to touch his hat, his face on the way down. "Don't be mad. Aren't you going to open it?"

"I'm not mad, *corazón.* Not at you."

"*Hrumm, hrumm,*" she said, reaching for the steering wheel.

Relax, Enrique Matos told himself, it's nothing—one of the old group who'd somehow caught wind of his return. Yet he knew it wasn't true. Those who still lived around there—more plantations now than people, the unmaintained roads dirt and gravel in most stretches—were as private as he was. Absentee owners. Not like the old days when neighbor stood with neighbor, no matter what their reputation. Days he'd only heard about: post-harvest whoops and table stomps, tango and samba and hot-blooded gypsy music. Knife fights over *mujeres* and cries in the night.

Enrique Matos swung a 360, saw nothing but bananas and still felt eyes. He'd been a fool to take this for granted. Incautious and stupid. From now on he'd wear his .40-caliber, already giving thought to how he'd explain it to Abuelita. Wild dogs and snakes were where you found them.

"Can I drive—*please?*" Anna, squirming around to look up at him. Black hair flipping the way only hers could, dark mischievous eyes, a flush in her cheeks. Pepper sauce on angel cake.

"May I," he corrected her.

"Matteo says I don't know how."

Enrique Matos wiped his palms on his jeans. He started the tractor, reset the choke and the idle, felt the wind again. "You may. But first, how high can you count with your eyes closed? No peeking."

"To one hundred," she said with certainty, and to prove it started counting. Which gave him an opportunity to release the envelope's prongs, run his thumb along the flap, pull out the Polaroid photographs taped between pieces of tablet backing. To feel what was behind his own eyes scream and twist on itself at the images pouring acid there.

Jesu-Maria.

"Papa?" a voice intruded. "What comes after twelve?"

He realized Anna still had her eyes shut. "Thirteen, *corazón*," he pulled himself together enough to say.

"Papa? Do you still miss Mama like I do?"

Mama...

Selena...

HER, to Abuelita.

Enrique Matos put the photos back inside the envelope, tucked it inside his shirt, levered the tractor into gear. But where Anna now stiff-armed the wheel to press tightly against his chest, he felt only the soulless cold thing between them.

4

Ben felt Kate leave bed at first light, heard her put on her running clothes and ease out the front door. Unable to get back to sleep in the whirl of thoughts that had started like a loud-firing lawnmower, he rose painfully and used the bathroom, glad at least that last-night's bloom of pink had been minimal. He spent a long time in the shower, toweled dry, eased into cords and a denim shirt.

Tiptoeing downstairs, he brewed coffee and filled his cup holder mug, leaving half for Kate. He then penned her a note: *New day. Gone to shuffle paper. Back noonish—B.* Adding when the thought hit, *Barbecue later?*

Hell, why not? People had barbecues, even people with one foot in the fire. He had a vision of Walter and Tommy in tropical shirts, rowing furiously after him as he blew air into becalmed sails. Chasing the image with coffee, he extended it to: *No blindfold, thanks. Real men face the firing squad.*

He checked his watch—seven thirty—saw Kate as ten minutes from gasping in the side door, no evidence yet of Shay. He was almost out the front when he spied the contents of last night's package on the dining table.

Guilt-curiosity-whatever pulled him toward it. The brochure was on top: stunning photos, poetically minimal text, Web site and an 800 number. With the Craig-and-Nancy connection, easy to see why Kate had jumped on it. Ben had another look at the prints, the Leary's ketch-rigged motor sailer. In fact, he vaguely recalled rolling his eyes at an invitation to see pictures of the new acquisition. Some months now. Nancy's gloat to Kate about how cheaply they'd gotten it down there from a charterman anxious to bail.

Angel Fire, her stern read, *Puntarenas.* Clean lines and a trim profile, good-sized foredeck and center cockpit. Another photo showed her under full sail, Craig at the helm, Nancy flanked by a boy and girl laughing and pointing at the camera. Jib, main sail, and mizzen heeling them at a pleasantly showy angle.

He flipped the shot, read the caption: *Learys and Morgan beating feet.*

Morgan: not a boat Hallenbeck Marine sold and not one he knew much about. Putting the print in his shirt pocket so he could research the make, he closed the door behind him and started the Cherokee.

Where the night had been damp enough to draw a pulse of wipers, the morning was blue-white with a ruffly little breeze, the kind Shay was always watercoloring. Mid-sixties expected around Newport, slightly warmer inland. Saturday excursionists already out in the channel as he eased down the hill.

A sailboat, he thought. Though Kate was a sailor by virtue of her breeding—proficient enough in college to fill in on Jeb's America's Cup team—Ben's experience was minimal. He'd known power boats. Flush one year from his winnings—not long after he'd fallen from grace and rebounded into an apprenticeship with Darnell Light—he'd nearly acquired one. A DEA-seized Cobalt with a cuddy cabin, Ben with an inside shot before it went to auction.

But then his mother called about the plumbing, the house where he'd grown up the proverbial black hole—money, emotions, name it—and that had been that. Now he *sold* boats. To nouveaux-riches types who viewed them as status symbols or sex toys or the flavor of the month. As Jeb put it, whatever it took

Passing a bakery, he stopped and bought a bag of scones. He was tempted to swing one by for Loren, but thought better—the way they'd left it and the fact that Kate would doubtless call after last night the clincher. He felt a wave of guilt, undeterred by rationalization. How different really was he from Deputy Thurman? The father who used to come home reeking of it and unapologetic, the son without the spine and sense to drift out the door he'd come in. Of course the old man had it nailed when he'd said once about Ben's indecision, "Have some respect for me, boy. Do *something.*"

So how's this, Dad. Four points within the spread, two minutes to go, his jumper clanking off the rim—not wanting to risk anybody else on the team shooting down the outcome. Knowing his coach could ill afford to take him out of the lineup. Winning within, Little Al had called it after the bets Ben made one spring led to praise about his scoring abilities and finally a cash offer to hold down the points. No big thing—a turnover here, a brick fired up there, a move telegraphed to an eager opponent. Refusing at first, of course. He was an athlete, a person of integrity. At least before Thurman's DOA routine, expenses piling up on his mother like the clinging wet snow that bowed the branch past elasticity.

Do *something*...

So he had. Until it spun out of control, the offers evolving into *losing* a key game, then a second. A goner by that time, just trying to find the sky. Finally walking into Norv Schander's office one afternoon and closing the door. On everything.

That is, until Kate and Shannon.

Ben crossed the bridge and made the turn toward West Lido Channel. Pulling into the parking lot, he saw Jeb's white Navigator plus a couple of other vehicles he recognized. He locked the Cherokee and, with his mug and the bakery bag, headed into the office part of the boutique-and-restaurant complex.

As Jeb said from day one, the location was by design. Newport was the largest pleasure-boat harbor in the country. And though it moored only a small portion of Hallenbeck Marine's inventory along the pedestrian walkway skirting the channel, being there was key—bar and restaurant decks filled with shoppers and oglers, brunchers there for the view. Spirit-lifting, Jeb liked to say. Rare when a number of prospects weren't lured in by the name and the painting in the window. Jeb at the helm of *Brigadier*, their late-seventies Cup finalist.

Speak of the devil, Ben thought, catching sight of the framed and spotlit homage: facing down the wind—Jeb's flamboyant personality dominant those years, if not his 12-meter.

Transferring the bag to his mug hand, he pushed open the door.

* * *

First thing after avoiding Jeb's cracked-open office door and handing the scones to Trudy to share with Arch, one of the other salesmen in today, was a call home. Reach out, as it were.

"Morning, sunshine," he said when Shay answered. "How you doing?"

"I'm eating breakfast."

"Not what—how."

"Okay..." That thing females did that died off, dripping with meaning, generally accusation.

"Is Mom there?"

"Not back from Tae-Bo."

The same Shay Metcalf who could spend hours talking on the phone about nothing. "Have her call me at the office, will you?"

"If I'm home."

"Write a note, Shay." Giving it a moment to sink in. "Everything else okay?"

"Peachy. Why wouldn't it be?"

Here it comes, Ben thought. "You tell me, Shay."

"Does a black Mustang sound familiar?"

Out of nowhere. Not Loren, if that's what she was thinking. More importantly, not Loren's style. "Not right off. Why?"

"It was driving around outside."

"You see who was in it?"

"The windows were tinted."

Ben made a mental note to ask Jeb if he was previewing the house, in no way unlike him. "Probably looking for the Pearson's garage sale. It's gone now?"

"Yes." There was a pause. "I hate it when you and Mom fight."

He let out a breath, leaned back in the chair. "That's why mornings were invented, Shay. So people could make fresh starts." Adding, at the sound of MTV coming through, "Hellooo...?"

"I'll leave your note."

"Thank you, Shannon Kay Metcalf."

He was about to hang up when she said, "What about the trip thing? It's off, right?"

"I take it you haven't talked to your mom?" Divide and conquer, the old standby.

"No. But the whole idea is so *wacked.*"

"Well, guess what..."

"You caved, didn't you—I can hear it in your voice. She pushed and you caved."

"Kind of pushing it yourself, aren't you?" he said.

"Mr. Example. Why are you doing this—some kind of punishment?"

Wrong time, wrong place, wrong guy. "We decided there was something in it for all of us, Shay."

"Two weeks on a boat? We can't even be in the same room for ten minutes."

"You look at the brochure and the photos?"

"I'm not one of your customers, Dad—remember?"

"So young and cynical."

"Perfect. Just forget it." Dial tone replaced her voice and a music video sounding like semis colliding.

To tamp the residual sparks, Ben watched a boat ease past the window and head upchannel, told himself to move on. Checking in with Jeb in front of the others seemed like sucking up, so he spent the next two hours packaging credit aps, completing orders and faxing them, logging in calls for the Monday sales meeting. No call yet from Kate.

With his *Boatwatch Master Guide*, he matched the Morgan to one called the Out-Island 415. Length in feet: forty-one-three; beam: thirteen-ten; interior headroom: six-four. To the net then: Ketch-rigged as *Angel Fire* was with jib, main, and mizzen, nearly eight hundred feet of sail. Mast: fifty-three-four; draft: four-two—things to interest Kate if she didn't already know them.

Of interest to him: aft master stateroom with private head and shower; guest stateroom—read Shay's—forward with additional head and shower; salon and separate galley. That big foredeck to catch rays on and fish from. User friendly. As if the Morgan were saying to him, *Come on: however you want to play it.* He'd printed out and was shutting down his computer, when he heard the voice. Room-filling, no matter how big the room.

"Thought I heard you out here. Planning on saying hello?"

"Sure, Jeb, I got busy. Figured you were, too."

"Can't argue with that. Join me, will you?"

Ben looked Trudy and Arch back to their work and entered, Jeb Hallenbeck standing six-three to Ben's just-over-six. Boat shoes, chinos, navy polo with the Hallenbeck Marine logo. Full gray hair, combed back and setting off a face like Sterling Hayden's—that same sunbaked, wind-swept, up-anchor intensity. Not that Jeb's voice altered the impression of a ship bearing down.

"How'd you like Kate's present?" he asked, shutting the door. "Something else, huh?"

"Total shock," Ben answered, wondering what next.

"You're a lucky man if that isn't clear by what's mine in your life. Kate and the weeks she talked me out of, for starters."

"Not a day goes by," Ben allowed.

"Sit down," Jeb said, waving him to a chair that Ben always swore he'd shortened the legs on so whoever sat there looked diminutive by comparison.

He decided to preempt. "If it's about the reports, I've been a little thin on closings. Nothing I can't make up."

Jeb looked at him as if he were evaluating a shift in the wind. Finally he said, "Any idea why a couple of unsavory characters might be asking Trudy about you?"

Son of a bitch, Ben thought. Little Al or no, you didn't do that—not to a long-time customer. *What* was *it lately*?

"Today?" he managed.

"So you do know them?"

"I didn't say that, Jeb. But I've met some leads who might qualify."

"Black lifter-type and a skinny guy. Yesterday, after you'd left..." The *early* unspoken, but there. The source, as well— Trudy aware of Ben's recent watering-hole habits, his leaving word where he could be reached if a high roller called or a deal went through. How Walter and Tommy had found him.

He glanced enviously at a couple strolling by—insouciant looks as they took in the masts and sleek hulls, the sun-dappled

26

water. Lido with its multi-million-dollar homes across the channel.

"They mention their names?"

"Trudy said no. And if you're thinking she should have said something to you, I told her I'd handle it."

Ben shrugged—hands raised, eyes wide. "Sorry..."

Jeb paused to twist a cigar wrapper around his index finger. "Anything you want to say to me, Ben?"

Jesus, Mary, and Joseph... "Now you mention it, I guess there is," he said, hoping the wetness he felt wasn't bleeding through. "You up for barbecue tonight?"

As it turned out, Jeb had something going with his current lady, even though Ben had composed himself long enough to include her in the invitation. He was stuffing the Morgan research into an envelope, not wanting to be there in case Jeb changed his mind, when the phone rang. It was Kate, back from errands and what-not. Almost croaking when he told her what he'd proposed.

"Them here? Merilee's younger than I am."

"Relax, they're busy," Ben said so softly he wasn't sure she'd heard him. Trudy gone, but Arch still there. Not to mention Jeb.

"All the same," Kate said, "I don't think I'll be taking calls the rest of the day. When are you coming home?"

A thought flashed: Loren—sitting on him. Rising and falling with his thrusts. "Just leaving," he said.

There was a pause. "If you still want to barbeque, get enough for two nights, salad makings and bread. And while you're at it, rum and daiquiri mix."

"Sounds serious."

"Eat, drink, and be merry."

He waited for her to hang up first, as she always did. When she didn't, he said simply, "Thanks for last night."

"Don't tell me you're starting to feel it?"

"It was never the idea, Kate, just about pulling it off." She didn't respond, so he added, "I don't know, maybe there's just a time to say screw it."

"And other things."

"What's that mean?"

Pause, and then, "Never mind. It's a start."

Halfway home, Ben stopped for gas and a pay phone.

"Hi," Loren said after he'd heard her say she'd take it in the office. "How you feeling?"

"Better, thanks."

"That's good news, at least." Asking him about his birthday dinner until he told her: Costa Rica, two weeks, Kate and Shay.

Long pause. "When do you leave?"

"Tuesday—early."

No response.

"Sooner gone, the sooner back," he said, trying to keep it light.

"Back to what?" Loren said. "Sorry, it's just my life—about which I stayed up most of the night. Want to know what I decided?"

"Sure." The sensation that goes with an elevator's sudden descent.

"One, you're an attractive man. Two, I love spending time with you. Three, therein lies the problem."

"What are you talking about?"

"Have a ball down there with the wife and kid." Fighting for control now. "And if I haven't hit it big, and you'll deal a game where I stand a chance, look me up when you come back."

Ben stood there in the March sunlight. Clouds and cars drifting by, feeling as if he were caught in a rip and losing sight of land.

5

It was nearly four when Ben pulled into his drive and set the brake. Shay was in the living room watching TV with Jennifer.

"Two more bags in the car, Shay."

"Hi to you, too, Dad."

Without looking at him, she rose and went outside, leaving the front door wide open.

"Hello, Mr. Metcalf."

"How's it going, Jenny?" he asked, shutting it to a crack.

"Better now my mom's up and around."

"How is she doing?"

Jennifer, who at fifteen was in the same class as Shay but more than showing her age differential, wore what they all wore: body-hugging mini-sleeve tees with low-rise jeans and exposed midriffs. She shrugged. "The bruising around her eyes is almost gone."

"Tell her we're thinking of her, will you?"

"Better not. Nobody's supposed to know but her plastic surgeon."

Taller and more statuesque than Shay, with loose-bobbed hair, she threw in a too-bright-by-half smile. "Cute," Shay confided once after Jennifer slept over, the house still echoing their *likes* and *I'm alls*. "Jen thinks you're cute." To which Ben had replied, "She's known me how long and she's just figured that out?" Getting a more-exasperated-than-usual *"Daaaad"* for his attempt at droll. Asking Shay now as she came into the kitchen where Kate was.

"Working on a report or something." Plunking her bags down.

"Costa Rica sounds so romantic," Jennifer said, throwing in a little cheerleader move. "Are you going to ride horses on the beach? We did that one time in Oregon, but it rained and we had to go back."

"Can Jen stay, Dad? Mom said if it was okay with you, it was okay with her."

Retrieving the olive oil, wine, and soy from one of the bags, Ben said, "Put the chicken in the big bowl, wash and chop some parsley, you've got a deal. Oh, and set the table."

Shay cocked her head at him. "Please, you mean?"

"Totally."

As they turned to, Ben put away the rest of the groceries, started making the marinade.

"Dad?" Done with the parsley and showing him. "We'll be in the pool."

"Jenny brought a suit?"

"I have one she can wear—the bottoms, anyway." Giggles as they ran upstairs.

Finishing the marinade, Ben poured it over the chicken. He made a batch of daiquiris, filled two old-fashioned glasses, and brought them into the den, where Kate was checking paper figures against a column on the screen.

"Hey," he said as she looked up and stretched.

"I heard the blender going. Kind of jumping the gun, aren't you?"

"Have a sip and tell me."

She took the glass, set it down. "Which credit card did you use?"

"The one the swiper didn't reject." He looked at the computer screen. "How's it going?"

"Don't ask." She checked her watch. "Damn, it's late."

"What about tomorrow and Monday?"

"It's due Monday. Anything else?"

"Jenny's staying, I won't put the chicken on for an hour, and I came up with this on the boat." Handing her the envelope with the printouts, he watched her slide them out, flip through, slide them back. "*You* I can see finding something like that. But how Craig and Nancy managed, I'll never know."

"But they did, didn't they? Besides, you give me too much credit. There's a lot I miss." Keeping up the look as he left her to her grids and numbers.

At five, the girls playing water basketball and Kate still ensconced, Ben rapped to let her know he was lighting the grill. He was repositioning chicken in the marinade when Kate came in and emptied what was left in the blender into her glass.

"Welcome aboard," he said.

"Watch your head, coming about." Eyes bright from his daiquiri and nosing into the chicken bowl. "Smells good."

"As do you."

"No comment." She was whirring another batch together as Ben took the chicken outside and set it on the grill, smoke rising in a fragrant plume.

"Smells awesome, Mr. Metcalf," Jennifer called. "Watch this." She attempted a half-court shot and missed. Retrieving the NERF basketball, she threw it up to him. "You try."

"From here?"

"Shannon says you used to play. Let's see you make one."

"Yeah," Kate said, coming up beside him. "Got a daiquiri here says you can't."

"How about my scholarship back?"

"Careful what you wish for."

Ben squeezed the absurdly light ball, rose in a jump shot, and released. It bounced soundlessly off the top of the backboard.

"Smooth, Dad."

"I always was overrated."

"Two out of three," Jennifer shouted.

"Jennifer..."

"Don't be a wus, Shay, he nearly made it." Swiping water at her for emphasis. Swiped at in return.

"Poor old Metcalf," Kate said. "Women fighting over him even at home." Adding after a pause, "Scary, isn't she? Fifteen going on twenty-seven."

Ben stopped lifting thighs to see how they were browning. "Am I supposed to cringe at that?"

"Whatever fits the shoe."

"Maybe you ought to have a cracker or something."

"You're the one let her in the pool like that." Then, "Time to change for dinner, girls. Shay? Jennifer? Out."

As they ran for the house, Ben took a gulp and tasted twice the rum he'd put in his batch. "How was the workout?"

"Lots of kicking and punching, thanks. How was Hallenbeck Marine?"

He smiled faintly, was turning a breast when she said, "Ben, have you ever wondered if your parents were proud of you?"

"Wheat Thins, onion flavor," he said. "Top drawer."

"Answer me. Have you?"

"The only game my old man saw me play, he fell into the cheerleaders he was so drunk. Is this going somewhere, or is it barbecue Ben night?"

On the verge of saying something, she let it go. "Never mind. I'm just buzzed and feeling sorry for myself."

"If you're talking about you and Jeb, ask him. Assuming that's him coming through the gate with what's-her-name."

"Merilee? Tell me you're kidding."

"*Whoohoo*," Merilee called as Jeb boomed out, "*Ahoy there...*"

"God, where's the blender," Kate said.

"We were going out, but the Club was so mobbed we came here," Merilee was saying as Ben ran another batch and Jeb sipped the Scotch he'd brought along, a pint of Glen-whatever. Navy blazer over gray slacks, an open white button-down that brought out his tan.

"It was so nice of Ben to invite us." Purple top and matching pants, dangly earrings and loose blonde perm. Three sheets to the wind and working on a fourth.

The girls came downstairs, Jennifer in a Mighty Ducks sweatshirt, Shay in jeans and the T-shirt she'd had on earlier with a Hawaiian shirt over it. Brown hair still damp, parted in the middle to wave below her shoulders.

"So how *is* my girl," Jeb asked after she'd introduced Jennifer.

"Fine, Grandpa."

"Time you started calling me Jeb, a young lady like yourself. Even your mother does when she's pissed at me."

Ben, serving chicken, caught Shay's eye. *There you go, kid. Now you see what I meant about Thurman.*

"She have the prettiest eyes, or what, Mer?"

"Look out, world." A knowing if off-kilter wink, followed by a slug of daiquiri and giggles from Jennifer.

"About time she learned to race, too," Jeb told Kate. "If you'd have brought her over the way I've suggested, she'd be set to chauffeur you two around Costa Rica."

"Is that true, Mom?"

Kate froze a smile at her daughter.

"Promise you'll take oodles of pictures."

"They will, Mer," Jeb said, winking at Merilee after forking in a bite. "Damn fine bird, Ben. Finally found something you're good at besides going to lunch." Bellowing out a laugh that Merilee echoed in falsetto.

Ben glanced at Kate, but she'd looked away.

"That's not nice," Shay said into the gathering quiet.

"It's all right, Shay. Your grandfather didn't mean anything by it."

"I know what he meant, and it's not all right." A flush had risen on her face, separate from the pool's glow.

In the quiet, Jeb said, "Might be time your daughter learned the difference between joshing and hurting, Kate."

"Maybe she does already—*Jeb.*"

"And maybe we'd best go where we're welcome."

Merilee in her frizzed hair and overdone makeup looked merely bewildered as Jeb rose. "Come on, Mer, the club'll be less crowded now." And to Kate and Ben, "Don't get up, it's under control. Unlike some I could mention."

As the door shut behind them, Kate's face a mask and Jennifer still staring at Shannon, Ben thought he'd never been so proud of anyone in his life.

They were in bed, Jennifer driven home and Shay in her room. Merilee and Jeb long gone.

"I'm sorry, Ben," Kate said, looking up from the printout she was trying to focus on after downing more Tylenol.

"Not your fault." Snapping off his end-table light. "How many you think they went through before our place?"

"Too many, and yes it is my fault. I'm the one he pressured it out of the other day."

33

"Forget it," Ben said. "It means nothing. Less than nothing."

But she wasn't about to let it go. "So to shut him up, I told him, right down to the sperm count. I was waiting for him to slip it in where he could. Some people never disappoint."

"You tell him there are other means, if that's what we decide?"

"Hard to hear when you're mouth's perpetually open."

Thinking of Shay's look when he thanked her for standing up for him, Ben didn't respond. Hearing her say again that wrong was wrong no matter who did it before shutting her door on him.

"At least he's right about one thing," Kate said. "You do make good chicken."

"Too bad we can't take it to the bank."

6

Sunday morning they slept late, Kate popping another round of Tylenol when they finally did get up, Ben joining her this time. Delaying his shower until she'd gone to put on coffee, not wanting her to notice his welts. Letting the water wash over him in the double wide that sometimes led to other things but hadn't since Shay spotted Ben and Loren at the Pelican.

Typical him, he thought—figuring that even if they were spotted, the sales prospect thing would fly. And probably it would have with anyone other than Shay, thanks to the Henri upheaval. Even Kate might have read it differently, given him the benefit of the doubt. The same doubt now swirling around them like last night's barbecue smoke.

He found himself wondering if he hadn't wanted to be caught, make a statement without having to make a statement. Poor Ben, forced to it because of his wife's commitment to her career. Competing with her old man, blah-blah-blah. *Shit...*

"Daaaad...?"

"Right out."

"Mom's putting on a scramble. She needs to know if you want some."

"Sure. Down in a sec."

Examining himself in the mirror—still fit from his workouts and the bruises already fading, a good omen for the trip—he had another thought. Maybe they'd like it down there...enough to chuck everything and start over. Find work on the charters or teach scuba at the hotels. Live cheap. Hell, he knew people who had done it.

Ben dried himself, put on fresh boxers and T-shirt. Emerging to finish dressing, he spotted the hamper Kate had left open across the room and rose, towel in hand, to can the jumper.

* * *

By ten, Shay and Kate were off to Fashion Island for bathing suits. Ben finished cleaning the kitchen and called Darnell Light from the den phone. At six rings, he heard the big man's voice, his familiar "Yo..."

"Darnell? Ben Metcalf. I wake you?"

"Very possibly."

"Sorry about that. I'll call back."

"Calling to apologize about it being so long, right?"

Ben went back years, pictured the man in his African big chair. African everything then, down to the braided hats his hero, Jim Brown, favored. "How about an omelet? The usual place, thirty minutes?"

"On you?"

"What isn't lately?"

He locked up, headed down to where Newport became Balboa Boulevard, their beachwalk meeting spot when he worked for Darnell Light following the point-shaving mess—the reason Dar had recruited him. Ben could still hear him saying, "Damn, I bet on those games and *I* couldn't tell." Hardly a ringing endorsement, but something when only ashes were showing up.

No other offers, certainly.

Getting their coffees, he took a sand-side table and contemplated the joggers and bladers, pier and water. A close-in sailboat roiled up Shay's dark observation: "*Two weeks on a boat? We can't even be in the same room for ten minutes.*"

"That you behind those Ray-Bans?"

Ben turned and saw gray in the wiry hair, that unexpectedly Moorish nose. Three hundred easy on a six-five frame—down at retirement, then up again after NFL knees hampered his old ability to shed pounds. That rolling, limping gait belying the ferocity with which he'd once come at quarterbacks. Cargo shorts, gym tank, Mexican sandals, Wayfarers. Out of Africa, evidently.

"Dar...way too long." Standing to return the grin, the bear hug, the handclasp.

Darnell eased himself onto the bench, popped the lid off his cup, dumped in half-and-half. Sipping the result, he said, "Damn, don't you ever age?"

"Day before yesterday. Thirty-seven."

"Oh to be again. How's the family, your mom?"

"Well, thanks. And more or less clear of the hole she was in."

"Credit where it's due, m'man."

Ben sipped his coffee. "How's beach life?"

"Lemme know when you want to trade property taxes."

"Not just yet, thanks." Taking the slack out of his aviators as he took in the lines around Darnell's eyes and how they'd spread; asking, after a beat, "Pancho make parole yet?" Pancho Light, the best number-three Ben had ever played with—how Ben first met his old man. Before the drugs rolled Pancho up.

Darnell shook his head. "Got turned down again. Hard to break free in there when the guards are taking cuts. Even if he wanted to."

"I'm sorry, Dar."

"Tell me about it. And speaking of you," grin replacing the frown, dawn shading night, "remember the time we peeled eighty large off the dealer without him blinking?"

"Ancient history."

"Yet here we are." Kicking sand out of his *huaraches* as the waitress came with the food Ben had ordered with their coffees. Never once knowing Dar to vary his order.

They started in. Three roller girls in shorts and bathing suit tops whipped by laughing, Dar pausing in mid-bite to follow them.

"Lord A'mighty," he said.

Ben waited until their sound was gone. "You recall a bookmaker and loan shark named Al Devore?"

"Little Al?" No expression now, viewholes into a tar pit. "Why? Somebody finally off the gentleman?"

"Not that I'm aware of."

"Too bad. How much you into him?"

Ben let his eyes take in the horizon. "Forty-three and compounding. Bets at first, then just keeping up. Way out of hand."

"Meaning he's leaning on you."

Ben nodded.

"Kate know?"

37

He shook his head.

Dar tossed a piece of toast to some waiting gulls, one taking off with it, the rest in squawking pursuit. "Shit," he said. "Learn the moves, then split on me, right about the time I'm thinking you got potential." Making a sucking noise with his teeth. "All right. What are we buying here?"

"Time," Ben answered. "May first, if it's doable."

"Time costs."

"It's not as if I have much choice."

"Why? You off somewhere?"

"Come hell or high water." Leaving out Loren, Ben explained: Kate's nonrefundable surprise; damned if he did, more so if he didn't.

"And you don't want Little Al knowing. Afraid he might think you not coming back or spending money that's rightly his. Want him to cut you some slack."

Ben nodded. For a moment neither spoke.

Darnell said, "I can see if he'll take five percent, maybe seven. All I can spare for what I'm gonna charge you."

"Thanks."

Shrug. "Man, don't you get tired of running up tabs?"

"With Devore? He's not usually like this."

"I'm talking why period, knowing what you know. Still trying to beat yourself?"

"There's a question."

"Least you know where the problem lies," Darnell said, glancing down at Ben's plate, up again at him.

Ben shoved over the short stack he hadn't touched.

Cutting into a hotcake, the big man said, "Any chance we might resume our mutually profitable relationship when you get back?"

Ben let a beat pass, a breath. "The line or the truth?"

"No, I didn't think so." Dar met his eyes. "One caveat in the other thing, though: Little and me, we ain't exactly on the best of terms. Had to educate a gentleman in his employ messing with one of my ladies." Digging back into the stack. "What I'm gonna do to you, you don't learn from this."

Great, Ben thought with a nod of acquiescence.

Bon Voyage.

7

Puerto Caldera, Twelve Miles South of Puntarenas, Present

The men fit the waterfront bar like the blue-greens in a lagoon. Reflective of neither the best- nor worst-dressed of the patrons, they had on loose-weave shirts with rolled-up sleeves, summer-weight trousers, baseball hats to shade and conceal. Each had slipped in around eleven, corresponding to the arrival of a medium-sized container ship, the bar rail already rowdy with crew. Bypassing the dice rolls and game machines, they'd chosen a table in the corner, away from the windows.

The younger of the two, who could pass for a dock worker were it not for glasses that gave his face a slightly academic look, waited until the waitress was out of earshot. "All right," he said to the more slightly built man in the woven leather suspenders. "Why are we here?"

"Given your sense of drama, I thought a public place best."

"Don't count on it," Enrique Matos came back.

The slight man rubbed a shoulder. "Rains are coming early this year. I can feel them."

Enrique Matos said nothing, the man always having reminded him of the brother of an ex-president of Mexico. A dapper, smiling man on whose property a number of embarrassing discoveries had been made. Political opponents of his brother. Buried alive.

"You're looking well, Rique," he was saying now. "No thanks for freeing you from that hellhole?"

By way of answer, Enrique drew out the envelope with the Polaroids in it, slapped it on the table.

Without looking down, the slight man smiled and said, "You know your father was like that. Never a moment for amenities."

"Explain this."

The man opened a cellophane-wrapped package, bit the end off a cigarillo, fired it with a match from a small box. "Her taxi went off the road and burned, didn't it? Very sad." He let out smoke. "And how *are* the little ones holding up?"

"Abuelita has been a rock." All Enrique could think of to say.

"Of course a grandmother can never replace a mother, can she? Forgive me...your late wife's name again?"

"Serena. The pictures—who took them?"

Smoothing the tuft of hair beneath his lower lip, the man said, "You know it's curious you were never charged. I mean, it's all there—unfaithful wife; volatile, possessive husband." He unfolded a piece of paper, handed it over. "Read it. It's just a copy."

Enrique scanned the familiar writing, the bar din as nothing now. Raising his eyes, he had the feeling he was looking up from a deep well.

"My point," the man continued, touching a match to the paper and watching it curl in the ashtray, "is that neither can an old woman replace a father sent back to prison. Especially when she could die, leaving the children to curse him for having killed their mother, exposed them to who knows what. Those things in the photographs, for instance, the originals of which will accompany the note."

He leaned closer.

"And tell me, did Serena really do those things to—"

Enrique had him by the shirt, eyeball to eyeball, the cigarillo rolling across the table onto the floor, when he caught movement. Two men—a beefy one and a shorter skinnier one in sunglasses—separating from their beers. He let go.

"Righteous is it? Your wife was a whore and you know it— hell, everyone knew it." The man stepped on the wayward cigarillo, lit another as the two sat at his nod. "Did you think I went to the trouble of getting you out of prison because we have so much in common?"

"You'd do that to my children?"

"No, Rique, you would. *Comprende*?"

"What do you want?"

"To do what you were born for, of course—taking things at sea." He smoothed thinning hair. "In this case, cotton and lumber, the usual arrangement. Plus a little surprise that will not be reflected in the manifesto. Copper ingots hoping to avoid their fate."

"This whole dance—just for cargo?"

"For your children's future."

"And if those aboard have other ideas?"

The man smiled, wove his fingers under his chin. "You're the smart Matos. Figure it out."

"The wrong Matos, you mean."

"I know my eyes, Rique. You can't hide it from me."

Enrique rotated his beer as he grasped at straws. "Others do this...the Panamanians."

"Young, unpredictable, and sloppy. Possessed of neither your qualifications nor temperament. I was going to save it for later, but there's something else. Something to make your old man rise from—"

"Caution might be a wiser choice in reference to my father."

"It involves a certain shipping company. Not to mention the same security force responsible for him."

Enrique felt a boiler firing deep inside. "You know this for a fact?"

"When have my sources failed?"

"You have a short memory."

"And you, Rique, have a choice. Either I am friend or enemy, something I'd advise against even without the pictures and the note." He chased a drag with beer. "One time and out—*para los niños*. In whose name it might be wise to pray nothing happens to me."

Holy Mary...Mother of God...Pray for us sinners.

Now, and at the hour of our death.

Enrique tapped a cigarillo from the box. "I'll do better than that," he said, refusing the man's proffered match and striking one of his own. "I'll light a candle to it."

8

The 737 broke through cotton-roll clouds into bright sun and blue sky—eight-forty, twenty minutes late thanks to the L.A. sock-in. For a moment Ben imagined himself out there barefoot, what that would feel like. Next to him, Kate scanned an in-flight magazine. Shannon Kay, in her window seat across the aisle, continued to stare out from CD phones as the airliner found its altitude and leveled off. Ben swallowed to adapt his ears, tried letting the sudden rush of sound and setting his watch two hours ahead to Costa Rica time be metaphors for escape, and came up short.

Monday still was *there*: Kate off early to submit her report and tie up loose ends—four when they finally saw her. Ben driving Shay to notify teachers and administrators. Ben's sales meeting after dropping Shay back home to finish packing, Jeb's absence not unexpected in light of the note he'd left on Ben's desk.

TAKE CARE OF THEM.

Or else, Ben presumed that meant.

Then the scramble: checklists on their checklists, items inspired by the Leary's faxed tips. On and on, until they *had* to get disciplined about it, Ben calming one crisis by making room in his duffel for Shay's art materials. Mostly, however, there was the cell call from Dar as Ben drove home from what seemed like his eighteenth trip to Payless. Starting with, "So what'd you do to piss off the white guy?"

"White guy..."

"Thin dude seems to have Little Al's ear."

Thin dude..."Tommy?"

"That's him," Dar said. "Drives a Mustang."

Ripples: anger-fear-anger. "Black? Tinted windows?"

"Hard to see how he sees through 'em. Why?"

The car cruising the house.

42

Son-of-a-bitch Tommy, right under the radar.

The thought was enough to make him pull over, a moped honking angrily as it passed his window. Ben said, "Walt pulled him off me Friday after he threatened Shay. I thought he was just mouthing off, trying to scare me." Going on to explain how Shay had spotted it.

There was a long pause, then Dar through his own traffic noise. "Is having this guy gone worth coming back to work for me? Because that's what it'd take."

Murder one plus *his old life: all he needed.*

"Sorry, Dar—bad connection."

"Best listen. Man's made you his personal crusade, Walt told me. Al's got himself cancer, I couldn't even get in to see him. Which explains Tommy, his hard-on for you, and no slack on the due date."

"Maybe I'll rob a bank down there." The joke empty-sounding to even him.

"One like that, looking to prove himself, take over from Al, you can see it in the eyes. Even Walt said so."

Fear-anger-fear: "See what, Dar?"

"What ain't there. You catch my meaning?"

Shay's eyes still hadn't left the plane's windows.

"She'll come around," Ben heard Kate say over the engines, Tommy's face Cheshire-like as it retreated around the corner.

He popped his ears again, forced himself to focus on Kate.

"Among other things," she was saying, "she hates the way she looks in a swimsuit. Compared to Jennifer, anyway."

"And maybe her mom?"

Kate shrugged. "Wouldn't be the first recorded instance."

Quicksand, Ben decided.

"I remember fourteen, if that's what you're thinking. Only too well."

"Not according to the pictures I've seen."

"Pictures don't show the inside, Ben."

"I know what they show. Why do you think I burned mine?"

"How'd it go with Jeb?"

Ben told her about the note.

"Jeb being Jeb. Nothing personal."

Ben was tempted to remind her everything was personal with Jeb, but he didn't, and Kate settled back into her magazine. Tommy at bay for the moment, he drew out the Costa Rica guidebook, started in on the text and color photos. Dawn-of-time jungles, dark- and pearl-sand beaches, *African Queen* rivers, islands, and postcard waterfalls. Splashy festivals and open-faced residents—*Ticos,* they were called. Boys and girls whose eyes looked dipped in hot fudge. And horseback riders...

Ben unbuckled, stood up to give it to Shay, waiting as she pulled off her headphones. "Speaking of riding on the beach," he said.

She looked at the photograph. "Jen's thing—remember?"

"Your mom still rides."

"Her, not me." Staring at it nonetheless.

Ben looked again: morning light gilding the horses, riders, and feathery palms. "On the other hand," he said, "not bad for a sketch. In the right hands, of course."

Shay seemed to brighten.

Which is when the bottom dropped out.

Ben was conscious of her high-pitched scream over a cacophony of them. Metal striking metal and the scattergun clatter of plastic. Of being flung like a beanbag as the plane impacted stable air.

Then, nothing...

He wasn't out long, the plane potholing like a jeep on a bad road as the attendant got him into his seat belt. He heard the pilot announcing in Spanish and English that they were almost out of the turbulence, beyond the *cordillera* thermals that had caused it, Kate's voice asking *"My God, are you all right?"*

"Ready to go, coach," he heard himself say while deciding if he actually was.

Kate took a deep breath and looked away.

Ben did, too, opened a hand to Shay, whose eyes were fixed on him from a face as white as her pillow. He touched the spot behind his ear where he'd hit, felt a good-sized lump forming, but no blood. He smiled, showed her, then Kate, then the passengers and the attendant hovering over him.

"Hit a Metcalf in the head, you better come with more than that," he said. "Really...I'm okay."

Sheepish more than anything, he spent the next twenty minutes waving off soft drinks and damp cloths, accepting ice wrapped in a towel and Advil. "I *must* be dazed," he said to Kate after downing the Advil. "Darnell'd have his lawyer on the Airfone by now."

But she was shaking her head as though seeing it again no matter where she looked.

"Kate...?"

"It's all so damned fragile. You, me, Shannon...one stupid thing and it's gone."

"It's a bump, Kate. Nothing to—"

"Remember that when you do things, what you stand to lose. I mean all of us, Ben, not just you."

He looked over at Shay gripping her seat, then at Kate with her arms across her chest. "Don't leave you to Jeb, you mean."

"*Goddamnit...*" Tears barely quenching the fire in her eyes.

Making out something he thought had said good-bye, if not in so many words, he said, "Sorry—you're right, of course. Downhill from here on in."

9

San José from the air looked about the size of Stockton, maybe a quadrupled, tin-roofed Santa Barbara. Urban but not L.A. urban. That impression left as soon as they cleared customs and caught a cab to the hotel the Leary's had recommended. Then the traffic more resembled Ben's recollections of Tijuana. Taxis, fuming buses, and trucks played bumper tag with equal relish; cars honked and darted, street-crossing pedestrians became matadors. Sidewalk vendors hawked gladiolas and newspapers, shave ice and pineapple slices, crepe-paper fans and piñatas, some working the idling cars like waterboys during a time out. But the twilight was dry and mild, the mountains stood up nicely, two traffic cops on horseback tipped their caps to Shay, the plazas looked green and inviting against a rosying sky, and handsome restorations spoke of a once-heated affair with neoclassical architecture.

One of which was their hotel, a former coffee planter's house.

As Kate and Shay cased the lobby, Ben phoned the Puntarenas-based driver the Leary's used to ferry them to the coast. *Porfirio: cheap, good, speaks English*—Porfirio's wife agreeing he'd pick them up at ten next morning. After paella they strolled the still-peopled streets and shops to Parque Morazán, where couples sat enjoying wafts of native pipe music, one another, and the soft night. All in all, it had the feel of summer vacation from the perspective of the first moments. Time stretching languidly.

It wasn't until later, Shay in her room and Kate breathing deeply beside him, Ben staring at the ceiling after another round of ibuprofen, that how it *could* have ended—face-masked figures picking through a smoking hillside nightmare—brought up the flashbacks, Kate's *Goddamnit, Ben,* and finally, in the bathroom down the hall, his paella.

* * *

Porfirio arrived forty minutes after they'd finished papaya, huevos and black beans, and set up outside with their luggage. Shay spotted a man driving an oxcart, Kate a flock of parrots, Ben a city bus painted to look like an island at sunset.

Then, Porfirio. Eighties blue Vanagon, painted-over dings, chrome hubcaps pitted from the coastal air. He wore a floral shirt tucked into cord jeans, lime socks, well-broken-in running shoes. A smile allowing ample room for self-amusement.

"First time, huh?" he said, tossing their bags in back, helping them up and in. "How you like it?" Navigating his way out of the city as though the horn were a rudder.

"Colorful," Kate said.

"What are those?" Shay asked, after the second roadside vendor. Glossy orange balls the size of small tomatoes.

"*Pejibaye*—palm fruit. Boiled in salt water and served with mayonnaise, not bad. You like fruit?"

"With mayonnaise? I don't think so."

"You wait: bananas, melons, mangos, guavas, star *carambolas, manzana rosa*...all you want."

They were into rolling grass-and-green-tree country now, the road in a gradual climb. Soon it began to wind and narrow, light and shadow the windshield. Which didn't stop Porfirio from passing a Coca-Cola truck they barely cleared, then a milk wagon. Prompting Ben to tell him to cool it, they were in no hurry.

At ridge top, they stopped for gas and a *jugo de cas* at a general-store-like *pulperia*. "Guava juice," Porfirio explained.

"You know the boat?" Ben asked him as the girls used the facility. Puffing cigars Ben had bought with the colónes he'd exchanged dollars for at the hotel.

"*Fuego de los Angeles?* Sure—local term for sunset. But not like you see most days. Special kind: *espléndido*, like angels." He raised his face, spread his arms to mimic heavenly singing.

"The kind you hear."

"That's it—think it can't get no better, but does. Like..." Making a circle with thumb and index finger, running the other index finger in and out of the hole. Winking at Ben as he gestured.

Kate and Shay appeared and they got back in the VW, the road beginning its descent toward the coast. Yellow-blooming trees began showing among the green; bougainvillea tracked rock walls dotted with hibiscus. As Kate dozed, they passed something blue and split along the gut. Long tail, black carrion birds working the carcass.

"Ick...what was that?" Shay asked.

"Iguana—big one," Porfirio said. "Vultures picking it over."

"*Gross.*"

"Hey, you like fish?"

She gave him a suspicious look. "Some."

"How about shrimp? You like shrimp?"

She nodded.

"Keep going," Kate spoke up from the back.

Porfirio grinned. "Remind me to tell you 'bout my cousin's place. *Madre de Dios...*"

They went by farms and smaller properties, the yards thick with banana and papaya, kids and dogs chasing soccer balls. Palm trees began to predominate, flowers and stucco, older pickups, outskirts that gave way to neighborhoods approaching modest.

"Port city, till they open up Caldera," Porfirio observed. "Big ships stop there now. You want my cousin's place first or boat."

"Boat," Ben said, as he read Kate's glance.

Porfirio looked disappointed. "Is no expensive, my cousin's."

"Later, maybe."

Puntarenas rose from an extended sand spit. Hotels, soda stands and tourista pulls, markets, stores, and promenades: a seen-better-days edge. Finally the boat moorage and a yacht club set into an estuary lined with mangroves, waterfowl in them looking to Ben like wind-deposited tissue.

"Storks and spoonbills, you into birds," Porfirio said, stopping in front of the moorings, where they piled out to humid and ninetyish. Whiffs of silt and salt, low tide. "So...you see her?" Looking down the row in front of them as he unloaded their bags.

Ben saw swaying masts, people aboard some of the boats, three dinghy'd-up workers pulling up decking on an old Chris-Craft.

Kate pointed. "There."

"*Su madre*, she got good eyes." Porfirio said to Shay.

"Tell me about it."

As Porfirio started that way, Ben picked up their remaining gear, rejoining them as they looked across a median of green water to *Angel Fire*'s starboard side. Sweep of white above her antifouling paint, oblong ports laid out three and two in the cabin stripe, center cockpit under a forest-green enclosure. Boom-wrapped mainsail and shorter mizzen aft under matching shroud, forestay-furled jib showing green as well.

Ben had the impression of bigger than he'd anticipated. Shittier, certainly: home sweet home from the bird splatters.

"When's the last time anybody had her out?" Kate finally asked.

Porfirio thought. "October...*Dia de los Muertos*. Rains come late last year. Early this year, I think." Raising his nose to sniff the air. "You want I come back tonight for shrimp?"

"How about we call you?" Kate said, breaking off her scan.

Ben asked how much they owed him.

"*Bienvenidos á Costa Rica*. Señor and Señora Leary, they take care of it."

"No need to ask why," Kate said as Porfirio was leaving the dock.

After ice cream Ben scored from a place near the yacht club plus a trek to a *mercado* for soap, Kate hitched a hop, got the motor going, and brought *Angel Fire* alongside the dock, where they spent till near dark cleaning her. Bird droppings and airborne crud abovedecks, four-and-a-half months of dust below. Finally, after trimming the enclosure to form a Bimini over the cockpit, topping off the fresh-water tanks and charging the batteries, hosing down the decks and each other, they re-moored her and collapsed.

"Remind me to get a fan when we go for food," Ben said.

"Some vacation," Shay put in.

"Nice color you got going there, kid."

"I've been working on it at home."

"And I thought we went through this. You're ten degrees off the equator here."

"*Daaaad.*"

"Come on, you two," Kate said from where she lay sprawled on the foredeck. "Look at that sky."

"Smell that dock."

Ben said, "Anybody else wrecked?"

"We can't go to bed now. It's hot downstairs."

"Below, Shay," Kate said. "In a boat, you go below."

"Can we sleep up here?"

"You and a zillion mosquitoes," Ben said as Porfirio shouted from the quay, "Shrimp lovers no' fear. Porfirio *esta aqui.*"

"Bite my tongue," Kate said.

It was a small place not far from the bus depot: ancient palm fronds and netting, desiccated starfish and cork floats, brightly painted tables inside a red threshold. The shrimp was fragrant with garlic and Porfirio's cousins were full of tips about where to go and what to see. Finally even he seemed weary, dropping them at their dinghy amid *cuidados* about the coming rain and the already-here *papagayo*, Kate telling him that was the idea, to harness some of it.

An hour later, Shay in her forward berth, Ben lay in their aft one, his shrimp doing backflips and the noise of a party spilling from the club.

"Ben...you awake?"

"Believe it or not." Rolling over to glance out the port.

Kate said, "This will be good for her. She doesn't get much chance to pitch in and have it mean something."

"I'm sure you're right."

"Are you? All right I mean?"

Hi, Tommy. No, I spent it on shrimp and antacids...you understand. "What's the *papagayo* he was talking about?"

"Northeast winds prevalent at this time of year."

They lay listening to the water lapping, shouts from the party, the boat creaking as it caught a wake and rocked gently.

"Still think we can handle her?" he asked.

"*Angel Fire?* Why not—there's always Jeb collect."

Ben glanced over, caught the grin.

"Of course we can handle it," she said. "You consider the Learys Einsteins?"

"Got us to clean their boat, didn't they?"

Ashore, a woman's high-pitched whoop preceded the sound of a bottle breaking. Kate said, "You feel it, too?"

"Feel what?"

"I don't know. That what's waiting out there for us *is* us."

Ben doubled his pillow and leaned into it. "Guess we'll have to see."

"Don't tell me the thought hasn't occurred to you."

Suddenly it all caught up. As if she'd pulled a lever on a vending machine—invalidation rattling from its slot to bang against the stay, Tommy grinning at him big-time now. "What, Kate? There's not enough pressure here? You have to dredge some up?"

"It was on my mind, Ben. Things happen when you're committed to making them happen."

"Shifty drifty Ben, blown about by life's winds. Any old port in a storm. Or should I say porthole?"

"And *we* are what you make of us," she shot back. "Otherwise we *are* lost." Turning from him to face the bulkhead.

10

Despite a restless night, residual heat from the boat's being closed up adding to their own heated exchange, they rolled out at dawn. Watching the sun light Puntarenas and the moorings, the mangroves across the lagoon and birds taking flight, Ben said, "Sorry to be so defensive last night."

Kate sipped the coffee he'd made, kept her eyes toward the bow.

"You were right. I just got crosswise of it. Fresh start?"

She returned the mug to her lap. "How's your head this morning?"

"Not bad. A little tender."

"Ben, you ever feel as if you're going under in your own life?"

Fresh from the in-box. "Maybe the trick is just to come up for air, Kate. Probably too simple a concept."

"Just let things happen..."

"I'm the last guy to ask. But maybe."

"Maybe what?" Shay, balancing up the ladder with a cocoa in one hand: aqua shorts, sandals, white tee. Baseball cap with *Backstreet Boys* in rock-concert script.

"Maybe we'll go ashore for huevos," Ben segued. "Sound good?"

Shay plopped down beside Kate. "At this hour? I don't think so."

"Hunger happens."

"I mean when did you two become morning people?"

"Since this morning," Kate said, glancing at Ben.

After showering ashore, they set out for breakfast and a trip to the *mercado*. Two hours later they were unloading bags of groceries, Kate by and large following Nancy's notebook suggestions: staples, fish caught with the aboard-ship tackle, fruit and vegetables from the locals where they'd put in, those

52

places also outlined. As she read the lists and thumbed through the ship's log, Ben got organized to hit the things he'd missed yesterday.

"Got some nice-looking iguana for tonight," he kidded Shay, at work on her sketchpad. Setting down his bucket and sponge to hand her a reddish-colored banana from the bunch they'd bought.

"Sure, Dad."

He slipped over to eye her sketch: a perspective on the sloop directly east. Mangroves across the estuary standing in as background.

"That's good, Shay."

"It's not finished."

"Great art is never finished, just interrupted. I read that somewhere."

"It's just homework. I'm supposed to draw stuff I see." Sticking the banana in her mouth finally to flip back a page for him. Two little kids beside a piling.

"How'd you get them to stay still?" he asked.

"Coins from where we stopped for juice. After it was finished."

"Like mother, like daughter."

"I heard that," Kate said. Emerging on deck in a bikini Ben hadn't seen before—one of the new ones, plumerias on a black field. Bottle of sunscreen and a big yellow towel.

"Well, now," Ben said.

"Time to get serious." Spreading her towel as Shay rose, and with her pens, charcoals, and banana, quietly went below.

Ben was almost finished cleaning the portholes when he became aware of a small craft trailing its blue-and-white painter drifting downchannel. Pointing and yuks starting up from the deck-pullers aboard the old Chris.

"All right," he said. "Who secured the dinghy?"

"Shay." Kate answered, rubbing in sunscreen. "Why?"

"Port quarter, two o'clock." Ben approximating forty yards and on-course for the main channel. "Cast off while I start the engine?"

"Don't bother," she said, getting up and heading for the rail. "I can make it faster swimming. Then again..."

The boat maneuvering toward the dinghy was a sportfisherman—dark-blue-hulled, upper-forties in length, her fishing outriggers raked aft. Some years old and no great beauty, but judging by the engine burble, a speed conversion of some kind. Likely a charter, though Ben could see no one else aboard. Just the man on the flybridge looking something like Antonio Banderas in black-rimmed sunglasses. Deftly working the props to bring her alongside the dinghy and cinch it to his starboard rail, then pull up alongside *Angel Fire*.

"Lose something?" he asked. Tipping his cap before removing it and his sunglasses to eyes the green of weathered copper.

Kate took the painter from him and secured it. "Yes—thank you."

"Welcome to my country. Americans?"

"How did you know?"

The man opened his hands. "Second home for many of you. I've noticed this boat and wondered who owned it."

"We're just guests," Kate said. "Vacationers."

"Bound for...?"

"New and exciting, we hope. I'm Kate Metcalf. This is my husband, Ben. My daughter, Shannon, is below."

Ben nodded as the eyes swung his way, took his measure before returning to land on Kate, glowing from the sun. No attempt to introduce himself.

"Experienced sailors?" the man asked.

"More or less," Ben said.

"Then may I take the liberty of suggesting you cruise close in? You'll be able to explore what few make time for."

"We appreciate it," Kate said. "Your English as well."

"I had good teachers. Also the opportunity to spend time in your—"

"Nice rig you have there," Ben said to draw the man's eyes from his wife.

They swung back to Ben. "You like fishing? She's available for charter. Nothing else like her."

"Not too likely," Ben said, leaving off the "*asshole.*" Determined to hold gaze despite the other's seeming ability to look right through him.

The man grinned, resettled his cap and sunglasses. "Then I bid you a pleasant trip and a safe one." And with a look back at Kate after he'd levered into gear and spun the wheel, "*Vaya con Dios.*"

They watched him. Engines sounding like muffled Shelbys, the boat picked up speed past the Chris, empty now of deck hands. Around the jut of land, and gone.

"*Whew.* I could get used to that," Kate said.

Ben stood there mute. As if he were ten years old and Kevin Furlong, the kid everybody at school was scared shitless of, had just hawked in his face.

"Probably ought to register the swimsuit," she added. "At least alert the manufacturer."

"Not funny, Kate."

"Oh, I don't know. When in Costa Rica, right?"

"You get her name?"

"The boat's? No—did you?"

Ben shook his head. Still feeling a rushing in his ears that only now was letting in sounds.

"Brings it home, anyway," she said, resuming her sunscreen.

"How's that?"

"You're a big boy, Ben. You figure it out." Winking at him before lowering herself onto the towel and releasing her strap as Ben watched the man's wake feather out and disappear.

At two, having run through functions, responsibilities, some basic commands, Kate ordered the mooring line slipped and motored them down the lagoon and into the gulf. Explaining as she did the heart of sailing: wind direction, points of sail relative to it, jibing and coming about on a tack. Things to expect tomorrow when they raised sails.

It was a beautiful day, the water silver-flecked, breeze picking up once they rounded the point. Ashore, development gave way to coastal lowlands: banana and coffee plantings, sugar cane, beaches spread out under rocky bluffs—Shannon at the bow sketching it.

Ben took the helm as Kate went below to make log entries and recheck the chart notes. Back on deck then with sodas.

"Ahoy the helm," she said, returning from giving Shay hers.

"Ahoy the skip," Ben answered. "She having fun yet?"

"Inching toward it."

Ben regarded her, now in blue shorts and a white polo, maroon Topsiders. "You thinking what I am? That she went below because of how you looked in that suit?"

"What I think is that she needs to feel a part of something."

He glanced at the digital readings on the binnacle, the wind having jumped from nine to fourteen. "Any idea what?"

Her own grin went wolfish. "Cut your engine speed and give me a bit with Shay. At my signal, head up and stand by."

As Ben watched, she went forward, talked and gestured for twenty minutes. Then she was signaling the new heading and Ben was coming to it, Kate guiding Shay through a raising of the mainsail. Winching the halyard tight before unfurling the jib and checking the sheet lines where they met at the cockpit, both sails luffing as Ben stayed head to wind, the reading at seventeen now.

"Here's the drill," Kate said after a final check, Shay looking flushed and wide-eyed. "Shay on jib sheets,"—holding up each green line to demonstrate its effect—"Ben on main,"—holding up the speckled white line from where it fed through the blocks—"me on helm. We'll be coming about to a port tack, the wind on our port beam." Lining up one arm to vector the wind, the other to the boat's new position. "Which means the sails will fill off...what side, Shay?"

"You're asking me?"

"The leeward or downwind side, in this case starboard. At which point, Ben eases the main to its optimal trim or set—which I will indicate—Shay the jib. With me so far?"

"Come on, Capt'n Kidd. Anything I can pick up, you'll be doing in half the time. Guaranteed."

"*Daaaad...*"

Ben felt his adrenaline kick in, the wind dispel Tommy, Walt, Little Al, the man in the sportfisherman—all else not of the moment. He felt Kate bring her about, the sails whump to life as he and Shay trimmed them to her command, *Angel Fire* take the bit and go, parallel again with the coastline on a southeast reach. He was aware that Kate had turned off the motor, that the sounds were their own whoops rising into the warm buffet, creaks sounding as if the ketch were casting off its long sleep and calling out to them, *Run...run with me.*

11

The man in the black-rimmed glasses looked up and into the eyes tracking his predicament. The knight he thought he'd accounted for had defied all logic to sweep in and take his pawn; worse, to straddle his king and queen. Good as over. Considering who he was playing.

For a long moment—as though he had options—he sat letting the tension build. Trying to escape with a vestige of pride, to snatch at least that from his adversary. And there it was: first a snort, then a giggle.

"*Estoro!*" he mock-fumed. "Is that any way to show respect for your old man when he's thinking?"

Still thinking was more like it. Imaging the *mujer* on the boat to the detriment of business at hand.

Matteo Matos, age eight, tried for his game face, but it was too much. "Give up?" he asked.

"*En sus sueños.*"

"English, Papa—remember?"

Poetic justice: nipped by his own maxim—closure after Serena, his wife circumventing him on the issue of tutoring Matteo and Anna in English because she didn't know it and refused to learn. "Of course I remember. What do you think?"

"That you forgot."

Enrique Matos looked across at the gray-haired woman weaving a table runner. "Is this what you teach them while I'm away, to disrespect their father?"

Without looking up, she answered, "If you would play more often..." Her inference clear: *With your son...let alone your daughter.*

"Abuelita doesn't speak English," Matteo offered.

"Abuelita knows more English than you think," Enrique said. "Besides, you have to learn it. Why...?"

"Because it's important?"

"It is where you'll be going." Leaning over to kiss his son's hair, to savor its warmth and boy smell.

"Where, Papa?"

"Places. Any more questions?"

"Yes. Are you going to move or give up?"

Enrique made a show of checking his watch. "Look at the time. Save the board and we'll finish when I get back."

"Anna wants a game."

"What else have I taught you? About just that?"

"Never give up, but—"

"Right."

"Give the boy his due," Abuelita said. "*That* is important."

Enrique spent a long moment rubbing his chin and pretending to think. "As you were saying, Matteo, never give up." Smiling at his son before toppling his king. "Unless it's to fight another day."

Enrique Matos drove over roads still not patched from last season's rains, his thoughts locked on the *mujer. Madonna de las Velas.* A woman of fire, but intelligence behind those eyes. Not like those he'd given thought to since Serena: waterfront women, the occasional cloud-forest type there to extract a life from the myriad around them.

This one, though...

Seeing her eyes again, he almost overshot his turn, the gate already unlocked and swung into the tangle. By design the lane was a mess—what the rains hadn't eroded kept interest at bay. Weeds scraped the pickup's undercarriage, vine and branches its sides. Farther on, the land slid off into the yellow-green of a small inlet, the air thick with tide and heat and insects, sunlight pelting the leaves and the structure ahead like warm rain.

Enrique banged over a final pothole to a raised area of crushed shell, where he killed the engine next to Pineda's last-legs station wagon. Always more fish-processing shed than storage facility, the warehouse sagged on pilings driven decades ago into the silt, *Pescados y Crustáceos* in once-red letters across the tin facade. Out beside the pilings where a boat was moored near his, a dorsal fin swirled after something.

Enrique stepped onto the weathered planks that served as an approach, inserted a key into the deadbolt, inside waiting for his senses to adjust. Ten degrees warmer, sunlight slanting through cracks in the roof and siding, that ingrained salt-fish smell. Fact was, he couldn't remember when the place was a going concern, customers strolling among the metal troughs on which tuna, roosterfish, jack, and *cubbera* lay iced and marble-eyed. Now the counters sagged as badly as the roof, the scales weighed only spiderwebs.

He ran into one, brushed it away, headed for the rear.

The four waiting for him sat around a rectangular base marked by burns and oxidation. Pineda, Chávez, Durantes, and Beltran—an up-and-comer according to Durantes. Smoke rising from their cigarettes toward the slatted light. Lap of water against pilings, the creak of a reluctant venting fan.

"Trying to burn the place down?" Enrique asked by way of greeting.

The men crushed their smokes, Chávez kicking his into a gap through which daylight spun. Enrique unfolded a metal chair between Pineda and Chávez, all leaning toward the aerial photograph and chart he splayed to the surface with lead sinkers.

"*Reina de Aconcagua,*" he said, tapping the photo. "Departing Guayaquil on the twenty-first, confirmation as the date approaches. Lumber and cotton, with a bonus of copper ingots."

"The climb?" Beltran asked. Oiled reddish hair combed straight back off a mottled face. Well-muscled, a St. Christopher medal showing under his half-buttoned shirt. At perhaps thirty, the youngest of them.

"Figure on seventeen, water to rail," Enrique answered. "Same as before."

"Hell with that same-as-before business. I was there, remember?" Durantes—bad skin and a shoved-back hairline, a nose that ran like a seagull's from a salvage job that once nearly claimed him. Machete in a scabbard on his hip.

Enrique met his eyes. "A benefit of which is that we'll be smarter and better prepared."

For a moment no one spoke. Then Pineda, a since-the-beginning associate of Rudolfo Matos. Mid to late sixties; loyal to the name, so far as it went. "No one questions that, Rique."

"What about the take?" Beltran put in.

"It goes well, we go home happy—same as always," Enrique said evenly. "Anyone dispute that?"

"Some happier than others?" Durantes.

Enrique regarded him. "You have something to say, say it now."

"Word gets around, I've heard it myself." Chávez put in. Closer to Enrique's age—thirty-nine—an orphan since grade school, where they'd known each other. Small gold stud in his right ear, blue shirt with leaping marlin. Along on Rudolfo Matos's last two raids. "About your release and what you might have given up for it."

"Talk is cheap. You think I'd be less to you than my father?"

No one spoke.

"*Do you?*"

"How broad is our window?" Pineda asked.

Enrique turned to the chart. "Three days, four at the outside." He tapped an area between Guayaquil, where the ship was being loaded, and an island off Colombia. "We strike here—far enough from the Canal, a straight shot across the gulf—up to...here, where we camouflage and offload. Same deal as my father made you. Questions?"

"What about communications?" Beltran, the up-and-comer.

"I'm working on a tape. Status quo reports to buy us time. Plus a device to jam her outgoing messages."

"Resistance?" Chávez asked.

He held his expression in check. "I was getting there. Our source assures me that an old friend is in charge of security. Venegas. And this time, he is ours."

"Big talk," Durantes said over the expected comments. "Considering."

"Four years ago, we paid to know his tactics. Four years later, he doesn't know ours." Bringing out envelopes he handed each of them.

Pineda spoke first. "It needs saying, Rique. We loved your old man, but personal works for nobody."

"It's not personal," he lied. "It came up. I thought you'd want to know."

Silence. Then one by one, they opened their envelopes. All except Durantes, who threw his down.

"Not like I don't need the money," he said. "But it sounds like revenge, and revenge always seems to get people like me dead."

"You're saying I'm lying to you."

"What do I know?" Durantes said. "What do any of us know? The prodigal son: one mission, where your old man gets it." Waving off Pineda's cautionary look. "How do we know you didn't plot it all along? How do we know you aren't setting us up now in exchange for—"

By then Enrique's .40 was out from the small of his back and between Durantes's eyes, the man's hand frozen on the handle of his machete. A red haze was over everything and Pineda was shaking his head, saying, "Put it down, Rique. This is not your father's way."

Enrique was conscious of the lapping water, dust in the rays of sunlight, the held-in breath of the men around him. Tightness like a steel band fighting his own.

"Those who are in, go over the plan, find the holes, get back to me," he managed to say. "There is much to do in three days." Releasing the hammer and walking toward the front and daylight, hearing "*Crazy fuck*" behind him and knowing it was true.

PART TWO

Kate

12

Kate eased out from beside the sleeping Ben. She used the head, put on her bathing suit and a T-shirt, then went up on deck where the sun was spilling from a notch in the mountain range they'd begun tracking. According to the guidebook, a transition zone.

Kate hoped it was true.

She removed the tee, felt the sun on her skin. Morning was such a golden time—as if everything were dipped in it. Shining promises unalloyed by the day's hard light. And yet who was she kidding: Kathryn Alice Hallenbeck was no romantic, no child of Jeb could be. Which doubtless explained longshots like Henri Dufresne and Ben Metcalf to anyone who cared. Different each, but hardly random in their selection.

Kate stepped over the lifeline and dove into the bright river. The water felt marvelous, cool but not cold. Smooth strokes distanced her, turned her for a look back after she'd gotten about fifty yards off.

Straight from a postcard: *Angel Fire* swaying at anchor; beach and jungle, green peaks rising beyond; water clear enough to see bottom. Even yesterday's sail had gone well, Shay reacting to her on-the-fly immersion with more enthusiasm than she'd displayed in weeks. And it had been a blast: racing the sun to anchorage, watching it go down, first one to spot the green flash wins. Ages since they'd done anything close.

She watched the clouds turning peach-yellow-white. Jeb wasn't going to win this day, the life she'd made after Henri. Not if she had anything to say about it. This time her gamble—that money wasn't time—would be the one that landed.

Thinking like Ben now.

She followed a flight of pelicans, then started a leisurely crawl for the boat. Midway, she saw him emerge from below, drape a towel, and dive in, so she pulled up and treaded water.

Despite Jeb's warnings á lá Henri, Ben had been fine. Until his little poke in the eye, that is, part of which she blamed on her own obsessions, or she wouldn't be there. And the man on the sportfisherman confirmed something for her—just as a number of spurned business encounters had. That months from forty she was still in the game.

Ben swam underwater, surfaced alongside. "You believe this?" he said, brushing water off.

Kate grinned back. "Not yet. Shay up?"

"Had her nose in one of your sailing books last I saw."

"Who knew?"

"You have as much fun as we did yesterday?"

"I'd forgotten how much," she said.

A fish jumped, the ripples spreading toward them. Ashore and under the canopy of trees, a rooster crowed.

"I think it's because I always equated sailing with Jeb."

Ben said, "Which is why you never pushed Shay toward it. Like you'd be giving her over to him. Close?"

Kate felt a chill as if she'd hit a cold current. "Ben, promise me something. That if anything ever happens, you won't let Jeb take her."

Ben lost his smile. "Where's that coming from? In the first place, he couldn't."

"You don't know him."

"She's smarter than that, Kate. And I promise, okay? Now, you have anything harder for me to do than that?"

Suddenly it was as if the current had turned and she were back again in warm waters. "Coffee," she said. "After I beat your cheeks to the boat."

They set out at nine, Kate wanting to augment: tacking and jibing, true and apparent wind, man overboard. Shay ate it up— as though all along it had been hers and she just needed to be led to it. Salt in the genes, Ben speculated, not without envy. Though he was proficient enough with repetition, she was instinctive, the proverbial fish to water.

Except when Kate handed her the helm.

It was after they'd put in for lunch at a small town with brightly colored stores, all of them feeling the street rolling from their time aboard. Half an hour after they returned and Kate announced she was going below for a nap.

"The helm is Shay's. First mate, B.D. Metcalf."

"*Moooom...*"

"Steady as she goes. Coast to port and don't hit anything."

"*It's not funny*," Shay said as she disappeared. "*What do I do?*"

"What you've been making look easy all along," Ben said. "Any orders for the deck?"

Shay glanced at the instruments, up at the telltales indicating wind efficiency over the sail surfaces.

"That a flutter up there in the main?" Ben inquired casually.

Shay checked her heading and bore off the helm. Immediately the windward telltale flowed aft to match the one through the clear-plastic sail window.

"I drifted during changeover," she said.

"I'll never tell."

"Won't happen again."

He shook his head. "Your poor boyfriends."

"You see me with any boyfriends?"

"I didn't mean this instant."

"Jennifer has three." She let a beat go by. "One of them, Barry Scherfenberg, she already did it with."

Ben was about to say talk is cheap, but decided to rephrase. "And you believe her?"

"Yes—no. I don't know."

"Might be something in that," he said. "Not believing everything you hear and letting it determine how you feel about yourself."

"Fat chance I have with *this* body."

"Watch your helm." Which gave him a moment to further shape his thought. "Look," he began, "I'm not long on advice and you're probably not keen on it from me anyway. That said, you interested?"

"What am I going to do, hide?"

"Okay. I didn't have a real date till I was eighteen. Sports were it, girls scared me to death." He rubbed the base of his neck. "Who you are is inside you, Shay. Some people go their whole lives without getting that."

Nothing.

"What I see is an attractive, talented young woman. And if I can see it, it's a matter of time before some undeserving does."

Eyes dead ahead, hands at ten and two.

"Besides, Jenny's older. Biologically, anyway."

"Mom's older than you are. I don't see any difference."

"Shay, I'm going to let you in on a secret. Growing up doesn't stop, it only gets more complicated." *Tell Loren about it...Kate and Little Al and Walter and Tommy and Darnell.* "And your leeward telltale is starting to luff."

Late afternoon, Ben and Shay dropped the jib and the main and Kate mizzened into the harbor at Quepos. After checking in at the Port Captain's office, they checked out a snorkeling beach, floating above angel fish and yellow tangs, orange trumpets, little blue ones they had to ask the name of later. Bits of rainbow in a gust. And in the bask of sunset, the lights of Quepos coming on and a waft of night blossoms, they ate the snapper Ben hibachi'd, Kate serving it with a chutney constructed from the recipe taped to a galley door.

Getting up early, they caught the bus to Manual Antonio National Park and, with a picnic lunch, set out to explore. Beaches first—white-sand crescents fringed by jungle and the darker green rising up behind. After picnicking accompanied by white-faced monkeys, Shay spotted an iridescent butterfly as big as her palm and several that looked like upside-down owl faces. They then followed trails hung with wild orchids and passion flower, red-tipped bromeliads, umbrella leaves. Which proved useful during a mid-afternoon shower that clattered away as quickly as the macaws that shared their grove.

At one fork, Kate checked out a tree frog with legs that looked glazed, matching it in the guide to one that, like the belladonna spider, the natives used to tip their poison darts.

The following morning, Kate had Ben head to wind and they anchored at the mouth of a river Nancy had noted. Taking the dinghy as far as it would go, they hiked to a stepped waterfall, iridescent little birds darting among the mosses, rocks, and ferns, monkeys in the trees above them. Shay spotted one with a baby on its back and that was that, breaking out her sketch pad as Ben and Kate swam and poked around downstream.

"Hard to take, isn't it?" Kate said, throwing back her head to gaze at green lace, blossoms against a China sky.

"See that pool down there? You think Nancy ever swam naked in it?" Slipping out of his trunks and waving them at her.

"Ben..."

"And miss making our own notes?" He let the current take him down a chute, around a bend, and into an emerald set with boulders. Kate joining him finally, slipping out of her own suit and tossing it up the bank with his.

"What if Shay sees us?"

"She knows more than you think, if that's what you're thinking."

"Thank you, Dr. Spock." Kate dove, kicked out across the pool, surfaced, butterfly'd back. "What more, huh?"

"I can think of something." Taking her hand and pulling her in.

"Ben, no."

He extended to arms length and waited, but nothing more came. "I see," he finally said. "It isn't about us and Shay seeing it. It's about her seeing what she thinks she did. Back on Pelican's deck."

"Not what, Ben. Who."

He ran a hand over his face. "Her name is Loren; she wants to buy a boat. And we've been through this, Kate."

Water lapped at her breastbone, dripped onto freckled shoulders. Parrots called from the trees.

"Done," Ben said suddenly. Hoping the water wouldn't conduct the pounding of his heart.

"As in it's over between you? Or done talking about it?"

"You've heard me on this, Kate. Whatever turns the key."

Seconds passed. "All right," she said quietly.

Boom, ba-boom, ba-boom...

"Maybe it's this, where we are and what's here, but I'm taking you at your word. *No más.*" Touching a finger to his lips before striking out for the rocks.

13

After lunch and a hunt for shells, they rowed back, theirs still the only boat at anchor. Ben used the on-board tackle to work a school of yellowtail, in half an hour catching enough for two nights. He was finishing cleaning them when Kate came up from below, Ben thinking she looked particularly good in white shorts and a sleeveless olive tee that set off her newly acquired glow.

"Radio said we might be getting some swells in from Alaska. Late today, they thought."

"Long way from home," he said, recalling a post-Dar, pre-Kate winter holeup from everything, the way the swells could storm in on Hawaii's North Shore. Nothing like *those* babies to take your mind off things.

Kate double checked the wind's direction with the masthead fly. "Meantime," she said. "Shall we dance?"

"Thought you'd never ask."

While she raised the mizzen, Ben handled the main and the jib, Shay perched on the bow. One of her homework goals, Kate told him from the helm—sketch a pair of whales to go with her monkey drawing—*too perfect.*

And it was: blue sky with brush-stroke featherings; wind steady at fourteen, capping farther out where it turned from blue-green to deep indigo. After a bit, he felt drowsy and went below to stretch out for twenty—even with his eyes closed, reprising their *no más* scene at the pool. Free and clear, the swimsuit edition without the swimsuit. What more, indeed?

So why didn't he feel better...?

He awoke to pitch-and-roll, the rush of water past the ports; emerging topside, he saw Shay had traded bow for helm, the way it was elevatoring. Spray plumed. Whitecaps stood out like foam.

As did their wake.

"*Hoochiemama*," she said, her face flushed, T-shirt patterned by spray and her cap now bill-to-back. "Have *we* been ripping."

"Swells arrived early," Kate said. "We wondered when you'd feel them. Let alone the seven-plus we've been making."

"Where are we?"

"Just north of Uvita."

Ben followed her point on the chart, saw sheltered bay around the horn from a pistol-shaped line of x-marks.

"Rocks," she clarified. "Meaning we'll swing around the barrel part, then the handle—above this second set of shoals, and in. Drop anchor up by the village."

Ben took a closer look at the barrel's tip. "Widow Rock?"

"A sense of humor these Ticos."

"How long has this been going on?"

"The wind just after you went below. The swells about thirty minutes."

Ben took note of the six-footers angling under them. Not what he'd call close-sequence, but enough to keep it interesting in the pitch department. He double-checked the wind, confirmed it with Kate at holding northeast, sail trim as she'd shown him. *Angel Fire* still running smartly.

There was a whoop from Shay. "Eight-and-a-half. How am I doing?"

"Like there's no tomorrow," Kate said. "But head her off about twenty. We'll need to give the rocks room."

Forty minutes later they made out the reef, a foaming line jutting a mile and a half from a wooded point. By this time the swells, heightened by the impediment, had almost doubled and were coming up sharply under Shay's new heading. Frothing water—incoming and receding—surrounded the cockpit as the waves lifted the stern and bumped them to nine knots. Followed by increasing roll as the wind hit thirty. Now the swells were heaving the boat onto its side: ghost waves, unpredictable in their collisions with each other and with *Angel Fire*. Wind shredding their tops into lacy white spume.

"*Moooom...*"

"Keep her off, Shay, we need more clearance." Kate said, fighting the roll, binoculars fixed on the rocks. In distance, max, a football field.

"*I'm trying.*"

"Kate, maybe—"

"Maybe what? She's doing fine."

The bottom dropped out as they burst through a crest.

"*Moooom...*"

"You're my daughter. You can do this."

"*I'm scared.*"

"You've got a job to do—*do it,*" Kate flared in a voice that pulled Ben's eyes from the reef.

"*What...*" she aimed in his direction. Then, "*Concentrate, Shay.*"

A ninth-wave prototype drove under them; for a second Ben lost track of the bow. Then the starboard rail went under, Shay screaming as a burst of white water sluiced over the lip and into the cockpit. *Angel Fire* shuddered, slammed out of the trough and into the preceding wave.

Ben was conscious of water to his calves but draining, Widow Rock way too close, Shay screaming "*I HATE YOU, I HATE YOU*" as Kate finally took the helm and the starboard blocks reappeared trailing seagrass. Eyes on the rock, he shouted, "Can we reef in?"

"Too dangerous right now," Kate shouted back. "And we need the power to get around it."

"One more like that and—"

"*You think I don't know it?*"

Too well Ben knew the tone: overload...at that moment, at least, too far from the sailor she'd been. Another swell almost drenched the spreaders, *Angel Fire*'s bow closing in on pitchpole. And—just as suddenly—it fed the solution.

"Surf us out," Ben said, barely conscious of Shay's moaning.

"*Talk sense.*"

"Our angle's wrong. Go with the swell, hard over, then to leeward. Ride it out and angle in." Zig-zagging the edge of his hand to demonstrate. Hoping to God he was right.

"With shit for clearance," she came back.

"Keep, this up, the rocks won't matter. At least try. Or let me."

Nothing.

Ben glanced aft, saw a huge one closing, and stepped in. Hard over before the swell could neutralize the rudder...digging it back when the swell had swept them a boat length toward the shoal. Back down at a less precipitous angle, the bow no longer buried and the roll lessening. Robbing the swell of its killing force before anticipating the next one.

At best, it would be thin: closer to the rocks this way, but closer to quieter water. Trying to sound confidant, he said, "A dozen more, Kate. Run us out."

Which she did, the wheel's motion and her ingrained knowledge reclaiming the moment. Back to the original reach, with the swells breaking on the reef they'd just cleared.

For a moment, no one said anything. Then Ben was wrapping his hands around Kate's, kneeling beside a white-faced and swallowing Shay to help her go below. Getting her an empty Dutch Oven before heading topside again.

"Ben, I couldn't..."

"Couldn't what, Kate?"

"You know what I—"

"We're safe. Anything else matter?"

Shaking her head, she headed *Angel Fire* around the south end of the pistol-grip—tacking upwind now. But in getting this far, they'd also reached the air foil created by the mountains around the bay. Already the wind had slacked. Half a mile in, Kate had Ben dump the jib and mizzen, and she started the engine. For perhaps a hundred yards, they loosened handholds—physical and mental—tried to focus on the bright day, the shoreline revealing its details as they closed. Then he was conscious of an *oh-shit* sound. Familiar drop in rpms. Idling down, revving back up.

Until it coughed and died.

Kate hit the switch to starter noise. Six more times and nothing.

Son of a bitch, Ben thought. For as little as they'd run her, there had to be fuel, and a check bore him out: primary tank right up, auxiliary topped out. Water in the line? Air? *Damn, damn, damn...*

"I'll go," he said, one foot on the steps.

"No time for that," Kate snapped, and she was right. Wind and current were driving them toward the rocks they'd just swung around. No way to clear, too close to drift beyond.

"Drop anchor?"

"Too deep, we'll have to tack in. You with me?"

"You and me, kid."

She smiled—the response he'd hoped for—and they went to it: Ben yanking the jib back out while they were still head to wind, aware, as he did, of his blisters, the stiffness in his hands. Backwinding it at Kate's direction until they'd swung to a course that would take them close enough to hit the reef with a stone before angling off. But this time when they tacked, they hadn't enough momentum to bring her around. Three boat lengths from it, *Angel Fire* stopped dead and began to slide.

Two boat lengths...

"Fall off," Kate yelled into the luff. "We're jibing."

"Running out of room."

"What room? Jibe ho."

At Kate's hard-over, Ben muscled the main around, then the jib. *Angel Fire* picked up way. And as they shoehorned through, Ben draped over the stern to fend off—uncoiling his legs into the nearest rock before swinging back aboard, barely making it to begin the trek downwind into the bay's heart where they could tack back safely—he was conscious of a head flushing below decks, how much he needed one about now, and, finally, of their widening grins.

14

Enrique pinned up the schematic revealing *Reina de Aconcagua*'s squat bridge and deckhouse. Engines, stack, rudder machinery, and crew's quarters aft in a single-island setup; pair of cross-treed working masts forward between hatches.

"Four hundred thirty feet, sixty-six hundred tons, twenty-plus knots, depending," he said. "Commissioned 1968, retrofitted '78. Panama flagged and, as we know, RouteStar owned. Holds here, here, here, and here. "

He turned to face them. Pineda, Chávez, Beltran, and a dour Durantes—smoking and drinking guaro in the main cabin of his sportfisherman: *Machacha*, after the local speedster gamefish, her poles and lines set out for effect, engines maintaining trolling speed into the wind. Last meet before intercept; final chance for bugs to be ironed out, details presented, responsibilities assigned, bitches aired.

"Word yet on when she leaves?" Chávez.

Enrique gestured to his cell phone. "Any minute now, one of the reasons we're here. Our source knows, we know."

"They don't publish these things?"

"In this case, not the correct information."

Pineda tossed off his guaro and poured more. "Sounds like Venegas."

Durantes said, "Which wouldn't mean anything, would it? Like he might be expecting us?"

"After what happened last time, he'd want whoever he suspected to get the word," Enrique said. "There's been no indication of that."

"But to clear the air, you wouldn't be sitting on such information." Pineda, acting to defuse.

"Once and forever, my father is dead. I've no wish to join him in a fool's mission."

Eyes met eyes; there was a murmur.

"You want to get to the details?" Durantes said.

Ever closer, Enrique thought. He replaced the schematic with a diagram indicating relative positions—large hull representing *Reina*, smaller one for *Machacha*, torpedo shapes depicting the assault craft—four blocked sequences. "Number one," he began, "Pineda, Durantes, and Beltran engage her starboard quarter. Chavez with me portside."

Beltran leaned forward. "Anyone mind if I'm with you instead?"

"Why?" Enrique asked to silence and glances.

"Youth, for one, speed where it counts, weapons. SEAL training on exchange."

"Pass or fail?" Pineda.

"What do you think, *viejo*?" Neither mocking nor afraid, just said.

Chávez shrugged, Enrique watching Pineda, who, after a breath, also shrugged. "See me later," he said to Beltran.

"You're the boss."

Durantes downed his guaro. "What about Venegas?"

"Venegas is a counterpuncher," Enrique said. "Starboard's job is to make him throw everything that way while staying out of range. The exception is Durantes, who, at my signal, runs hooks in under your covering fire. Sequences one, two, three, and four. Twenty minutes."

"And if we don't have him by then?"

"Break off and re-form. Tow the assault boats to a location on your sheet and ride it out. Same goes if anything happens to me. But we will have him." No one spoke. "Which reminds me, *Numero Uno*: Venegas alive. Clear? Nobody dies who doesn't have to."

Beltran shifted on the bench seat. "You tell Venegas that?"

Tense laughter. Cigarette smoke wisping out into wind still kicking up whitecaps.

"What about the weather?" Chávez asked.

"Shouldn't be a factor. Wind's due to drop and no moon."

Beltran said, "And we have hit targets this size?"

The others looked at each other, then at Beltran.

"One," Enrique said. Imaging Rudolfo Matos's boat disintegrating in a hail of machine-gun fire, all but his son following orders to scatter and regroup...three interminable years his payoff for insubordination. And, as his cell phone began to trill, "Another reason he won't be expecting us."

The man sporting the tuft of a goatee under his lip replaced the receiver, into which he'd relayed to Enrique Matos *Reina de Aconcagua*'s time of departure and her projected route, courtesy of the official with whom it had been filed at the last moment. Putting his feet up, he recalled their conversation.

Him: "You're sure that what we discussed is aboard?"

Official: "You think I want to give up living?"

Him: "Not the way I'd handle it."

Reputation, he thought: What was a man without it?

Prey to anything that came along.

Buzzing in to his receptionist, he gave her the rest of the afternoon to be with her twins down with summer bronchitis. He then used his untraceable line to dial two numbers. One was to a Colombian exchange; the other was to a local number with a distinctly northern flavor. Someone who had been trying, along with his compatriots, to locate items of importance massed for shipment, then judiciously rerouted. Someone who might be receptive to a sizable fee, the surest way to an American's heart.

He let the parts come together in his mind: players on a board, none but him seeing the entire picture. Like the son of a father who'd tried pulling the same stunt on him four years ago. Smiling at the symmetry, he lit a fragrant Havana, a gift at lunch from the deputy commissioner of something-or-other who had presented him with the plaque he'd already added to his wall collection.

CON LAS GRACIAS AGRADECIDA DE UNA GENTE.

With the thanks of a grateful people, indeed.

15

Kate opened her eyes to Venus low in the west, a scattering of persistent stars and shore lights. Not a whisper coming in the ports. Four hours after Ben finally got the engine running, a pressure system had snuffed the wind like a candle flame. Not the least of her headaches, either—no response from Shay, even when Kate had tried apologizing through the bulkhead.

She'd raised up, was bracing herself to leave the berth, when Ben said, "Some night."

"Sorry to be so restless. You notice the wind?"

"Umm-hmm." Yawning.

"Think somebody might be trying to tell us something here? Like cool it awhile?"

"No. And yes, she'll be okay, if that's what you're referring to. Wait'll she tells her pals at school. Instant celebrity—thank you, Mom."

Kate leaned against the bulkhead, Ben and the arm propped under his head just visible in the faint glow from the ports. The atmosphere thick and close in the cabin from the lack of circulation. "You want to know what I was out there yesterday?" she said. "Twelve years old in a rental twenty-seven, this goddamn squall on Lake Erie I couldn't handle. Hands so cold I could barely feel them, water turning my feet to ice, Jeb's voice cutting through me. Hell, they could have been the same words I used on Shay."

"Bullshit, that's Jeb talking. Miss Perfect." Sitting up and putting his legs over. "And who gives a rip beyond a guy who wasn't there and never has been except to view you as somebody to give him a run for his money? Makes me want to puke."

* * *

78

Shay finally emerged in drawstring shorts and a sleeveless *N'Sync* T-shirt as Ben was taking his cereal topside to watch Kate Australian crawl back and forth as if a great white were chasing her.

"Corn flakes and a banana left," he said to her.

"No thanks."

They watched Kate swim.

"You know how she feels about yesterday. Why make it worse?"

"Excuse me? I'm the one she owes an apology, and you know it." Rubbing her toes and not looking at him.

"And that depends on when you decide to accept it?"

"That has nothing to do with it."

"Then we agree," Ben said. "What happened out there, what she said in the heat of it, had nothing to do with you. You were simply in the way."

"I give up," she said. "In the way of what?"

"Your mom and lovable old Jeb. It wasn't you she was laying into, it was herself at your age."

"Give me a break."

"Metcalf's law," he said. "The brown stuff flows downhill, no matter how old. Better to learn it now than find yourself up to your ears, wondering how it got so deep."

By now Kate had pulled up and was floating between ship and shore. Watching them talk about her, Ben could see; waiting as though for thumbs up or thumbs down, her fate somehow in their hands. Breeze beginning to ripple the surface.

"Some choice, you know that?" Shay said, raising her hand in a small wave that brought one in return.

"How's that?"

"You and her."

They made Isla del Caño—a Nancy starred review—by midday. Twelve miles offshore, the island was dotted with perfectly round lithic spheres, mossed guardians of a native burial ground. As Shay sat getting a bead on one with her pad and pencils, Ben and Kate wandered among philodendrons the size of boats, epiphyte-hung evergreens, gnarled trees thought to have been planted for their sap and seeds by those buried there. Snorkeling, they spotted roosterfish and grouper, lobster and giant conch, octopus and brittle star. And as they were nearing the mainland later, a sea turtle, plodding in with a white bird on its carapace.

"Whatever you told Shay this morning, I'll take it," Kate said as they waited to fire the fish Ben had caught. Sky turning pink and crimson, twilight cries floating out with the perfume of flowers no one would stand before in wonder. Shay finishing up her sketches below in better light.

"Nothing much. I just colored in some grays."

Kate sipped her wine. "Did Jeb come up?"

"As little as possible. Why?"

"In some ways she's like him."

"Happy thought. What about Henri? You see him in her?"

"That way she squints into the sun, maybe, the tint in her hair. It's getting harder to remember." She fell silent again.

Ben took a swig of his beer. "Where'd you meet him?"

"Henri? I've told you all that."

"Maybe I wasn't interested until now."

"And now you are..."

"I asked, didn't I?"

"Squaw Valley. I was up from Stanford on a ski weekend. He was there...competing." She took an extended pull on the wine.

"This being the abridged version."

"I just don't think I want to go there, Ben, not tonight. Some other time, if you really want to dredge it up, which is hard to believe."

16

They left the warehouse at dawn: four boats that had entered the overgrown inlet the night before, plus *Machacha*. Enough men so that each of the cigar-shaped assault craft—outrigged to either side like canoes, with 100-hp outboards and towed under shroud behind all but *Machacha*—could carry at least seven.

Beyond the inlet they fanned out, then settled into the long haul that would take them to the Gulf of Panama and beyond. As they sped on at slightly differing rates, the men slept, drank coffee, read magazines and paperbacks. Smoking and raucous at first, later subdued.

At midpoint they cleaned and oiled their weapons: Commandos looking like cut-down AR-15s, well-used Astras, Llamas, and Czech-made semi-autos with taped-together grips. They checked ammunition belts and clips, battery lanterns and walkie-talkies, grappling hooks with explosive launching devices. They grew restless, smoking with greater frequency, yet talked out. Knees bounced and fingers popped; a few did push-ups. Somebody started a dice game that within a short time folded.

Under cover of darkness, the boats rejoined: one at a time over perhaps an hour. By nine-thirty they'd lashed together into a floating island, the men lifting the shrouds on the assault craft and testing the outboards. They had one final meeting before joining in a prayer said by such men: out-of-work gold miners from the Osa; fish, banana, and palm harvesters; mustered-out Panamanian conscripts; jail-hardened types who craved the adrenaline, the payoff, the opportunity to strike back at something. Finished, they lined char under their eyes, final-checked their guns, and settled in to wait, their cigarettes resembling fireflies in the night.

17

Next morning, Kate slept in while Ben and Shay explored the coastline. They nosed up a waterway past herons and egrets until the overhanging branches nearly brushed them out of the dinghy, cruised back for *pan dulce,* tried communing with the statue of Francis Drake, purported to have put in there and buried treasure enough to buy Central America. When they returned, Kate was on deck with the guidebook, letting her hair dry in the sun.

"I've been reading about the pirates who sailed these waters. You guys find any buried treasure?"

"Forgot our shovels," Ben told her.

Shay said, "We asked Drake, but he wouldn't tell."

"Henry Morgan once led his men over from the Caribbean side and took Panama City—did you know that? What the Spaniards didn't burn first to keep out of his hands." She took a bite of sweet bread. "Those that didn't hang or die from their self-inflictions wound up stealing for the government."

"Hasn't changed much in three hundred years, has it?" Ben said.

Shay looked up from her sketch. "What self-inflictions?"

"Congressional," Ben said. "The nongovernmental variety."

"I don't...oh."

Two-and-a-half hours of milking a modest breeze later, it died completely. Ben, his line having been run out twice and chewed through, sat up from half-doze and thumbed back his cap.

"Is it me, or have we stopped?"

"What now, Mom?" Shay said from behind the wheel.

Kate glanced at the chart, then the jungle and river tributaries to starboard. "Okay, here's the deal: We're about halfway to where I thought we could put in tonight. One: We can start the motor and lumber up there. Two: We can wait for the wind. Three:"—rechecking the chart—"we can putter around the inlets, then tie up to one of these mooring buoys."

"Buoys," Ben said. "Out here..."

"Check it out." Pointing to markers roughly four miles into a wide shallow bay. "National Geographic Explorer *and* a night off from the mosquitoes. Yeas...nays?"

"Too far from Disneyland," Ben said, scanning the chart's broken delta of indented coastline, uninhabited land veined with blue.

"Maybe see a boa constrictor?" Shay asked.

"If he doesn't see you first."

"Cool."

"I can see how you'd get lost in here," Ben said.

Having slid *Angel Fire* past sunning iguanas, crocodiles looking like old logs and giving Shay the shivers, islands so dense with vegetation they could have been made of gold, mangrove roots rising from bird-tracked mud—they were into their fourth inlet, Shay and Ben on the bow checking depth. Twice they'd come close to being stuck, mud and sand swirling as Kate backed the motor or feathered off.

"Any second now I expect to see Bogart and Hepburn asking for directions," she said.

"Asking us? Good luck."

As they cleared an overhang, Ben caught movement, or thought he did, on an indentation bisected by creek. Not moving so much as undulating, the forest here quiet, no bird or monkey calls.

"What *is* that?" Shay said.

Suddenly grasping what it was, Ben tried waving Kate off. But her attention was on a sandbar, and Shay already had the binoculars up.

"*Omigod...*"

Ben forced himself to look at the thing coiled and coiling around whatever it was in the dappled shade, its head lost in the snake's girth. One leg twitching through coil as thick as his thigh.

Finally Kate saw it and veered off.

"Mom, where are you going?" Shay said. "We have to help it."

"Most likely it's dead already," Kate answered.

"You don't know that."

"Sometimes there's nothing to be done, Shay. I'm sorry."

"No you're not—you're not sorry at all." Storming aft to go below. For a moment they heard her rummaging, tossing things to get at others. Then as suddenly, she was back on deck, holding a black snub-nosed revolver.

"Where did you get that?" Ben said.

"You're wasting time. Go back."

"You don't fool with those, Shannon. Give it to me." Extending his hand to her. "Before one of us gets hurt."

"*Go back.*"

"So you can do what?" Kate said. "Shoot it? It's doing what it needs to survive."

"Then I'll scare it off." Both hands around the grip, the barrel edging closer to her mother—as though each was fighting for control.

Kate kept her voice calm. "And maybe kill it trying to save something that wouldn't make it anyway. Snakes crush their prey so they can feed, Shay—you know that."

"It's because I wanted to see one, isn't it? You're making this my fault." But it was delivered without force, as if she were playing a part without the juice necessary to charge the performance.

Gently, Ben loosened her grip on the revolver and took it, and for a moment Shay stood rooted. Then she headed for the steps, pausing at the opening to turn on Kate, this time with heat. "Did you ever think that might be me out there—that *that's* what it feels like being your daughter? *Like I can't breathe?*"

Arms around tucked-up knees, Kate said, "I can't believe Nancy would allow a gun on board."

"It was clipped to a bulkhead Shay was cleaning."

"But why...?"

"There are worse things when you need one."

"Says Deputy Thurman."

Ben kept his eyes on a fading sunset lidded by clouds.

"Sorry—it's just the last thing I expected in the hands of my child. Can you do something with it?"

He felt the .38 in the cargo pocket of his shorts, where he'd stashed it. "I'll think of something."

They were on the stern watching the light fade, Shay in her cabin, nobody feeling like food. "Want to know something?" Ben said at length. "I came that close to shooting it myself."

"You aren't the only one."

"You did the right thing, Kate. She knows that."

A moment passed in silence. "Then why's she so stifled by me?"

"Take it with a grain. She doesn't remind you of anyone?"

Kate rocked gently.

"She wants to be you—even if she doesn't know it yet."

The clouds had become chain mail, sea the gray-green of marble. A freshness rode the breeze that had sprung up about the time they'd secured *Angel Fire* to the buoy.

"Nice way out here," Ben said after further silence. "Being the only ones, too."

"It has been good, hasn't it?"

"The kind you look back on, Kate."

She loosened the grip on her knees. "You mean that?"

"Yes, I mean that."

"I'm glad."

He bent to kiss her—softly until he felt it returned, then firmer, back to soft again. Her hand touched his face, pressed his lips to hers, their teeth clicking once to involuntary smiles. Resuming then: warmth of skin, fragrance of tan and sunblock, salt-sweet wetness. Presets bringing in *their* frequencies, playing *their* sounds; thermostats slid to familiar settings: welcome to the days before being owned by your treadmill—each day faster by increments, until you looked down and the ground was a blur and getting off meant breaking something. And when Kate pulled back for breaths that sent his pulse racing, nipples taut against her shirt's damp cling, Ben had the feeling that maybe— no matter how many shots he'd tanked to this point—this one might beat the buzzer.

18

Instead of drawing fire from *Reina*, none came. Which was enough to encourage Durantes to keep his boat in and send up five men. Halfway to the rail, the ship came to life. Spotlights lanced, fire from two angles, and before the others could distract it, one of Durantes's men had been picked off the rope, another chewed up in the screws after losing his grip to the squall that had surprised them.

Then Chávez, Pineda, and what remained of Durantes's crew took on the lights, rained down glass on the defenders, ran feints. As they did, Enrique and Beltran swept in on the port quarter. They engaged their hooks in the silence of the starboard din and, after dangling and banging for an eternity against a rain-slick hull, made the deck and split up.

*Radio shed: move, move...*Seconds later, Enrique had his .40 trained on the operator, a Filipino who looked as if he'd just rolled out. Handing him the recorder with the taped status reports, he ordered him to hook it up. But as the Filipino was complying, a man in fatigues burst in, was able to raise his submachine gun a split second before Enrique fired, the *soldado*'s burst catching the Filipino instead.

Sucking air, still seeing the man ragdolled and the Virgin deserting him, Enrique tracked Beltran, spun him around, asked him if he'd found Venegas.

"Venegas is done."

Enrique's sweat turned to ice.

"Over—finished," Beltran added, inserting a clip into his assault rifle. Rearming the breech.

"Venegas alive: That meant nothing to you?"

"He was lining up on Chávez. You don't believe me, ask Pineda."

Nothing to add. Just that whoever had ordered Venegas to pull the trigger on Rudolfo Matos four years ago—assuming someone had—now was frozen in a dead throat. He heard, "You're the one told me after the meet to guardian-angel Chávez. Well, guess what?"

Enrique fought an urge, brushed passed, made his way to where Venegas lay crumpled against the rail. Staring down, he felt fatigue like a hand unplugging him from what was happening, the shouts and pounding feet. Until Durantes rushed up breathless.

"*Fire*—lumber's burning like a sonofabitch. Venegas must have set charges."

"Put it out," Enrique told him.

"The systems don't work. They've been disabled."

"Smother it, seal it off."

"We'll try, but the holds are interconnected."

Durantes was right, of course. Surveying its spread, intensity fanned by the pitch in the lumber, Enrique figured if they salvaged half they'd be lucky. Unlikely the way the ship was configured. Making his way up and aft, he mounted the bridge in time to hear shots, entered the wheelhouse to see a figure standing over not only the bodies of the captain, but the helmsman and a crew member in his skivvies.

"*Beltran...*"

Beltran turned, eyes bright with a fever Enrique had seen before in prison fights. Enrique jammed his pistol under the man's jaw.

"Drop it."

"The fuck you doing? They came at me."

"Outside. Now." Following Beltran onto the bridge walk, Enrique backed him to the wing rail, black water speeding by thirty feet below. Rain spinning down in the remaining lights.

"Think it through. You don't want to be doing this."

"Jump," Enrique said.

"Bullshit, I got friends in—"

Enrique swung left and fired, brought the .40 back to dead center. Beltran unflinched, slowly mounted the rail, stood gripping it outside as rain coursed his face. "Man, man," he said. "Big mistake."

Enrique fired right, aimed back, and this time Beltran leaped, flailing as Pineda and Durantes burst from the wheelhouse.

They saw the pistol, the radio Enrique was talking into, the escort boat looking small as it swerved toward the splash.

Durantes blistered him with a look, turned on his heel, clanged away down the steps.

Pineda said, "The one shot off the ropes was Durantes's cousin."

Enrique looked at him. "You saw the bodies inside? Venegas at the rail?"

"Enough to know Beltran put an end to it."

Enrique swiped at rain "You've seen what we face in the holds?"

Nod. Eyes on the smoke boiling up forward.

"Why, Pineda? Why fight this hard? For lumber and copper?"

"Maybe Venegas understood who'd taken him on."

"Beltran never gave him the chance," Enrique said. "And why only a few *soldados* for crew?"

For a moment there was only engine vibration: all ahead flank. Then, "Figure it out, *mi capitán*—and while you're at it, a plan to save *us*. We're going to need it."

Running flat out, they made Costa Rican water ahead of schedule, the ship nowhere near maximum load. And despite the temptation of Golfo Dulce, the thumb of water Enrique knew from childhood—now a one-way-in-no-way-out trap—he passed it up, relying instead on the taped position communiqués to buy them time.

Pineda entered the wheelhouse, dripping rain. "Fire's through the second hold and into the third," he said.

"The copper?"

"Plus some spaces I haven't checked."

"What about the men?"

"Despite Durantes, too scared of the fire to jump you."

Enrique looked out to where it was shooting through the hatch covers—a blowtorch whose roar permeated the bridge and, with the increasing rain, made it impossible to see beyond the forecastle. He caught sight of *Machacha* on the starboard quarter, the other boats having taken the assault craft and the wounded, some to rejoin the salvage operation, others to await their cut. Provided there was one.

"Would it help if we blew the hatches?" he asked Pineda.

"Not if that was Noah's rain. Blowing hatches will only feed it."

Hoping to reach the ache behind them, Enrique rubbed his eyes. "Then we'll have to drown her. Someplace shallow and remote. Only question is where, given the time we have left."

"Three hours. If that." Soot giving Pineda's face a demonic cast as he lit a cigarette.

Enrique ran a dead-reckoning off their speed and position, tapped a finger on the chart. "Here," he said.

19

It was like their first time only better, Ben thought.

Not only what had led to it, but the way they took it...slow and discovering. Kate gently pushing him back, her eyes roving and settling; lips and breasts, tongue and fingers hovering like the butterflies at Miguel Antonio...touching down with an arching lightness. Longer each time. Back and forth until their sounds so filled the cabin Ben was concerned that Shay might hear.

By then, however, the rain that had begun as drizzle was coming in earnest: white noise. Plus, concern at this point was far back and losing lengths to the bright spinnaker that had billowed to breaking and was now sweeping him—Kate with him—off the edge of the known world.

For a time, Ben lay listening to her breathing and the rain. In that frame of mind, he eased from bed without waking her, dressed, and found the cigars he'd bought. Tiptoeing past Shay's cabin, he climbed to the cockpit, settled against a cushion, and put his feet up.

Here, the rain was immediate—that was the word—the way *he* felt. As though his sensors had dialed in all the channels at once. He lit the cigar, savored it, put a hand out to the rain. Warm, just up from the Gulf of Panama, maybe South America...over by morning to a fine day. He could picture it: jungle pulsing with sounds; turquoise water veined with light feathering out to the deeper blues; whitecaps, if they were lucky. Everything clean and new.

He began a pinball trip through the things he'd bounced off just to get here—Tommy, Walt, Al, Jeb. After all, his thought went, without Jeb there'd be no Kate, no Shannon, none of it. Least of all, Ben Metcalf, the lost highway he'd been headed down.

Ben let the smoke caress his senses, carry off another thought: What if he had prevailed on Kate to not spend the money on anything so frivolous—however he'd put it the night of his birthday. Merely their lives: the music of her that still rang in his ears.

Later, somehow, for everything.

Now wins.

And it was then, through the drumbeat of rain, that he picked out an altogether different sound.

20

So far, so good—Isla del Caño almost off the radar, wide berth given to Bahia Drake. Not as if anyone could have seen the flames from either, Enrique Matos thought. Nor he beyond them, the fire having burned itself into his vision—a condition that, as they neared land, spelled increasing peril.

Running aground was not an option.

Pineda dipped his head in, rainwater running off to mix with what they'd tried cleaning up. "Have we started the swing inland yet?"

Enrique nodded, checked the depth sounder again. "Eighty meters. Seventy-eight...five—getting there."

"What are you shooting for?"

"There's a thirty-meter line paralleling the coast that shallows up. Barge access, if we're where I think we are."

"How current is the chart?"

"Ninety-one."

Pineda made the sign of the cross.

Despite all, Enrique smiled. "*Machacha* still out there?"

Pineda spoke into the portable. A response crackled back, and he clicked off. "Ready."

"What about the seacocks?"

"What they can't open because of the fire, they'll blow."

"Order it at the first thirty mark."

Pineda nodded. "Durantes found charges that didn't detonate."

"Luck, imagine that." Enrique said, donning his rain shell. And to Pineda's look, "I'll be forward. Maybe I can make out the coastline, keep us off a bar. Anything's better than this." He turned to Chávez working helm, his face red from the interior illumination. "Monitor your shore bearing. Keep us in the thirties, then swing her north, all stop at my signal." He slipped the radio into a pocket. "Depth readings every thirty seconds."

"Done, Rique."

Enrique took a minute studying the best route to the forecastle: portside judging by the flames, less damage there as well. Then he was out and off the bridge, thinking that the roar was what hell must sound like, the rain on his nylon shell as warm as blood.

21

Ben could tell the sound was building.

Engines, the deep churn of props—big and coming their way. But from where?

He could see no running lights, just the glow from their own masthead unit. Grabbing the battery lantern, he stepped out into the rain.

It was like stepping under a waterfall. Drops danced on the decking, peppered the sail covers, sluiced into darkness. At the starboard shroud, Ben snapped on the lantern, held up his hand to see better. Nothing...port shroud the same. He went forward, swept the beam through wide arcs for a glimpse of anything, and saw only water. It was a siren playing tricks, making the sound come from all directions. Ben swiveled, craned, swept his beam again. He was about to beat on the deck, yell for Shay and Kate to get up, when he turned his head and saw it.

Starboard side, *Lord God...*

Like a mountain sliding out of the night to fall on them—a mountain on fire—the bow of a ship speeding dead amidships. And at the bow's knife edge, backlit and looking down on him, the figure of a man.

"*NOOOOOO...*"

Ben was aware of raising his lantern, the raw sounds he was making, seemingly into a vacuum. Of Shay's .38 in his hand. Firing it again and again to warn the thing off them, knowing, of course, that it was too late.

And then it was.

He had a last glance upward, then the thing with the man on its bow sliced through *Angel Fire* as if it were driftwood.

He came to in the water, Kate's scream echoing behind the roaring, a numbness in the scalp behind his right ear. Unable to tread water with his left arm, he still gripped the lantern; switching hands, he was able to point it at the disappearing stern. Then it was gone, and he swung the beam through debris and washboard water, the bow section settling fast, no sign of the aft.

Then the bow, too, was gone.

Pain began to factor in, the effort of staying afloat. Chill from being wet this long. He was able to spot something that appeared substantial enough for support and one-armed to it. Deck cooler, still sealed. He managed to get his good arm through the strap, swing his light in a slow 360, spot the dinghy bobbing twenty yards off.

Thank God.

Ben kicked out into the rise and fall, making it in what seemed like days, the way it kept receding. Gritting his teeth against his shoulder pain, he abandoned the cooler, forced himself to lever a leg over the inflatable's side, roll in next to what was lying curled and sodden and shivering.

"Dad…?"

That and the rain slacking were the last things he remembered.

22

The slight man reached into the pool of light and picked up the phone. Five-thirty, gray showing outside the louvers, cigarette going among the dead ones crowding his ashtray. Already two dumps into the basket from the wait, two crumpled packs at the bottom.

"*Digame.*"

"And you to me."

High-powered boat engines, the man guessing *Machacha.* Bracing himself for whatever, he asked, "You're not at the drop point. Why?"

"Venegas had the ship set to burn."

"*Say that again...*"

"Fire—the forward three holds."

No! No, no, no, no, no: machine-gun rounds that served no one; no situation, surely. "And Venegas?" he asked, forcing himself to focus.

"Dead."

The slight man drew in smoke. "You see how it comes round? You of all people should—"

"I'm not finished. We were lucky to get as far as we did."

"Which is where?"

"The bottom. To save what we could."

Breaths, slow and deep. Thinking it could be worse, it could always be worse, the slight man said, "I'm trying to understand. Just tell me where."

"When I've thought some things through."

"Rique, you are trying my patience."

Engine drone. "The deal was the money. Which you'll get."

"We'll talk about it after you've slept. What about the others."

"Two dead, three burned but expected to make it.

The slight man felt a chill. "Their names?"

"Curious you should ask."

"What does that mean?"

"That knowing you as I do, I find the question out of character. And incendiary charges in *this* cargo? What does that say?"

The slight man lit another cigarette, let gravity and fatigue sink him deeper into the chair. He blew smoke upward. "You tell me."

"It says there are things that don't add up. It says that Venegas knew we were coming."

"How?"

"My thought, exactly."

"Rique, this has cost us—don't make it worse. We'll talk when you're clearheaded." Picturing what his contacts down south would do with this bit of news.

"There's something else..."

"After everything that's made this such a rewarding night? What possibly?" Listening for a moment to what was said before realizing he was inhaling the cigarette's filter and crushing it out. "You struck and sank a *what...*?"

Someone said something in Spanish, and Ben opened gummed eyes to blur, then gradual focus. A hospital room: sun pouring in through miniblinds, pastel colors, machines he was hooked up to, I.V. and monitors. And something else: short-length wrist straps.

A face bent down, round-faced and hairnetted, with a nurse's cap. The face exited, replaced by another: dark eyes behind rimless glasses, black hair pulled back, yellow shirt under a white smock. Thirtyish...*F. Ayala* on her name tag.

Then *they* flooded in: the night, the rain, knowing the thing was out there. Hearing it but unable to see it. Seeing it then.

Ben tried to rise and felt it everywhere; gently he was pushed back. "*Mi...*"—trying to think of the Spanish word—"*...esposa.*"

"The nurse has gone for your daughter, Mr. Metcalf," the new face said in lightly accented English. "I am Dr. Ayala."

"I meant my wife. And why am I tied up like this?"

Checking the machine that indicated blood pressure and pulse rate, other things Ben couldn't make out, she said, "Your daughter is a resilient young lady. You must be quite proud of her."

"Shannon's all right?"

"It was your daughter who brought you to the attention of a fishing boat by waving her shirt at them."

"Shay did that?"

"Three mornings ago, four counting today." Noting something on her clipboard as she checked her wristwatch.

God Almighty... "Where is this?"

"Hospital de San Vicente—San José. The boat ran you to a town with an airport."

"I want to know what room my wife is in," he said. "And why am I strapped in like this?"

Dr. Ayala stopped writing and took a breath. "In addition to bruising and abrasions, you've sustained possible damage to your right eardrum. Perhaps you feel also the stitches we put in to close a laceration in your scalp. And while your shoulder is unbroken, we were concerned enough to—"

"*Dad...?*"

She was all over him, then: tweaking his shoulder, moistening his gown as he kissed her hair, smelled the institutional shampoo in it. Finally she pulled back, and he couldn't recall ever seeing a face as beautiful as her tear-streaked and sunburned one.

"You okay, kiddo?"

"My wrist was sore and I couldn't get warm, but I'm better now."

"Dr. Ayala said you saved the day. Sorry I wasn't more help."

"*Oh, Dad...*"

"What is it? We're okay, right? Mom, too..."

Shay turned—just as Ayala's dark eyes met his...that's when he knew. And the moan that wrenched up from deep inside him sounded like *Angel Fire* as the ship hit her, and whatever it was they were adding to his I.V. swept in like seawater into a teak-lined aft cabin slipping down into blue-green depths.

* * *

It was night when he finally came out of it and saw her sitting there, a book in her lap.

"Shay...?"

"Dad, you slept all afternoon."

She'd been crying again; either that or the light on her flush made it look that way. He took a breath, felt it in his ribs and obliques, his hurt shoulder. Get a grip, he thought...at least for her sake.

"I was dreaming. We were eating ice cream and your voice was coming from somewhere, saying guava was your favorite."

She bit her lip, looked small in the chair under the light—a little girl putting off going to bed. "Those men made me talk to them," she said.

"What men? About what, Shay?"

"The ones who came to see if you were awake yet. They wanted to know about you and mom."

"Did they say why?"

"No. Only that they'd be back. I think they were police." She tried to off-hand it, but her expression betrayed her.

"Hey, it's all right," he said, wanting to hold her but unable to because of the straps. "That's who the hospital would think to call, a policeman. They're just making sure we're okay."

"Dad, I was so scared out there. I didn't know what to do...whether you were going to—"

"You saved us, Shannon Kay. Dr. Ayala said so."

She reached out for his hand, held it as she pulled back from the edge, and for a while neither spoke. Then she said, "I forgot. Grampa flew down, he's at a hotel. He'll be back in the morning."

Jeb, naturally, Ben thought. And yet, comforting: like the cavalry arriving to save an embattled fort.

"And a man from the Consulate," she added.

"What man from the Consulate?"

"The one Grandpa's been talking to. I guess the hospital notified him, too. He brought me these clothes."

She straightened to give him a better look: jeans and a *U.S. Marine Corps* tee under a pale-blue guayabera shirt. "Not bad, huh? Considering what I was wearing." She put a hand over her eyes. "I couldn't find her, Dad. I tried, but the lantern wouldn't work."

"You did everything you could, I know you did. Mom does, too." The bubble in his throat expanded to almost beyond breaking.

"Do you think she suffered?"

God... "I don't see how, Shay. It was over too fast."

"I couldn't stand it if she suffered. I just couldn't."

"All we can do is remember who your mom was and what she wanted for us. The best."

She thought a moment. "Grandpa wants me to go back with him."

So much for the cavalry. And yet...

He took a breath. "We can talk about that later, Shay."

"Dad, can I ask you something?"

"Anything."

"You didn't do something to hurt Mom, did you?"

Ben felt as if he'd fallen through ice and it had glazed over. "Who told you something like that? Those men?"

"Not exactly. They more asked questions about the ship."

"What did you tell them?"

"The truth. That I never saw it."

Inch-thick now, impervious to his blows as he pounded on it from below. "But you heard it? You heard me yelling..."

"I had my headphones on. Then there was like an explosion, and all this water, and—"

"It's okay. Let it go."

"Dad, they were asking about you and Mom. If you'd been having problems. Stuff like that."

He didn't have to ask what she'd told them. Her eyes said it.

23

They showed up the next day, two of them. A florid cop type with oiled hair who basically stood in the corner and a thin-haired, slightly built man in woven leather suspenders holding up tropical-weight trousers. White shirt, darting eyes, and a habit of raising a knuckle to his lips, as if to suppress a belch.

"Valentin Torrijos," he said, extending a hand to Ben's strapped right one. *"Policía National."*

Trying to keep his anger in check, Ben said, "My daughter mentioned you spoke with her. She recalled seeing some of your finest on horseback, directing traffic."

Torrijos pulled the lone chair close, seated himself. "Different, but the same idea. Your adopted daughter is a spirited young woman, Mr. Metcalf. And may I add condolences about your wife."

Ben felt the roaring return to his good ear—as if someone had turned the key on a compressor. "Do you mind an observation?"

Torrijos waited.

"I'm impressed at how versed in English everyone seems to be. Why is that?"

"For one thing, we teach it. For another, I was educated at your University of Southern California."

"Ah," Ben said.

"I perceive you're feeling better."

"But still strapped in. Any idea about that?"

Torrijos raised the knuckle to his lips. "Assuming you're ready to make a statement, Armando will start the tape recorder."

"Whatever."

Prodded by Torrijos's questions, it was as if he'd gone through it again. He felt clammy and his head ached and the stitches behind his bad ear burned and his hospital gown was sweated through, its odor like a ghost presence. "Trouble you for some water?" he finally asked.

Torrijos raised the glass with the straw, watched him sip. He lit a cigarette, nodding to Armando that he could do the same outside.

"You mind not smoking?" Ben said. "I tend to throw up."

"As you wish." Dropping it into a half-full glass of pink liquid.

"Glad that wasn't gasoline."

Torrijos took no note. "This ship you say hit you."

"Did hit us. What about it?"

"Your adopted daughter. She claims she neither heard nor saw it."

"I believe my daughter explained to you why she—"

"Plus, what I really find puzzling..."—air-conditioning whispering on as he paused—"there was no report of such a ship. Either on fire or missing that night."

"Visibility was not a high point."

"And yet," Torrijos went on as if Ben hadn't spoken, "you'd expect that if such a ship were in distress, its owners it would be aware of the fact."

"I'm not following you."

"Not one company has reported a ship like it missing in the area, let alone on fire. Odd, don't you think?"

"How do you explain the name I saw?"

"Partial, you said. *Reina* something or other..."

"You have my statement."

"For your information, Mr. Metcalf, *Reina*—which if you didn't know means *queen* in Spanish—is a common ship's name throughout Latin America. *Reina de* this, *Reina del* that...easy to recall from somewhere else. Now, as to the man you say you saw..."

Ben clenched a fist, unclenched it as he saw Torrijos home in. "I told you, the man on the bow was the same one I saw in Puntarenas. On a fishing boat."

"Sport or commercial?"

"Sportfishing. Looked like a charter."

"With no one aboard..."

"Just him."

Pursing his lips, Torrijos said, "And your adopted daughter can verify this sighting?"

"She was below."

"As she was the night you were struck."

"That's right."

He tapped the knuckle under his chin. "Amazing how you were able to see these things on such a night and with so little time."

"As I said on tape, I had the lantern. Plus our masthead light."

"Which the ship disregarded."

"Obviously."

"Because the battery was dead..."

Ben leaned to his right hand, touched his scalp where the bristle-like stitches had begun to itch. Shay's words echoed: *I couldn't find her, Dad. I tried, but the lantern wouldn't work.* "It worked when I was using it, Torrijos, I spotted the dinghy with it. It must have quit after I blacked out."

"An unhappy combination of factors."

"Tell me about it."

The eyes narrowed. "Better, I think, that you explain the gun in your pocket. How it came to be filled with spent cartridges."

The revolver...Unaware of putting it there, only of firing it, Ben said, "I used it to warn the ship off."

"Not on your wife?"

Red lit the room. "Release these straps and say that."

This time Torrijos smiled fully; crossing a leg, he smoothed the crease in his trousers. "Your adopted daughter was quite frank with us. The result, I'm told, is a woman named Loren Sanders, who has admitted the affair."

God, poor Loren; Ben's mouth felt as if he'd just spit sand.

"You told Shannon that?"

"Should I?" Torrijos rose and walked to the window. "You're an interesting man, Mr. Metcalf. Marijuana and car theft as a juvenile...a betting scandal in college...two scam implications. Hardly a distinguished criminal history." He turned to face Ben. "I have known men who simply desired to be caught. Would that apply here?"

"You honestly expect an answer?"

"My sources tell me you owe money to an odds maker not unknown to Latin as well as American authorities. They further turned up a substantial life insurance policy listing you as co-beneficiary."

"It's Kate's," Ben said with what force he could muster, which wasn't much. "She's owned it since before we were married."

"Yet she added you to her daughter's name in 1996, five years after you were married. You responded by looting it to support gambling debts."

Ben tried to recall having seen anyone following him around Newport and gave up. Which didn't mean Jeb wasn't capable of it.

"With her full knowledge."

"Before she revoked the privilege when her equity kept shrinking." Lighting a cigarette anyway when Ben said nothing. "You see how all this looks, don't you, Mr. Metcalf? A remote and distant professional woman. A philandering, debt-incurring husband. A great deal of money if someone shot her and set the propane tank to go off, thereby eliminating your adopted daughter as well." He shrugged, raised his hands. "Oh, and we've located the bow half of your friends' boat. It's on a ledge above a drop-off, no sign of the stern. But guess what it shows—evidence of fire."

"The ship was on fire. Add a direct hit on the propane, and—"

"You sell boats with propane systems, don't you Mr. Metcalf? Meaning you'd be versed in their workings?"

Aware of chill where the sweat had been, Ben just stared.

"Shall I call in Armando to amend your statement?"

"No, but you could bring me a phone."

The man followed the curl of his smoke. "Ordinarily, a lawyer would be the next step, Mr. Metcalf, but I don't see you being here that long. As your father-in-law put it, you'll be going back to face charges there rather than here. And trust me, *there* is better. Where else can you acquit yourself by blaming the police?"

* * *

Jeb descended the next morning. Ben's mouth was dry; his eyes burned from lack of sleep. Twisting in the straps, he'd just dozed off when the round-faced nurse swept in to change his bags and chart vitals. Then Jeb with Shannon—same jeans, tee, and fading sunburn, but an orange guayabera. Jeb in tan slacks, white polo, summerweight navy blazer, spit-shined burgundy loafers.

"I'm relieved to see Torrijos posted a guard," he said without preamble.

"Good of you to be so open with him," Ben said.

"I'll be open with whomever I goddamn please."

"How about having some regard for who's present, Jeb?"

"As if that mattered when you were taking my money and plotting against my daughter."

Ben was conscious of the jacaranda trees outside the window, how delicate they were in their movements: pale green filigree against the white clouds and blue sky.

"Dad, what's he saying...?"

"What I'm saying is that you'll never have another opportunity to hurt my granddaughter."

"*What is he talking about?*"

"Shay, your grandfather seems to think—"

"You mean the police think."

Ben started again. "He believes I had something to do with what happened, Shay."

She moved back—an inch, but enough. "Did you?"

Eyes fixed on her face, anything to burn it in, Ben said, "Not in a million years."

"You lying sack, tell her how truthful you've been about everything else. This woman you were screwing and—"

"Watch your mouth—"

"Your phantom ship. This man no one saw but you."

Glaring at each other, they fell silent.

"What man, Dad?"

Ben tried to focus. "The one I saw on the bow, Shay. I was going to tell you about it after I spoke with Torrijos, but it was late when he left."

"Come along, Shannon." Taking her hand. "Learn from this—what can happen when you give everything to men like these. Something my unfortunate daughter never did."

The casual way it was tossed off triggered a return of Kate's words: *"I just don't think I want to go there, Ben,"* when he'd pursued the subject of Henri. Henri and Jeb...

"What men, Jeb? Who besides me?"

His look was pure contempt. "Every boyfriend she let her hair down with to screw me over. Well, I won't have to buy *you* off. The prosecutor up there is a personal friend."

*Bingo, you SOB...*Ben said, "You know, I never understood why Henri Dufresne just gave up. *'But that old man,'* he told me. That's what he meant, isn't it? You buying him off."

"One more chisler in debt. Predictable as sin."

Shannon pulled her hand from Jeb's grasp. "You paid my father to leave me and my mother?"

"Three hundred thou—which he took. Time to grow up, Missy. We have a plane to catch."

She looked at Jeb, back at Ben.

"I don't know...maybe it is best," Ben said feeling like a fighter after too many blows.

"To be rid of him, it is," Jeb added. "Now, let's go."

"Did you hurt Mom?" Flat and even, her eyes holding Ben's.

"Never intentionally, Shay." Hearing Torrijos's again about wanting to be caught; doubt following as sure as water behind a finger withdrawn from a dike. "The truth."

Jeb snugged what looked to be plane tickets in a leather fold-over. "We're not listening to any more. Those animals you owe money to took sledge hammers to the house—*my house*—for which I intend to sue if you ever do get out of jail. After you reimburse me for the sailboat your friends the Learys already have contacted me about."

Shay said, "Is that all you have to tell me? That maybe it's best?"

"I loved her, Shay. I love you."

"Come along, Missy. Our plane leaves at ten."

"DON'T YOU TOUCH ME!"

It was so sudden, so jarring, Jeb stopped his hand in mid-grab. Which is when Shay stiff-armed the stainless-steel stand with half-filled glasses into him and Dr. Ayala rushed in with Armando.

The man from the American Consulate stopped by that afternoon. Pinstriped shirt and repp tie, attaché, the bottom half of a tan cotton suit. In his short haircut and designer hornrims, he looked about twenty-five, but had to have been closer to Ben's age.

"Mr. Metcalf," he said, extending a business card Ben took. "How are they treating you?"

Alan Killfoile; Ben flipped the card on the stand. "You've met Inspector—or whatever he is—Torrijos?"

"Chief Inspector Torrijos is an important figure in law enforcement here."

"Then you have some idea what I'm facing."

"Do you mind if I sit down?"

Ben waved toward the chair.

Killfoile spent a moment adjusting to it, perhaps finding the words, the partly shut blinds banding him with light and shadow. "You do appear to be in a spot, Mr. Metcalf," he finally said.

"Can they do this? Railroad me out of here?"

"I should think you'd be glad to be going home."

"Then you either misunderstand the situation or choose to."

Killfoile ran a nail along the line of his jaw. "There's no need to take that tone with us, Mr. Metcalf. We're only trying to be helpful."

"That may be," Ben said. "But I've lost my wife—*my wife,* Mr. Killfoile. Torrijos all but accused me of murdering her."

"I'm sure there are—"

"Plus, I nearly lost my daughter, first to the ship that hit us, then to my pirate of a father-in-law."

"We've talked," the man said guardedly.

"This while strapped to a hospital bed in a foreign country." Ben paused while he still had brakes. "Am I wrong, or would this seem a good time to step in?"

Killfoile opened the attaché he'd set down. Drawing out two passport-size folders, he laid them next to his business card.

"We were able to rush these for you. They'll suffice until you receive your permanent ones. And I've already made inquiries."

"Inquiries..."

He cleared his throat. "I trust your daughter is pleased with her clothes?"

"I don't see what—"

"We provided basics, as well, toiletries for each of you. Along with some men's things your size."

"And to the issue at hand, Mr. Killfoile?"

"Yes." He tapped the attaché, drew a long breath. "There is, it would appear, very little we can do."

"Other than cooperate with Torrijos," Ben said.

"That is correct." Adjusting his hornrims. "You see, this is a sensitive time involving certain expectations regarding hurricane aid. At the moment we're trying to keep a low profile. And from what I've seen, Mr. Metcalf, things in your case do look rather cut and dried."

"No shit," Ben said.

As Alan Killfoile rose to go, he tightened his tie. "Well, if there's nothing else, I believe Chief Inspector Torrijos has you out on tonight's red-eye."

24

Armando and another plainclothes in sunglasses showed up at four o'clock to supervise Ben's release. They stood by as he was freed from the straps, dressed himself in chinos and yet another guayabera—a pale green one also in the carry-on Killfoile had left. After signing papers brought by the round-faced nurse, Dr. Ayala extended her hand.

"Good luck, Mr. Metcalf. Your shoulder should feel better in a day or so."

"I look forward to it."

Lowering her voice, she added, "I hope you understand the straps were necessary at first."

"My daughter and I thank you for your help."

Armando and the other man then flanked him and Shay out to an unmarked brown Caprice where Torrijos waited.

"It's good to see you two on your way," he told them as they stepped inside and shut the doors. That was it for conversation as they hit late-afternoon traffic, Ben dwelling on the surreality, three going home as two. As if it were yesterday Kate surprised him with the reservations, seconds ago they'd arrived to the kaleidoscopic variety outside the windows.

Now it simply looked leached of color: ominous, a bad tape in place of what had been their life. Clouds had moved in on the mountains, many of the vendors and the traffic cops wore ponchos and hat covers. A few cars had their headlights on. As the city fell away and the airport loomed, rain pelted the hood. Ben put a hand over Shay's, found it as warm as his. But her face held no warmth, looking neither at him nor Torrijos nor the two in the front. Just out at the rain.

They stopped in a loading zone, Armando staying with the car as Torrijos and the one he addressed as Rosado escorted them to the airline desk. Through security, then, and onto the plane, already the better part of full. Leaning over Ben in the aisle seat after Rosado shut their carry-ons into the compartment, Torrijos said, "Confession is good for the soul, Mr. Metcalf—I recommend it. You'll also see I took the liberty of having what money we found sent home with your credit cards. And now, good-bye."

At least the attendant smiled as they left.

"Excuse me," he addressed her. "Is this flight on schedule?"

"Soon as we finish boarding." Light and carefree, café con leche skin—young and full of the promise of a weekend in L.A. As she continued her rounds, Ben leaned over to Shay staring at the raindrops, the mountains brooding under their clouds.

"You holding up?"

"I never want to see rain again." Not looking at him.

"Shay, it's important that you understand your grandfather."

"I never want to see him, either."

"He loves you. If he didn't, he wouldn't bother."

"Some way of showing it."

"It's what fits him. The same in your mom's case—protecting her from what he thought was wrong."

"Tell somebody who cares." Sinking deeper into her seat.

"I'm telling you because he'll be there to meet you."

For the first time, her eyes left the rain. "What are you talking about?" as Ben unbuckled his seatbelt. "*What are you doing?*"

"I can't leave it, Shay. Not like this. I have to find out what happened." Looking down the aisle before rising and pretending to stretch. Glancing around as he cracked the compartment and took out his carry-on.

"And leave me to Jeb and Big Bird? No. *No, no, no.*"

"This isn't about you. It's about your mom and what I owe her."

"Which didn't stop you from cheating on her."

"Shay, sometimes all you're able to see in the mirror is yourself."

"Then you admit it."

Now or never, right or wrong, but sick of the lies, Ben took a breath and plunged. "And there isn't a day goes by I don't regret it. You were right. I didn't deserve her and I don't deserve you, and you sure don't deserve me. Time to cut your losses."

"What—so you can cheat me, too? Dumb little Shannon you can just kiss off? Well, forget it."

Ben looked off the people who'd swiveled in their direction, sat back down with the carry-on. "Will you keep your voice down? Just do as your grandfather says. I won't be here forever."

"They'll catch you."

"Maybe." Transferring the temporary passport from the carry-on to a pocket. "At least you'll be safe."

"I mean once I start screaming."

Ben looked at her. At the hot blue eyes boring into his.

"You want me to prove it?" she said. "I'm the one who mouthed off that I hated her, who threatened her with a gun. Try leaving without me."

Sticking to groups, scanning for Torrijos-Armando-Rosado, they found an off-thoroughfare phone where Ben was able to make his *Hallenbeck Marine* credit number work. After six rings, hearing Darnell Light's voice: "*Leave your number and the time you called and we might get back.*"

"Dar, you there? Pick up, it's me."

There was a click and, "Trouble in Paradise?"

Something in the big man's tone. "You could say that."

"Well, I got enough trouble without adding yours to my bill. You understand me?"

Ben got it then—*tapped*, their working code from con days. And no time to worry about it. "Dar, I need your help."

"Yeah—when don't you?" *Keep a distance.*

"Guess it seems that way lately."

"You hear about your house? I went by there. Smashed toilets on the lawn, wet rugs, the whole bit. Smelled like an army had been shitting for a week. Some tradeoff."

Though he tried plugging in, Ben felt nothing—zero in comparison to everything else. "Jeb mentioned it," he said.

"Point made is what counts with people like Tommy, that and the vig. But that house for that debt? *Hell.* Next thing I know the cops are at my place. And what is with that?"

Ben took a breath, then another, not enough air in the terminal. "Kate's gone, Dar...while we were at sea. The boat, too. Somebody wants them to think I did it."

There was a pause. Then, "*Lo siento*, man. I didn't know. Your girl all right?"

"Good as can be expected."

"So what can I do?"

"Whatever you can spare would help."

Dar whistled softly, more alert code: *Read into my next.* "Putting me on here? I'm getting too old to have cops looking up my hole."

"I'm sorry about that."

"Sorry means shit when you got a son in prison and they know it."

Which explained the lack of an offer, even in code, to come in person, Dar's normal MO. At any rate, the man would stand out head and shoulders, a giraffe among the wildebeests—what he and Shay least needed right now and Dar could ill afford.

Thinking *Bye-bye Cherokee*, Ben said, "Lot B, area E—key under the rear bumper, ticket under the mat. Take it. Cash it out."

Darnell let a five-count pass—another system they'd worked out that Ben nearly forgot. "For what? You'd just piss it away and want more. Tough about your troubles, but you need to come north and west. First thing you do."

"What did he say?" Shay asked.

"Tomorrow morning, Western Union," Ben said over foot shuffle, a PA announcement in Spanish as they walked. "I don't know how much."

"So what do we do till then?"

"Did they leave you any money?"

"All I had on were my underpants and a T-shirt."

Ben thought a minute. "Can you fit what's in your bag into mine?"

"I suppose."

"Good. Do it in the women's room while I make one more call. Then we'll scout out the busses."

"Anything else?"

"Yeah," he said. "Cross your fingers Porfirio's still on the Leary's tab."

Porfirio was, it turned out, having heard none of any of it. Change of plans, Ben told him—only that much. And after forty minutes of offering to trade Shay's carry-on for bus fare and a few extra colónes, they found a taker and settled into the Friday night arrivals headed for San José.

By now the rain had stopped, clouds parting to reveal stars through the glow of city, a sickle of new moon. Ben found another phone and looked up *Ayala,* pausing at the nearly half page of book listings, the eleven Fs. Fortunately, just two had the designation *Dr.* before the name, no addresses given. With the remaining colónes he called both and heard her voice on the latter answering machine. He then called information, asked for the address of the *F. Ayala* number that had been hers.

Following a discarded *tourista* map, avoiding policed intersections, Ben's stitches and shoulder throbbing, they finally limped up to a mid-scale three-story apartment building with a buzzer entry. Pushing the intercom opposite the name, he heard a voice come on: "*Quien es?*" Scratchy, but hers.

"Ben Metcalf, Doctor. From the hospital. I need your help. Please don't hang up."

Surprised pause. "I have company, Mr. Metcalf. Why are you here?"

"Because you're a good person, I know that. Because I have an exhausted daughter who hasn't eaten in too long."

Shorter pause: classical music in the background, but no voices—most likely, no company. "I don't want trouble," she said.

"There won't be any, I promise. I'll even stay outside if you prefer."

Yet another pause as she thought that over, the drip-drip of a still-draining gutter off to their left. Then the buzzer.

25

The boy in the glasses kept staring at her. Not glancing away even when the girl came to stand solemnly beside him. Eight and maybe six years old.

"*Papa*," the boy shouted, making Kate wince.

"*Papa*," the girl echoed, running out. "*Sus ojos están abriendo.*"

And then Kate saw him. Behind the girl...tugged along by her. Clearing her head took a moment, blinks and opening her eyes a final time to *him*—the *Twilight Zone* impossibility of it. Perhaps an inch shorter than Ben's six-one and touched by recent sun; thick, dark hair; intense face offset by eyes the color of weathered copper.

The man from the sportfisherman in Puntarenas.

As he stood there in drawstring pants and faded Batik shirt looking down at her, nothing made sense. Who he was...who they were...why and how she'd gotten here. As if landing in someone else's dream.

"How are you feeling?" he inquired.

"Like I've been hit by a truck," she said hoarsely. "Why are these pans by the bed?"

"You swallowed a good deal of seawater. We've been returning it to the sea."

"*You've been throwing up*," the girl chirped as it all came back: impact, darkness, water flooding in as she groped for balance and the life jacket she knew was under the berth. Failing to find it as the world turned upside down. Fighting her way to the surface, breath giving out, determined to live for Ben and Shay but not finding them. Swimming for what seemed an eternity.

Which explained why her gut felt as if someone had been at it with a baseball bat, a throat that ached from retching.

"That's Abuelita's nightgown," the boy said.

"Abuelita..."

"Our grandmother."

"Papa's mama," the girl put in.

Kate struggled to sit up, the boy reacting to his father's *"Matteo"* to assist her. "What is this place?" she asked, fighting nausea. "Why am I here?"

The man gestured to the children. Reluctantly they left the room, but not before Kate caught sight of a white-haired woman in a rocker glancing up from something she was working on, male hands holding a newspaper closer to the door. Then it shut and she was left with the man from Puntarenas.

"Where is my daughter? My husband?" Lightheaded.

He leaned against a hand-painted chest, folded his arms. "I'm sorry," he said. Only that.

Kate felt a spreading cold, molten tears forming. But the cry hurt so much, she nearly doubled over. Drawing her feet up, she crushed her face into her knees and tried wrestling it back inside.

"You were fortunate," he said. "By the time my man circled back, all he saw was you—swimming as if four miles from shore meant nothing."

"You were there?"

"I was in command of the ship that struck you." Neither blinking nor looking away.

"*You what...?*"

The door opened. All concentration, the boy walked a mug and a plate of thick tortillas over, the girl clutching her hands until the boy set it down. As if it were important for the man to know, he said, "Abuelita thought she might be hungry."

"Thank her. And next time knock, then wait for someone to say enter. Is that clear?"

Though he nodded, it was as if the boy hadn't heard, so fixed were his eyes on Kate.

"*Matteo*," the girl whispered, pulling at his arm. "*Venga te.*"

"Excuse Matteo," the man said when they'd left. "He's talked of little else since you arrived."

This is not fucking happening, Kate thought, closing her eyes long enough to know from what she saw *that* wasn't going to work. Not sure what was. "And that would be your daughter?"

"Forgive my manners. Anna is six, Matteo eight."

A bubble in her throat prevented a response. Not that she had one.

"Do you feel like some soup?"

Kate tried swallowing, but the bubble was growing too fast. "If you want to know how I feel," she managed, "imagine *them* under that ocean and you in this bed. And before I eat any of your goddamned soup, *I want to know why.*" Wishing it hadn't sounded so much like a sob.

"Let me get this straight," Kate said. "You ran a ship without lights, full speed at night in a squall, into our boat—then left my husband and daughter out there?" With the soup, she was feeling a vestige of her strength, but at the same time, a numbness: rapid-fire images of Ben and Shay. "Is that how someone responsible for two children and his mother honors them?"

"You have no idea what you're talking about," he said from the deep-set window where he'd been pacing, Kate deciding from his look that she might have hit a nerve.

"Where is your wife in all this?"

"My wife is dead."

"Besides that, what have I wrong?"

"I told you, we had no time. What happened was regrettable, but I could not endanger my men in a fruitless search."

"*Fruitless...*"

"That's not how I meant it."

"The many for the few, in other words." For a moment, Kate couldn't speak. "Where is this ship now?"

"I think that will be enough questions for one day," he said.

"And I'm supposed to accept that?"

"That would be up to you."

"Like my coming here..."

He ran a hand through his hair, stopping briefly to rub his temples. "Strictly speaking, you are a complication. And I assume the sarcasm means you're feeling better."

"You haven't seen the half," Kate said looking beyond him to wrought iron fronting red hibiscus, what looked like banana trees beyond them. Cloudless sky where a hawk wheeled. Somewhere in the house a radio was playing faint Puccini: *Madame Butterfly,* she decided. "Who are you?"

He regarded her, took a breath and let it out. "Enrique Matos," he said finally. "Wiser to forget if anyone asks."

"And those bars would be meant to keep people out or people in?"

His eyes darted toward them and stayed.

"Put another way," she said, "when are you releasing me?"

"When I determine it's safe."

"Safe for whom?"

No response.

Kate said, "People will wonder where I am. My father, for one—a man of some influence." A mistake, she thought after having said it: liking neither the way it sounded nor its connotation of ransom. Yet much as she hated the idea, it could be her way out.

"You have an odd way of referring to him," he said.

"My father is who he is. Where are we?"

"Perhaps I've been unclear. The less you know, the safer it will be for you."

Not without pain and dizziness, Kate threw back the covers and set her feet on the floor, her words coming in a rush, as though from a POW film. "My name is Kathryn Hallenbeck Metcalf and I am an American citizen. I demand to know why you're holding me against my will."

Enrique Matos paused at the door. "You demand? *Mujer,* had it been up to my people, you'd still be swimming naked in circles."

Later, after she'd used the bathroom, sat on the edge of the tub until her dizziness passed, Kate returned to the clothes he'd set out: underwear, indigo skirt and peasant top, belt and matching sandals. What appeared to be a fit, though the top seemed generous.

The wife's clothes—and no way in hell was anyone dressing her. Surely not the man who'd left her husband and daughter to drown.

Kate went to the closet and, in the diminishing light, rummaged until she'd found the only black garment, a simple dress hemmed below the knee. Form fitting, but at least it made the statement *she* intended.

She'd put it on, was regarding herself in the mirror—the sallowness of her skin, shadows under the salt-stressed eyes— when the door eased open and Matteo stood there, a rectangular wooden box under his arm. Light and dark squares...a game board.

At first, in the light, he didn't see her, and her eyes went past him to the newspaper man, leaning around Matteo from chair height—as if to say *I'm here: understand that.* Then he pulled back and she was left with Matteo gaping, eyes huge through his glasses, one hand covering his mouth. As if he'd just seen someone he knew had died.

PART THREE

Shay

26

The Western Union affiliate opened at ten. As they approached it from across the street, Ben could see the clerk inside, readying for the day's business.

"Look all right to you?" he asked Shay.

She looked up and down the street, humming with traffic and light streaming through the jacarandas. "What am I looking for?"

"Plainclothes or uniformed police. Same with cars."

"It's a busy street. And you're making me nervous. Let's get our money and get going"

"You see a phone?"

They looked. Finally Shay said, "Outside and to the left. Corner of the building." Pointing it out under the shadow of a blue awning.

Ben sized it up as too close and no view of the front desk. Timewise, though, it was that or nothing. "Okay," he said. "You watch the clerk. If he acts like it's routine, wave with your right hand. If he goes for the phone or signals to anyone inside or out, use your left. Got it?"

"Sure, Dad." As if talking to a simpleton. "You really think this is necessary?"

There's very little I'm sure of. That must be obvious.

"Just be looking my way."

Ben adjusted the sunglasses Dr. Ayala loaned him. Before they left, he'd insisted on noting costs: food they'd eaten, a fanny pack from her closet, four thousand colónes in bills and coins—about twenty dollars' worth. Extra windbreaker, shorts, and sandals that fit Shay. Telling the doctor they'd send her a check when they got clear of what she asked about not once. On early call, she'd even been trusting enough to leave before they did.

121

Still, Ben hustled the protesting Shay outside almost the moment Ayala left for the bus, and for the better part of four hours they'd kept to the busying sidewalks. Then, when it opened not far from the Western Union office, a restaurant: morning hustle, left-behind newspapers, café con leche, cautiously building optimism.

At least they weren't tired and hungry, Ben thought, threading his way through the boulevarders, rising heat steaming out the last of the rain. Once on the other side, he approached the office from the phone corner, glanced across at Shay, and slotted his coins. One ring...two...Then the clerk was on—telling Ben that, *si,* they'd received a transfer of funds. Just come to the office with identification to complete the paperwork.

Ben hung up, was nearly at the window when he remembered to look across at Shay. Realizing through the traffic that she was waving and waving and waving: short sharp movements with her left hand. Pointing at it with her right.

He was back, Shay closing fast, when the unmarked brown Caprice pulled up and the cop in the sunglasses—Rosado—got out and entered the Western Union office. Guiding Shay behind a kiosk, Ben watched Armando circle the block and pull into a space, ease back and begin casing the sidewalk traffic.

"*Damnit,*" he said, shaking his head. Then he saw the fear in Shay's face, her eyes welling.

"The guy dialed a number off a card after you hung up. I thought you'd never look." Swiping angrily at tears, then at him. "Don't *do* that to me, *scare* me like that again."

"I'm sorry. Believe me, I'll try not to," he said, thinking *Kate,* that way she had when she was scared-mad, the times he drove too close or too fast. Pulling the surprised Shay to him against the memory's paper-cut suddenness before entering a leather and shoe store and steering her toward the rear entrance.

* * *

The walk to their original hotel—the square across from it, actually—took longer than Ben anticipated. When they finally got there, Porfirio, hat thumbed up against the heat, was reading a magazine.

"*Aaay*...thought you'd gotten lost," he said.

"Who, us?" Ben said as Porfirio awaited an opening, then shot into traffic ahead of a bus with waves painted on the sides. For a while he watched the mirrors for possible tails, finally conceding there were none. That, or whoever was tailing them was very good.

"You expecting company?" Porfirio asked casually.

"Not exactly."

"Anything I should know about?"

"Later, maybe."

Stone and wire fences began appearing as the city thinned. Cows with egrets on their backs. Coral trees with spiny red blossoms.

"And *la madre?* She is with the boat?"

Ben did his best with the basics, nothing about the *policía*. But they were past the ridge and on the downside before Porfirio ran out of questions and Shay came out of her implosion brought on by the original one. Asking him to pull in at a store they saw so she could buy pencils and a tablet. Same tone she'd used on the plane.

"I'm not too good with faces," she said to Ben, hers set tightly as Porfirio gunned them back onto the road amid a welter of horns. "But the man you saw..."

"The one you think is following you?" Porfirio spoke up. Directing his attention to the highway once his eyes locked onto Shay's in the rearview.

"*Perdoname*...just trying to be helpful."

By Puntarenas, she had something resembling him, some to go and not much eraser left. But they decided to give it a rest, let Ben's subconscious take over. Find someplace to hole up.

Over lunch at his cousin's, Shay passed the drawing around, though it was without detail, and Porfirio, the cousin, and his wife shook their heads. But when they volunteered their home, Porfirio translating, Ben refused as best he could.

"Why?" Shay asked when they were out of earshot. Porfirio silently unlocking the van.

"You familiar with aiding and abetting—being an accessory?"

"Who's going to know?"

"You don't subject people to things they don't know about that could get them in trouble. Same with Porfirio."

"And if they knew?"

"They won't. Not from us."

She was silent a moment. "Then we need to get some money. Like yesterday."

"You're the bank. What are we down to?"

"You don't want to know."

Ben had Porfirio drop them in front of a prosperous-looking hotel, then walked them through the heat to a group having seen better days. One three-story run-down in particular, Ben had thought out of a novel when they'd driven through before. Close to the pier and the charter boats.

As they registered for the least expensive room, bath down the hall, he asked the man where a cardroom might be, any bar with a game going. Having to pantomime the act of dealing before the man got it and drew them a sketchy grid with an X on it. Looking them all the way to where a threadbare runner led up a dim stairwell.

"Suspicious type," Ben said to lighten things—nothing he felt. "Probably a narc."

"You don't play cards," Shay said as they topped the third landing, started down a torn rosebud hallway with a lone light fixture. "Why a cardroom?"

"Relax and unwind?"

She looked at him. "Whatever you have in mind, don't do it."

"Okay."

"I mean it."

"That's what I like, confidence."

"Dad, I know you."

"Do you?" he said, inserting the key and opening to twin beds on rust-pitted frames, single chair, chest on which the ring-stained and cigarette wormed veneer was delaminating. About a hundred-twenty degrees before he could get the stuck window open a few inches.

"Think you might have found a cheaper hotel?"

"Consider it an adventure," he said. "Something to broaden your classmates' horizons."

"I'm being serious. We can't afford this."

For the first time in what seemed as long as he could remember, Ben smiled.

"I checked, Dad. There isn't one."

"Am I missing something?"

"TV—the lobby," Shay followed up. "I'm not staying in this room, and I am not going to a park to watch some stupid soccer game while you throw away our last thousand colónes or whatever."

"Children do not belong in bars."

"I'm not a child. But if I were, I've seen kids younger than I am coming out of them with their fathers."

"Those were midgets." Cracking his knuckles and bending back his fingers to loosen them, conscious of how sweaty his hands felt. What he used to take for granted—the no-limits feeling that had been his trademark—gone as sand through a hole. Aware now only of the stakes...how long it had been since—

"Midgets. Why didn't I think of that?"

"The answer is no."

You can do this, he told himself. *Kate would...*

"Sure, Dad."

The bar was up an alley between two shed-like structures looking as if they depended on it for support. Boarded-up windows fronted by *Bohemia*, *Imperial*, and *Carta Blanca* signs, rust streaks from a metal one that had spelled out *Pollo Frito* before *Coca-Cola*. Nobody around outside. Inside, however, the place hummed: long bar crowded with working men hunched over chicken in baskets or yelling at the two bartenders, the waitresses running beers. Stamped wainscoting painted aluminum, blade fans stirring up the smoke, kibitzers surrounding a pool game. And in back, a table where Ben reluctantly led Shay—asiding to her as they ran a gauntlet of eyes, "Tell me again why I agreed to this?"

"Because I'm going to behave and spot things you might not see alone?"

"Not it."

"Because I refused to stay in that awful sweltering room, and outside might not be safe?"

"That's the one," Ben said. Pulling out his colónes and wadding them to look like bankroll, plenty more where that came from. Smiling at the unsmiling men around the table. "*Gentes...habla Englais?*"

Two hours later, Shay over his shoulder nursing a root beer the waitress brought her along with a bar stool, Ben figured he'd won about a hundred and ten American. Bluffing down, running hands, counting cards, sizing up. Surprising himself with how close to the surface it had been. Heat rash from a still-potent allergy.

Not to mention the flush he'd put to his cover: a baby-sitting gringo in for a lark while mama shopped. Knowing Dar would shit at his no-prisoners lack of caution, but not caring. Needing only to win the next one and the next one and the next. For Kate...

"*Pinche momento,*" a competitor who'd been eyeing him snapped after tossing in his hand. Coming up with a scaling knife he set next to his dwindling stake. "*Jundio* got his girl flashing him our draws."

"*I am not,*" Shay insisted.

"It's all right," Ben said, shuffling the cards preparatory to his deal. Figuring from the man's unaccented English, lighter skin, and chin scruff, an expatriate or maybe half-American. Fisherman or charter crewman from his knife and a blue-ink spiderweb radiating from his elbow.

"Wrong idea, friend. Just killing time."

"Killing us, you mean," the man said. "Taking it out of my kid's mouth."

"*Daaaad...*" Not Shay's usual chip.

"Then maybe you shouldn't be here," Ben said, looking around the table for support and finding none, the others beginning to murmur. What plowing through yellow lights turning red, sparking off the speed bumps got you, he thought. Hearing Dar say again, "*Never let 'em feel you didn't sweat for it. Ebb and flow.*"

"No hard feelings," he added.

"*Cabron's* working us. Probably ain't even his kid."

"I am, too," Shay said.

"And I say we get it back." Repeated in Spanish.

The murmurs grew louder; pool and bar patrons began to take note, their noise gradually subsiding. Ben saw one of the keeps walk a baseball bat over to the corner and leave it there, the other slip a two-by across the front door.

"You want it back, earn it," he said, glancing at the bat. "One cut—winner take all."

"Dad, that man locked the doors."

"I saw him, hon. It's to scare us."

"Leave the money...it's not worth it."

Scaling Knife said, "Good advice, sport, you want to leave with what's still in your jeans."

"Cut the deck," Ben repeated. "You win, you pick who gets the take. I win, we walk with it. Fair and square."

"Like we believe that."

"Suit yourself. What's it going to be?"

The men hesitated. Buzzing in Spanish, they leaned toward Scaling Knife while Ben sized up their chances of bolting without serious damage as nil. After some rapid-fire exchanges, the man was back in his face.

"I say the alley, but *mis compañeros* are old and willing to play it out. Go ahead."

"Your call—you first."

The man glared, decided, reached for the deck. Lingering there, he turned over a jack to a murmur of assent.

"I get to shuffle?" Ben asked, gesturing.

One by one they shrugged.

Eyes on the man's, Ben shuffled: once, twice, three times...

And cut to a queen.

Curses flew, and groans, but the men let it go as he stood. And on their way down the length of the bar, Shay looking straight ahead, Ben feeling the wad in his pocket and a target on his back, he actually expected the beer bottles to reach the unbarred door before they did.

"Did you know you were going to win?" Shay asked after they'd circled the hotel to make sure they hadn't been followed. Beelined in and up the stairs to their room.

"That was the idea, anyway."

"How did you know?"

"Don't sound so impressed. It's nothing I'm proud of."

"Shut *up*. I never even knew you played cards."

"Let alone bent the odds? Like the man said, it's work." Regarding the pile of bills spread out on her cheap coverlet and trying to get past the lie. "What did we end up with?"

"A hundred twenty-two—that is, if I have it figured right." Checking her calculations again. "And you were great."

"No," Ben said, aware of the slickness on his palms again. "I was stupid—way too anxious. Playing like that, I nearly got us hurt. And that's your last time in a dive like that."

"Will you please not do that?" she said after a pause.

"Not do what?"

"I don't know—make me feel less or something."

"Sorry. I'm winging it here."

"So what do we do now?"

Wondering if that were the genie he felt bouncing off its cork or just his stomach doing flips, Ben went to the window, tried to let his adrenaline blow out into the humid night. His fear of what he'd opened up and might not be able to put back in clammy on his neck.

Trying to keep what he'd exposed them to out of his voice—willing it out—he said, "I was watching the faces in there tonight, comparing them to our man. Can you sketch in this light?"

***

Two in the morning, the umpteenth tracing, pencil shavings all over the money, she had it. At least as near as Ben could come: that arrogance he'd seen in the eyes, the set of face and jaw. Not art-class perfect, but close. Enough to do what he intended.

Lying in the dark, unable to sleep, Shay breathing across from him and a wind rising outside, he could feel the cards again: old friends willing to forgive and forget, take him back unconditionally. And yet Ben knew there was nothing unconditional about any of it. A knife next to a hand that would have used it had the others been more encouraging or Shay not been there was all the proof he needed. One thing certain: She was not going his route—that little flare he'd seen in her eyes when she'd spread out their winnings.

Maybe it came down to Jeb, about the battle he'd be sure to wage for her. About the right thing and the long run, never Ben Metcalf specialties. But that was about tomorrow.

Already the sky outside was showing him today.

27

Enrique saw Anna take the stuffed toy the man offered her. He watched her go inside as the man shut the door with a last sour glance at him. Policy: instituted because of last time, when Enrique lost it and broke some things, nearly the man's arm. Just something he had to live with until they gave him another chance.

He was returning to his truck when the cell phone rang. Pineda, he hoped, telling him the barge was in place, that they'd start diving tonight. That more of the cargo remained than they had estimated.

"*Pineda...?*"

"You can put to rest a disturbing rumor I heard," Valentin Torrijos said. "Involving the sailboat you hit and the woman who was aboard. One Kathryn Metcalf."

Enrique said nothing.

"You sent a boat back. You have this woman now. Or so it goes."

Enrique took a breath. Picturing him in his leather suspenders, rolled sleeves, and tuft of beard, he said, "You base your actions on rumors?"

Torrijos said, "Don't play games with me, Rique. Are you out of your mind?"

"To be in this deep with you? No question."

Long pause. "And what have you told her?"

"Nothing she didn't know or deserve to know. That is, before—"

"First the ship's location, and now this. How am I to trust you?"

"This from you?"

Enrique heard the sound of a lighter being struck. Deep inhale, a matching exhale. And traffic noise...a pay phone.

"There is a way out, you know," Torrijos said. "Put the woman out. Tell her the *policía* will escort her to safety. That's all you have to do."

Enrique let his silence speak for him.

"Read me. It is not a suggestion."

"The woman is dead."

"Dead..."

"Too far gone—pneumonia from the seawater," he said. "I've already disposed of the body."

"You'll show me the grave, of course."

"*Con gusto.* You can order the sharks around."

There was a longer pause. "Then I suppose you have nothing to fear. Except for one small thing."

"If you're referring to yourself, don't bother."

"Rique...we're business partners. Remember?"

He watched a pair of mallards chase a drake around the clinic pond, then give up as she joined a group preening on the bank. "You plan on getting to it?"

"*Que vida*," Torrijos said. "First the ship, then the sailboat, now the husband."

"What are you talking about?"

"A fishing boat found him and the daughter. They were flown to San José, where I learned of it—fortunately, in time." Torrijos rustled paper. "Benjamin Metcalf, small-time hustler...believable to no one, even the daughter. He did, however, elude my men at the airport before looking up the doctor who treated him—a softheaded sort who agrees her position at the hospital is important enough to inform us if he recontacts her."

"You mean you underestimated him."

"Once. Still, I wonder..."

"Don't stop there."

"How it feels to be him," Torrijos said. "Knowing that only you can clear yourself by finding the man who caused your wife's death." There was a long exhale. "From pneumonia, you said?"

"You're saying he saw me that night."

"Not only you, *compa*. Guess what Spanish word for queen he also remembered."

* * *

Kate watched Matteo closely; Matteo watched Kate. She was reaching for her bishop, preparation for a strike down the right side, two moves and maybe snag his rook, when she saw the hand creep up to his mouth, the crinkle at his eyes.

"What...?"

Matteo had come in after knocking and, though checking out the indigo skirt and peasant blouse she'd put on in place of last night's black dress, had stuck to his daylight mission. Asking her was she up to a game of chess. And she'd agreed. Mostly because anything beat sitting there—agonizing—wondering what it had been like for Ben and Shay. If anyone had looked for *Angel Fire*. Where they'd even look. If anyone had contacted Jeb. What her life had become in a hellish instant.

So there they were, locked in here-and-now, her mind embracing the diversion, rising to it. As yet no sign of the self-appointed arbiter of her fate. No idea who the son of a bitch was dealing with, but about to find out.

"*What...?*" she said again.

Matteo pointed to his knight. At which time she realized at least one of her bishops was lost, likely the game.

"Do you always treat guests this way?"

Shrug—his eyes going to slits behind the glasses.

"And who do I thank for your expertise?"

"Abuelita taught me," he said. "But I use a chess page now."

So they had a computer. And a Web site meant a phone line.

"The better to beat your sister, I suppose."

"Anna is getting better," he said brightly. "Yesterday we played two hours."

"And your father?"

Matteo's snort was her answer.

"I heard an engine earlier."

"Anna's appointment..."

Sounding so normal to her it almost brought tears. "Oh? What appointment is that?" Not expecting his response.

Hesitation, then, "I'm not supposed to talk about it."

"Talk about what?"

132

"Will you play another? I'll be black, if you like."

There was a knock and Enrique Matos entered. "Matteo," he said, "go see to your sister."

"Can't Abuelita? We're playing—"

"Anna needs you."

Matteo sighed, looked at Kate to no avail. But before the door closed behind him, she heard the sound—indistinct, yet identifiable.

"Why is Anna crying?" she said to Enrique.

"Anna misses her mother."

"Matteo said..." Before she could stop herself.

"Matteo said what?"

"Nothing. That he wasn't supposed to talk about it."

Enrique went to his spot at the window, bent over the sill, gazed out at the banana leaves. "You have other children?"

Kate let it go.

"Once a month Anna goes to have her blood cleaned. Soon it will be twice, then four times, then every day. It hurts her. She cries."

"I'm sorry."

"I am, too, for what good it does."

Kate tamped anger at all of it: the injustice of not being able to fight back. Which as far as she was concerned, as of this moment, excluded her. "So far, I'm willing to overlook this episode as well-meaning," she said. "But only if you end it now."

He looked at her without speaking.

"Me...here. This incarceration."

Still nothing.

"*Perdoname.* What would *you* call it?"

His gaze left hers, drifted back outside. "You want to know about incarceration, spend time in a Latin prison," he said. "You'd be surprised what you take from it."

"That's useful. What, exactly?"

"Like it doesn't end. Just wraps itself around and drags you back if you threaten the bond."

"Everything has chains. Is that where you got the tattoo?"

Enrique Matos touched a spot high up on his shoulder before glancing at the hummingbird on his forearm. "What do you do in life that gives you such a tongue?"

"Telecommunications equipment and networking. Vice president of marketing." Speaking, she thought, of chains—golden and otherwise.

"A name like Kathryn Hallenbeck Metcalf, I thought it something like that."

"Kate," she corrected him. "So you could set ransom?"

"That's what you think this is?"

"What I think is that you've been to prison."

He didn't answer her.

Engage and process; keep it going. "I assume you're aware of the ramifications. The risk to Abuelita and those children?"

He seemed to catch himself. "What concerns me now is keeping you alive."

"Oh? And why would that be a problem?"

"I need to tend to Anna." Heading for the door.

"Leave it open on your way out. Tell your friend out there to make a sandwich. End of complication."

Enrique Matos paused to look back. "For once, try understanding instead of just opening your mouth."

"For once, give me a reason."

She could almost see the wheels turning.

"It's very simple," he said before letting himself out. "People more than capable of it want you dead."

Enrique was listening to Anna read and wondering about the woman in his wife's bedroom, Serena's retreat from *him*—the symmetry of that—when his cell phone rang.

"How many times," Abuelita said from her rocking chair. Not looking at him: "*Teléfono* is not welcome."

"*Si, Abuelita.*" Canceling the ringer as he set Anna down and told Pineda to hold.

"This is still my house. Even your father respected that."

"*Por supuesto.* I'll be outside."

"Not soon enough." Then, "Bring your book, Anna."

As Anna was relocating, Enrique left the house and walked among the banana trees. Silver glints just visible through the shifting green.

"You need to be here," Pineda said when he reconnected.

"Just tell me the barge is in place and you've been down."

"It's not that. It's about what I found."

Here it was, Enrique thought—the final shitload through the fan.

"No lumber, no cotton," Pineda came back through static. "Some of the copper's fused. No surprise."

"What, then?"

"It's the sub-holds. The ones I hadn't been able to get to before?"

He vaguely recalled. "What about them?"

"Not so much the holds, as what's in one. Watertight containers. About three dozen of them."

"Can you bring them up?"

"That might be a mistake, Rique. How soon can you get here?"

"Look, is there some problem I'm—"

"Just get here. So far, I'm the only one who's seen them."

28

Ben left the mercado with the coin-operated photocopier in back, Shay downing a sugar-patterned *concha*.

"How many of those does that make?" he said.

"I don't know, three or four. Why? They're cheap."

"You should be having milk with it."

"Your point...?"

"What we can't afford are slumps."

"What about you?"

"I had something before you got up," Ben said.

"Yeah? What?"

"Never mind."

They found a bench and split the copies he'd made, the man's face having reproduced better than Ben could have hoped. Just one afterthought: a tweak of the eyebrows following his five AM walk, unable to sleep. Still sore, though much improved over the day before.

He held out a copy, the inscription translated for them by the night manager, Shay's neat writing under the face. *Recompensa—10,000 colónes para la información que conduce a esta hombre. Contestaciones terminantemente confidenciales: Reward—10,000 colónes for information leading to this man. Replies strictly confidential.*

Four spaced reply lines underneath.

Fifty dollars American the bait.

Which left them precious little once the cost of the room was factored in, the copies, what food they could get by on without Ben having to go back to cards. Just enough to function. Let alone avoid whatever police effort Torrijos had mounted.

"One more time?" he asked Shay.

"Show them to people leaving and entering, anyplace the locals patronize. No gringos, cops, anybody in uniform.

Judgment with caution. You'll be working the street fronting the water."

"And if one responds?"

"They write their information and a point of contact. Hang onto the turn-downs and *Yo no sés*."

"And if they don't speak English, maybe we can get Porfirio to translate." Then, to her troubled look, "You okay with this?"

"It's not that..."

Ben waited, struck by how achingly young and pretty she could look without the filters. The occasions to which she'd risen and was rising, the lines charged across without a look back. At the same time, sad at what was retreating in the distance.

"Dad...do you ever wonder if...I mean, if Mom..."

"Might have made it?" he finished.

She nodded.

"If anybody could have, it was your mom, the swimmer she was." *And try every waking minute.*

"Which means no, doesn't it." Toeing the ground.

"More that it would be a miracle." He smiled to drive the point home, the possibility in it. "But then, look at us."

"Right...look at us."

"Shay, I'm going to tell you something I barely admit to myself." Taking a breath to steel himself. "I heard her scream that night. Your name."

"*Oh, God. Are you sure?*"

He nodded, hearing it again: *Shaaaaaaaay*...like a rip in the heart. "I've tried not to delude myself, give *you* false hope. But it's there. More to the point, she'll always be inside us. Especially when I look at you."

"You mean that?" Eyes wide with shine.

"You *are* her, Shay. More than I could dream."

He held her to him, kissed the top of her head, saw the tears as they broke. She was starting toward a man and woman getting out of a truck, the flyers under her arm, when he added, "Plus you can draw faces like nobody's business."

Shay paused, turned and faced him, brushing at her cheeks.

"Dad?" she said, backing up.

"What is it?"

"Don't get carried away."

Finally losing sight of her around a corner, Ben crossed three streets, started in on the waterfront bars and hangouts, in three hours getting back not so much as a glimmer. He crossed *Paseo de las Touristas* to the pier and tried there, watching the expressions of those who at least made eye contact. Another hour of head shakes, shrugs, and *no hablas,* he tried some of the charter boats. He was getting nowhere when he heard, "Still pushing your luck, I see..."

Ben turned and saw Scaling Knife on a deck in the shadow of the commercial fishermen he'd just polled, the men already back to work as if he'd been a cloud passing between them and the sun.

"Where's your accomplice?" Scratching the elbow radiating his spiderweb tattoo. "Before I use you for bait."

Ben said, "I didn't come for trouble. I came to show you something."

"How you fucked us at cards."

"I need your help."

"You'll need more than that, you don't haul ass out of here."

Ben handed him a sheet, watched for reaction, saw something in the eyes—lightning in daylight periphery on a far ridge. Thinking you saw it, but not sure.

"Your idea of a death wish?" the man asked, looking up. "Working us on our own turf, then shoving some *pendejo's* face in mine?"

"You know him?"

"Why's it important?"

"Ten thousand colónes says so."

"Fucking fifty bucks," he said. "Got to be worth it to mean anything. Go home, and take your young stuff with you. Either that or drop her off for a real education."

He was bending for a coil of rope when Ben charged, using his angle to drive the man down into the open cabin. Like going for a loose ball: using an opponent for cushioning, driving the wind from him.

Flailing, the man got his knife free of its scabbard. But Ben had the leverage and jammed the blade between the deckboards, snapped it off at the haft.

"Now," he said, trying to focus on his pulled-back fist and not the pain in his ribs. "Who is he?"

"*You just landed...in deep shit.*" Half-smile, a half out-of-breath grimace.

"*Who is he?*"

"I don't know."

"Then who does? Your nose in trade for a name."

Three blocks up and six over, sweating from the heat and limping, Ben stood outside the alley bar where he'd won the money. Short breaths as he stepped in from the sunlight, let his eyes adjust. This early, none of last night's crowd was around: couple of guys nursing beers, two women playing pool. The bar waitress who'd gotten Shay her root beer.

"*Perdoname...*" he said to her back. "*Habla Englais?*"

The waitress turned, flashed on him, smiled slightly. "Not much choice in a place like this. Where's your daughter?"

"Helping me with these." Handing her one of the flyers.

Handing it back after a look, she revealed nothing. "You must be insane coming back here."

"Do you know this man?"

Her eyes left him for the room. "You have any idea how many men come in here? Most I stay healthy not knowing. Those I have known were too many."

"The guy with the scaling knife..."

Slight nod. "Delura."

"Your name did come up."

"*Boca grande.*"

"Please. It's important."

"Look," she said, her eyes coming back to him. "I got a daughter, too—younger than yours. And you want a beer or something? They ride my ass for talking."

"Glass of water, if it's no trouble."

With a glare from the bartender, she went and drew it for him, brought it back.

"Thanks."

"*Por nada.*"

"This man is responsible for my wife's death."

Glancing over her shoulder, she fished out some coins, put them in his hand. "Pay phone's in back. We have *policía* here."

"Thanks. I've seen them in operation."

"And everybody has a reason." Starting to wipe down a table.

He said, "Look, if it's the money, I'll go fifteen. I just don't have any more."

"That's why you were here last night?"

He nodded.

"Loco then, loco now," she said, shaking her head. "Keep it up, they'll be fishing you out of the estuary." Without looking at him, leaning closer. "Look, this town's rough and getting rougher. Why not take that girl of yours home instead of this—"

"*Louisa...*"

Ben followed the voice, saw the bartender's scowl. He ran some fast odds and decided to gamble. "We're at the San Felipe, room 304. Her name is Shannon, mine's Ben."

"Why tell me?" the waitress said, a *there-in-a-minute* wave at the barkeep.

"Call it a hunch," he said.

Shay was at their spot, the bench where they'd been that morning. "Sorry about the time," he said, joining her. "You about ready for some food?"

"Not really," she answered vacantly. The stack of flyers beside her seeming to Ben about the same as when he'd left.

He reached over to feel her forehead, then his own, and shrugged. They both felt hot and sweaty—five o'clock and still about ninety. "Let's go," he said. "I'll pick up something we can eat in the room."

"Dad, it's not that. It's what I saw when I went into a restaurant to use the bathroom." Tears forming in a face the picture of fatigue.

"What, hon—what did you see?" That flutter: watching a wave you thought you could bodyboard suddenly become a monster. Knowing it was too late as you kicked like mad.

"Us," she said. "Pictures from home on television. Our names and everything." She took a shuddery breath, failed to stem the tide, and let out in a teary rush, "I kept wanting to ask somebody what the announcer was saying, but I was afraid to. *Just so afraid...*" Letting Ben draw her in as the wave slammed him off the bottom and an image of Jeb turning over family photos answered *that* question.

29

Ben was dreaming of water rising in their room. Not being able to break the window as Kate beckoned to him, her face jolting him upright, gasping for air. Which led to a five AM haunt of the waterfront while Shay slept, the bar district and backstreets. Stopping short of the north end, the estuary where *Angel Fire* had been moored. Knowing he'd have to get to it sometime. After all, it was there the man's eyes had nearly burned a hole in Kate. There must be someone who either knew him or knew of him.

As he walked, it flashed: the other half of what he knew. *Reina* some-damn-thing...flogging his memory but unable to get a hit on the remaining letters. Just the incessant churn of fire, water, darkness, hurt.

But memory might not be his only source.

Waking Shay, he invested in a breakfast both agreed was necessary, then passed time with the flyers. At ten they found the library, asked the girl for the newspapers, waited as she found someone speaking better English who helped them with papers as far away as South America. And, when they found no mention of a *Reina* listed in current departures and arrivals, the back issues.

While Shay searched them, Ben asked the silver-haired man who'd helped them if he could cross-reference the word *Reina*— a ship's registry or something. Moments later, the man was back with a thick volume Ben scanned until he realized it was printed in 1992.

"Would there be anything more current?" he asked.

"The question is, is your ship?"

"I don't know that."

"I see," the man said. "We are somewhat down the list, sir. San José would be the place."

"Any chance you're linked by computer?"

142

"When they run."

"The more things change, right?" Ben said, sensing the man's frustration and easing up a notch.

"Our salvation and our cross—and so much for that. Vacationing?"

"Researching. I'm a writer." Seeing Shay emerge from the stacks flashing a scowl and newsprint hands before entering the ladies room.

The man's eyes lit briefly. "Retiree from Garden Grove and an avid reader. Anyone I'd know?"

"It's doubtful. Would there be a better time to check back?"

"As you're a writer, shall we say four o'clock?"

"Much obliged," Ben said as Shay came out of the ladies room shaking her hands.

"No writing, no books," the man replied. "No books, no readers. No readers, no library."

The rest of the day they worked the estuary side: yacht club employees, working docks and boatyards, service facilities, the *mercado centrál.* Each yielding similar results: momentary interest in the reward, hesitation, headshakes or shrugs. As if the man in the sketch had simply motored up the estuary and vanished.

At three o'clock, their agreed-on meeting time, Ben was glancing around for Shay, one eye on the ice-cream vendor dispensing cones under a blue umbrella, when he saw her.

Parking lot across the street...

Two *policía* holding copies of the flyer.

Cooked, Ben thought, approaching as casually as he could under the circumstances—*end of the line.* Surprised as he walked up, sweating, at how calm Shay seemed.

"Hey, Dad," she said brightly; then to them, "*Mi padre.*"

Ben forced a smile, up close saw the *policía* looking eighteen or nineteen, began breathing again as they nodded respectfully to him.

"Sorry you lost relative," the nearest one said with coaxing from the other. Smoothing a line of mustache that looked applied with pencil. "We keep look out." Tipping the flyer he'd rolled up to his cap and letting his eyes drift back to Shay.

"Passport, *por favor?*"

Hoping his sweat was understandable in the heat and figuring they'd already asked for Shay's, Ben handed over the temporary document to the mustached one, waited until it was handed back with a "*Gracias.*"

"*De nada.*" he managed.

"We find," the one with the flyer said. "But next time, us first."

Last smiles at Shay, they headed off to resume their beat.

"Give me heart failure, why don't you," Ben said as he and Shay wasted no time in the opposite direction.

"They just wanted to practice their English."

"Lost relative?"

"I had to make up something after telling them the name of our hotel. They kept asking and I couldn't come up with another," Shay said. "Besides, they were sweet."

He cocked his head at her.

"*What...?*"

"Just wondering," he said. "Of all the girls walking around, why they picked you to approach." Seeing her color rise, the twinkle and spreading little grin, and taking pleasure in them. "As if I didn't know."

The librarian-retiree from Garden Grove wasn't there. "Left early," the girl pronounced smilingly in English when Ben and Shay stopped back at four. "*Esto es para usted.*" Handing Ben a folded printout. Seventeen *Reina* candidates listed by shipping firm, six constructed after 1992.

He handed the list to Shay, who'd dropped into one of the chairs lining a planted divider. "Recognize any of these from your newspaper search?" Sitting down beside her with an atlas he'd asked for.

She unfolded a piece of paper from her pocket, worked her way down a short list. "No. One maybe, but the date's wrong."

"How so?"

"From the...Guayaquil paper...Ecuador. *Reina de Aconcagua*—however you say it. Wasn't scheduled to leave until three days after we were hit. See...? March 24. I went past our cutoff by mistake."

"And it was in port then?"

"Arrived...March 14, same day we did."

"At least it's on the west coast. Any other possibles?"

"Four. *Reina del Santos*—Recife bound for Lisbon. *Reina de las Islas*—Montevideo for Malta—"

"Hold on," Ben said, turning pages. "Okay..."

"*Reina del Rios*—Buenos Aires for Dakar." Pausing to let him catch up. "A second Buenos Aires, *Reina de las Pampas,* for Kyoto. All earlier departures, but—"

"The wrong direction," Ben said closing the atlas with a thump. "Or too far south, or some other damn thing, or *every* other damn thing."

Shay looked at him. "You want to know about this other *Reina?*"

"No point if the dates are wrong."

"You're sure you got the name right?"

"Thank you, I can read."

"Being dark and all," she said. "Could it have been—?"

"You heard me."

"So?"

He swiped at it, but it was out before he could kill it: the rat carrying the flea carrying the Black Death. "So *you* didn't hear the ship."

"I had the phones on." As if he'd slapped her. "*And what is it with that?*"

"Shay, wait a minute."

Even the girl behind the desk looked up as Ben put down the atlas, followed her out into the heat. Clutching herself as if she were cold and refusing to look at him.

"I'm sorry," he said to her back. "It just seems like everything we try, everything I do, puts us farther out. Just zero luck."

She turned to face him. "Don't you think I wish I hadn't shut her out? That I could have done something—anything?" Crying now, her shoulders shaking as two boys on their way in glanced discretely away.

"We are doing something, Shay, the best we can. That's what we have to remember."

"Well, it sucks," she said vehemently. "Every bit of it."

"No kidding and so what," Ben said, putting his arm around her. "How about something to eat, then another crack at it?"

Feeling better after some *gallo pinto*, the least expensive thing at a street stand, they hit it again. But the library yielded nothing other than more frustration. They were walking through the hotel lobby when the night manager handed Ben an envelope from their message slot.

Upstairs, after he'd tried the window for more air and failed to budge it, he took out the note and read, *Two cops were here. The big ships and cruise liners put in at Puerto Caldera. There's a bar off the docks called Papagayo. Ask for Xochitl (pronounced So-she). I never saw you—L.*

Thanks, Louisa, Ben thought, Shay's eyes wide after he explained who'd written it.

"What do we do now?"

"Caldera's about ten miles south," he said, gathering up their things. "I saw a bus stop beyond the depot, sailors waiting there this morning. There's less chance they'll be watching it."

"What about our bill?"

"They have our deposit. I'll send the rest later."

"You've done this before, haven't you?" she asked him on the way down the stairs.

"Makes you say that?" he asked.

"Just a feeling."

"Whatever you're thinking, I resent," Ben whispered as they hit the first floor, edged around to all clear: front desk clerk reading a magazine, exit sign above a door at the end of the hall off the lobby. Checking for alarms first, he eased the door shut behind them before starting down an alley heading east.

"Jen always thought you'd make a good Badboy," Shay said.

"That's encouraging."

She glanced over her shoulder. "Are you sure about this? It's so dark already."

"You read the note," he said. "It's a matter of time until they show up. Besides, I've got a feeling dark is better where we're going."

30

Enrique eased *Machacha* in beside the darkened motor barge. He threw her into neutral, came down off the flybridge to toss a stern line to one of Pineda's people, the same man who'd secured the bow. After five hours in wind-driven swells, the drop in decibels was dramatic. Four miles off, land rose in the afterglow of a sunset like the sparks from a spilling blast furnace.

He killed the big Volvo-Pentas and looked over the side. Aided by the clarity and underwater lights the divers had placed inside the hull, he could see a blackened crosstree, its metal boom twisted by the fire. Air hoses fostered a welter of bubbles; a crane operator maintained tension on the cable disappearing into the froth. Apart from the winch and an air compressor, none of the usual noise and chatter prevailed.

Torpedo-like and a quarter mile distant, the assault boats maintained watch—he could just make them out. Meant to intercept the curious, engage interlopers, or get everyone off the barge should the need arise, they showed no lights beyond the occasional flare from a match head or lighter.

Pineda dropped onto *Machacha's* rear deck.

Enrique followed him into the cabin, shut the hatch, drew the curtains as the man poured guaro into two glasses. "Later for me," he said.

Pineda shrugged, downed one and half the other, gasping from their fire as Enrique watched him, the tension in his face.

"You doing all right?"

"Nothing a week asleep wouldn't cure," the man said, shaking loose a cigarillo from a pack and lighting it with a plastic lighter. "So far, we're about a quarter through. The heat's twisted everything inside and the crane's too small for speed, but it's the best we could come up with. Not being able to salvage in daylight doesn't help."

147

"Other boats or planes?"

"Two choppers headed south. Beyond that, nothing out of the ordinary."

Enrique thought a moment, tempted to try and halve the timetable by running day shifts as well. And throw *all* caution to the winds..."Probably best to stick to what's working," he said.

"Agreed."

"Beltran been heard from?"

Pineda shook his head. "And Durantes said to send his cut to his wife. How's Chávez doing playing nanny?"

"I don't think I'd mention that word to him."

Pineda's grin lasted almost as long as his host's. Then in a serious tone, "What about your *niña?*"

Enrique felt a tightening. "Braver than both of us, Pineda."

"*Pobrecita.* Makes you wonder what God's so distracted with." Nipping a finger off the guaro. "And your mermaid? *Reina del mar?*"

"Kate, I'm to call her."

"I see," Pineda said with some amusement "And that's all you're going to say?"

"You remember the name Torrijos?"

"Heard enough about him. Enough to know your old man never trusted him. He's behind this?"

Nod. "Plus he found out about her."

Pineda exhaled smoke toward the hatch. "What'd you tell him?"

Enrique related what he'd said: the woman dead and disposed of—*comida de tiburón*—hoping the lie had held water. And as Pineda tossed off the remaining guaro, poured himself another, he tried to fathom the turning of it. Not that things still couldn't work out, *had* to work out. But it was like a ship the men were convinced was jinxed, nothing able to change their minds, only to reinforce. Even the most innocuous of incidents.

"So what are you going to do?"

"Mark time, lay it out for her at some point. Already Torrijos has a watcher. Abuelita's seen him."

Pineda sat a moment before draining the glass. "And how is she?"

"As ever. Told me to tell you she thinks you should have run for the hills when you saw her son coming."

"I do love that woman," Pineda said. Shaking his head and squinting against the smoke. "Rique, what's really brought you back to all this *tripas*? With your background."

"You ever try applying for my kind of work with a piracy rap?"

"Not in this life."

"Been to the house lately—seen the way she lives? What the place has turned into?" Rubbing his temples.

"Couple of times before you were released," Pineda said, tamping ash into his hand. "You know there's no shame in asking for help. Sometimes people like to know they're respected enough to *be* asked. You weren't the only one paid a price when Rudolfo went down."

"And you have a big mouth."

"Damned if you can't sound like him, too." Pineda's sudden grin showed gold as *Machacha* rode a swell.

"My point is, some things you get to refuse, others you don't."

"Which means what? Torrijos pulls the strings, you dance? Good thing Rudolfo ain't hearing it."

"Nobody has to like it, Pineda"

"And nobody takes the risks you are unless there's more to it—even a crack at Venegas. What's he got on you?"

Enrique tried taking it on, but his eyes slipped to the bottle and he reached for it. "This why you were in such a sweat to get me here?"

"Rique, I used to take you out to piss in the creek behind your house. Even then you used to make me turn around. Like there was something only you knew about the process. That's how I'm feeling now."

"Look, I know you mean well, but—"

"Forget it, I know." Pineda tossed off a last belt. "So what's she like, your mermaid?"

Enrique was conscious of the winch straining as something heavy cleared the surface and was lowered to the barge.

"You're aware a fisherman picked up the husband and daughter?"

Pineda nodded. "Word came down. Though nobody's seen the fisherman in a while."

"They were lucky to be in hospital when Torrijos heard. But they made a mistake. He'll kill them both when he finds them."

"Not to mention your mermaid. You tell her they're out there trying to find you?"

"And watch her tear down a wall so she can die with them?"

"You still haven't answered the question." Winking at him.

"You called, I'm here. Get to why."

But it was as if Pineda were plucking her from the water again, filling his eyes with her. "*Manolete*, what a sight," he said. "Little thin for my taste, but—" Jerking up from his own glass as Enrique smashed his against the bulkhead.

"The men are due for a break," Pineda said. "We'll go then." Cabin lamps catching the beads of sweat on his forehead, droplets on the wetsuit in his hand—an hour after he'd left and come back.

Enrique began rechecking his own gear: fins and half-wetsuit, BC vest and tank, weight belt and dive knife.

"You still mad at me?" Pineda's face like a moon in the open hatch.

"No. How long we going to be down?"

"Twenty minutes. Unless you want to sightsee."

"What I want is to be back by morning."

Pineda grinned and ducked back out, leaving to him the stars, the winch idling down, low voices on the barge.

Enrique slipped out of his clothes and into his suit, checked the gauges a final time, then stepped to the fishing deck where Pineda was spitting into his mask, dipping over the side to rinse it. Strapping on the knife and his dive watch, he saw shadows assisting two divers aboard the barge. Then Pineda, raising his face from putting on his fins, his doubled-over gut looking like a black basketball.

The guaro gone from his voice, Pineda said, "I want you to understand something before we check out what's below. Love, I get—except where it endangers my people. We clear on that?"

"What do you think?"

"That I've seen too much not to spell it out."

Enrique looked up at Venus. "Now one for you," he said. "Am I going to hear any more about this?"

"Just that it's good to see something besides Serena written all over you. And don't forget your torch." Grinning as he swung into his tank. Taking in the mouthpiece, a sample breath before sealing the mask.

Enrique did the same. Then over the side, last check before starting down, trying to remember the last time he dove. The water still held residual heat; as one, tiny fish flashed and were gone. Equalizing the pressure in his ears, he followed Pineda toward the greenish glow. Past the blackened crosstrees and a twisted catwalk, *Reina*'s discolored hull extending fore and aft beyond his vision, what was left of the boom and a cargo winch that had melted of its own weight through the decking. Despite his impatience, able for the first time to appreciate the fire's effect.

Already the plating and bulkheads were abloom with rust: dried blood in the light. Debris from the salvage work floated like dust in sunlight. Shadows traced the jagged tears in the holds. What was left of the coamings hung like wry smiles.

Grouper, sea bass, and parrotfish swam in and out of the openings, toward his mask then leisurely away. Enrique checked his depth meter: eighty-eight feet. As it always did, the otherworldly sound of his released breath reminded him of a science fiction film. That feeling of isolation—as if he were the only human alive on a hostile planet.

Pineda led him into the ship, past the main burn-through. He shone his torch into holds marked by what had once been lumber and now was charcoal—fire-desiccated twigs scattered by the inferno. Over, then, to a pile of loose and fire-bonded ingots showing raw marks where the divers had been at work. Pineda pointed, picked up an unfused copper ingot, let Enrique feel its weight, then led him aft through the burn to a door he levered open with the prybar on his belt.

They entered to chaos: boxes, shelving, tools, crates—tipped and piled atop one another by *Reina*'s impact with the bottom, Enrique thinking cause and effect. Sickened by the part he'd played in bringing a ship similar to the ones he'd trained on to this. Trying instead to focus on Anna leaving the clinic, Matteo playing chess, Abuelita laughing and smiling with them. And someone else if the candles he'd doubled in the Virgin's alcove at chapel interceded for him.

They swept their torches, no exterior light penetrating this blackness, the working hold well behind them now. One more stop, Pineda gestured: through yet another sprung door, bubbles rising to collect against the I-beams and plates. As if collaborating their reentry into a world of cloud and breeze.

At first Enrique didn't pick out the bodies. Two of them— wide eyes peering from inside the steel-meshed area Pineda had forced open and was now inside. Shirtless, in fatigue pants, the one nearest the door still gripped a combat knife, while the other hovered like a guardian angel above the things Pineda was moving toward.

Enrique made a sign of the cross, broke from the horror to see Pineda playing his beam over elongated olive-green shapes strapped to pallets ringed to the deck. He ran his finger along one's flange and gasket, felt the regularly spaced snap-locks before directing his torch again to the white letters repeated on every container. First a thirteen-digit serial number, then, stenciled in English:

NOM GUIDED MISSILE SYSTEM
W.A.S.P. II
INTERCEPT AERIAL M43

Amid thoughts not unlike a darting school of bait fish, Enrique looked up to find Pineda's eyes locked on his.

31

Kate was awake and staring at the ceiling when Anna slipped in with their breakfast tray, plus a book they'd been reading in English. *Charlotte's Web.* Kate swung out of bed, took the tray just as their juice glasses were about to tip into the bowls of cornmeal and brown sugar.

"I'm not too early, am I?" Anna said brightly. Pink pants, blue sneakers, faded purple tee with cartoon characters on it.

"No, sweetheart, I was awake. Just let me use the bathroom."

After she'd freshened and dressed, Anna asking about or commenting on each step, Kate relocated Matteo's game board and they started in on banana and milk. The routine to date: Anna in the morning, Matteo or sometimes both in the afternoon. Diversion, but not unwelcome, allowing her to learn things that might prove useful. Because one way or another she was getting out: the right instant, a combination of things breaking her way—not even that many, she thought. Just a crack to slip through and the will to do it.

Out to what she could only speculate, though she was sure Enrique's comment about people wishing her dead was fabrication. Logic dictated he'd have killed her already—easier still, let her drown. Not entangle himself with this bizarre arrangement.

Kidnapping, she reminded herself. Engaging family or no.

She had a breath-catching flashback: a book she'd read called *The Collector,* in which a twisted young man abducted and imprisoned women like butterflies, with similar results. However, any relation to that scenario vanished when she met Anna's uptilted face.

"Matteo says you play chess," Kate said.

Her mouth full, Anna nodded vigorously.

"And Abuelita taught him?"

153

Another nod, light threading her homemade page-boy. "She used to play on a team."

"But Matteo uses a computer?"

"Only at Jaime's—his friend. Abuelita doesn't let Papa have a *teléfono* in the house."

Find the phone, call for help or connect out...And so much for that plan.

Anna leaned over, beckoned her down to whisper, "But he has one in his pocket. He calls people with it. Outside."

Some hope there, Kate thought.

Anna took another bite, chewed reflectively as wind rattled the banana leaves. Suddenly she said, "Matteo's mad at me." A little smirk behind it.

"Why would Matteo be mad at you?"

"Because I hit him with my flute when he was trying to take it away. Right here..." Reaching out to touch Kate above her ear.

*Jesus Lord...*Kate masked her horror at the underside of Anna's forearm. She was about to ask where a bruise like that had come from, when she saw the puncture mark in the center and remembered: *It hurts. She cries.*

"I'll bet you were brave," she said. "Want to tell me about it?"

Anna shook her head, but a smile lurked, Kate marveling at how of the moment kids were. She felt a wave pass through her: similar small moments with Shay when *she* was growing up. Which threatened to become a tsunami unless she rode it out. Almost getting away with it.

"Why are you sad?" Anna said. "Is it because of me?"

"No, hon. It's because..." Almost losing it, then. *Damnit, not now.* "Have you been outside yet? It's such a nice day."

Anna put down her spoon and put her arms around Kate's waist. Held on tight as Kate tried to keep her shoulders from shaking and the tears off Anna's neck.

Gradually, it passed. They were through breakfast, Kate drifting as Anna labored through the story of Charlotte and her friends, when Kate sensed that Anna was building up to something.

"I'm sorry," she said. "Did you have a question?"

Anna's hands left the book, began fumbling with each other. Suddenly she blurted, "Are you going to be our mama now?" And to Kate's stunned look: "It's not my fault. Matteo made me ask."

The worst had passed by the time Kate heard a knock and Abuelita entered. Faded print housedress, red-and-white kerchief, mud-spotted walkers, Kate guessing that she'd been outside working. Perhaps a garden beyond Kate's window view of the sagging plantation.

"Is okay?" she asked from the door.

"Why not?" Kate said.

Despite a thin frame and a lined face that must have marked her once as striking, she looked radiant. From doing, the exertion that went with it, Kate figured; beyond that, however, something in her eyes. A knocked-down-got-back-up quality. An intelligence.

Abuelita seated herself in the wicker chair Anna had occupied. "You are better," she said.

"And ready to leave."

"Is dangerous to leave. Enrique not say so?"

Deciding that avenue was futile, Kate said, "My people believe I am dead. How do you think they feel right now?"

"Enrique, he knows." Tucking up a fallen wisp of gray. "He get back early this morning. Sleeping now."

"Back from where?"

Abuelita undid the kerchief, wiped her face and throat, dropped her hands and the kerchief to her lap. She let her eyes rove before returning to Kate's. "Anna tell me what she ask you. She is sorry."

"It's not her fault."

"I am sorry, too. For your loss."

Kate was about to ask why thus far Abuelita's had been the only apology, but she settled for a nod. A moment went by in which she was aware of the birds outside, Anna playing in the swing mounted in the big guanacaste tree, Matteo thumping a ball against the porch. Freedom sounds.

Abuelita got up and whistled lightly from the window. Immediately the thumping stopped. Coming back to the chair, she said, "They bother you, *los niños?*"

"No," Kate answered truthfully. "Anna said you played chess?"

A smile lit the woman's eyes. "Long time ago."

"And you've lived here a long time?" Trying for something she might use.

"Enrique's grandfather and I build when banana *muy bueno*. None here then. Long way from town."

"How long?"

"*Siete kilos.*" Catching herself as she said it.

Fifteen miles, Kate thought. *Damn.*

But the old woman had her eyes down a different road. "Banana, they get sick then. No good no more."

"And Enrique's grandfather?"

"He becomes fisherman—hard work. One day, he go out and not come back." Her eyes taking in the room as it might have been then. "Forty-one years—longer than Enrique born."

*Forty-one years...*Watching the room blur, Kate felt a hand on hers, heard Abuelita asking, "*Quantos años tiene su niña?*"

"Fourteen," Kate said finally. "Fifteen in July."

Abuelita's gaze softened. "I am that age when I become lost to my mother. *Mi familia.*" Pausing as though seeing it again, she said, "Enrique worry about you. You listen. He is a good man, good to *niños* and to me. Good to his father, my son—too good, I think." Pushing up from the chair and tapping on the door for the guard to let her out. "Good to you, you think about it."

"I'll keep it in mind," Kate said to her back.

32

They found the Papagayo, but no Xochitl on duty. "Day off," the bartender shouted to Ben over the music while Shay regarded the stripper gyrating under a color-alternating spot. Try tomorrow when the morning shift comes on.

"She wasn't much older than I am," Shay said, walking back to the hotel they'd found nearby—that virtue, at least. A step down even from the San Felipe, their monetary situation worse each time they looked.

"Don't get any ideas," Ben told her.

"How I made money on my vacation, which I then gave my dad?" Grinning and giving his shoulder a rap.

"Especially the last part."

The grin faded. "Are we safer here?"

"Nothing I'd count on."

"What about changing our look or something?"

And how obvious is that, Ben thought.

Finding a store still open, they purchased cheap tropical shirts, brown hair color for him, a pair of scissors they used to cut Shay's shoulder-length into a parted bob, Ben careful to dispose of both trimmings and dye plus Alan Killfoile's donated guayaberas.

"How do I look?" Shay asked tentatively.

"Gidget goes Costa Rica." Rubbing his hand across the week of stubble he'd also darkened, checking it out in the shard of mirror. "Me?"

"I don't know—you in a beard?"

"That's it?" Ben said.

"Too bad Jen's not here."

"Never mind, I'll take it."

Settling in then, he feigned sleep, waited for the deepening sounds of her breathing before easing out. At sidewalk level the air was heavy with impending showers, low clouds giving the lights a surreal bloom. Save for small groups of late revelers on their way back to the ship whose profile stood out against Puerto Caldera's tanks and cranes, its spotlit waterside freighters, the streets were largely empty of people. The place itself reminded him of a small-scale Long Beach or San Pedro...hustling to catch up like the taxis running double shifts to the restaurants, bars, and clubs. Cash as cash can while the liners were in town.

The Papagayo was still crowded: *cruisistas* three deep, margaritas in hand, while a rougher trade off the freighters and docks whooped it up from center tables, the fringe of booths against the louvered windows. At the opposite end, behind more louvers and a palm tree, service staff folded napkins around tomorrow's place settings.

The stripper finished her routine and left the stage. Ben ordered tonic water dressed as a collins and started playing with dice left by the man before him. In roughly an hour of give and take, hook and reel, he'd won about forty bucks from an accountant who was finally dragged off by his wife. He then put the colónes and three more pseudo-collins to work, launching first into challenges with the loud group to his right, then his left, the entire bar, and finally the table trade. Double the dice take from the way his pockets felt: entertainment value, the money feeling like tips after a performance.

Trying to look soused, Ben glanced around, thinking Darnell would enjoy this. On second thought, remind him that whatever was going to make or break the evening would happen soon, if at all, a certain attrition having taken place among the *cruisistas*. He let an elbow slip, righted it as a Latin man in a booth with four others detached himself and came over.

"Having fun yet?" the man said in a light accent.

"This? Coupla high school tricks is all."

Saluting Ben with his empty whiskey glass, he said, "My friends and I were wondering if you played *fiero*."

"S'late. Should be getting back to the ship."

The man drew a fat clip of bills from his pocket.

Bingo. Ben gave him upraised eyebrows. "Might if you tell me what it is."

"Like blackjack, only with two up. We start a game when the *nortes* go back to their pillow mints." Close enough for Ben to smell his citrus cologne. "We thought you might want to give us a chance to win some money back."

Ben winked broadly. "Or lose some more."

The man tried, but his smile looked run through a mangle. "*Con su permiso.*"

"Well, hell," Ben said, draining his mock collins and eyeballing them, in general a cut above those in Puntarenas. "How hard can it be?"

The man snapped his fingers toward the bar, pointed at Ben, and shouted, "*Uno más para mi amigo y todos nosotros.*"

"Same for me," Ben slurred. "Only make it a double."

Thirty minutes into the game, the bar empty except for one woman with her back to him nursing a drink, Ben was up a good hundred. But it had been too accommodating, too smiley—too facile. Yet with no crowd left for cover, the trick was to disengage without getting your head bashed, a talent Darnell always insisted came first. He was about to tell the five about his fellow shipboard gym staffers coming to pick him up when he felt in spades whatever'd been put in his drink.

He was getting to his feet, the room going psychedelic, floor rising like a Waimea swell, when the one who'd recruited him to the table said to laughter, "*Borracho* Yankee shithook. Who's the sucker, now?"

He was choking. In a puddle formed by the rain that had started while he was in the bar, dragged to it by the men who'd gone through his pockets as he attempted Beatle songs and they poured rum over him.

But it was okay. It would all be okay.

If he could just sleep...

Bobbing up, however, a child's toy that wouldn't stay submerged, was the nagging idea that this was *El Stoppo Grande.* That the puddle might as well be the Pacific for all the effect he was going to have on it.

He felt himself rolled to the side, a snort of air.

"Get up," a female voice said.

"*Goway.*"

"Now. They may be back."

"*Wanna sleep,*" he mumbled, proud to be so erudite under circumstances clearly calling for repose. He was conscious of being muscled against a wall, of coughing until he threw up, of being lurched down the alley. Leaning and walking, walking and leaning. A door closing. His head under a shower that felt like needles before landing in an oversize chair.

"I know you," he managed after his second coffee stayed down. "You're the stripper. Without your—"

"Louisa called me. I am who you came to see."

"Xochitl..."

She nodded.

Ben finished with the towel she'd given him, draped it over the chair. "The bartender said you weren't—"

"They do that."

Ben focused harder. Shay had been right to a degree; she was young, but not as youthful as the lights made her appear. She wore a green tube top, light denim jacket cut above the waist, black capris. Lipstick to match her auburn hair, a gold navel ring.

Wary eyes caught the light and fired it back.

Ben said, "You're strong, I'm glad to say."

"Years of practice with drunks."

They spent a moment regarding each other, the last of the rain tapering off eaves near the window. Ben's mouth tasted like the alley had smelled, the headache he'd felt when he came to having localized behind his left temple.

"Would you have any fruit?" he asked, massaging it with a palm. "It doesn't matter what kind."

She came back with half a scored mango and four aspirin tablets.

"Thank you," he said, downing them with the last of the coffee then starting on the mango. Letting it soak in and root out. "You from here?"

"Brownsville."

"Thought I heard Texas in there. Better money here?"

"Relatives. Which is why this is going to be a short conversation."

"Louisa tell you who I was looking for?"

She nodded.

He said, "I didn't bring a sketch, but I can get one."

"Doesn't matter. Go back to your ship or your hotel or your country. This is no place for you, asking what you're asking."

Ben rubbed the mango off his hands. "Sorry. I can't do that."

"Louisa said you have a daughter. If you can't do yourself a favor, do her one."

"I'll be going now," he said. Getting up unsteadily, then thinking to ask, "Where are we?"

"Six blocks east of the bar. And I won't ask where you're staying because I don't want to know."

"Thanks," Ben said. "For everything."

Xochitl bit her lip, appeared to come to a decision. "Look," she said. "The only reason I'm giving you this—" reaching under the cushion he'd been sitting on and handing him an envelope—"is because one of the relatives I mentioned went out a few years ago and never came back, except as something they had to X-ray to find the bullets." She drew a cigarette from her purse, put it in her mouth without lighting it. Removing it then as if she had no idea how it got there before throwing it aside. "That's who you're dealing with here. If not him, then somebody like him."

He turned the envelope in his hands.

"One more thing. You made it out of that alley yourself."

Ben said, "I want to pay you something." Reaching into first one empty pocket then the other. Thankful only that he'd left his passport in the room.

The best things in life are free.

But you can give them to the birds and bees...

"Just go," she said. "Okay?"

But he already had the flap up on the envelope, had seen what was inside. Colónes—some twenty bucks' worth. Plus a folded piece of paper.

He was sitting there trying to find the words to thank her when Xochitl walked over and opened the door, stood framed in the false dawn. "Call us even. It's what they paid me to dope your drink," she said. "And don't look at me like that. Life's tough enough."

Setting out through an offshore breeze laced with passion flower, the sweetness of *copa de oro*, Ben located the bar, empty and dark at this hour, then backtracked to their flophouse, praying that Shay hadn't wakened while he was gone. Not knowing what to do or say if she had. Checking his watch and seeing he'd shot almost seven hours.

It was only when he'd slipped into the stale warmth of their room and she'd resumed the rhythm of her breathing that he came down long enough to unfold the piece of paper. Able then in glow from the window to make out the letters forming the single word printed on it.

M-A-T-O-S.

33

Later in the morning, over *huevos* and melon, Shay having forgiven him long enough to eat, they agreed to split up, meet back at the café at one.

"You *will* be here?" she said.

"I will be here."

"No more wild hairs?"

"Earth to Shay, I was a hundred up," Ben said, his mickey head not completely gone, despite the additional aspirin he'd purchased and wolfed down.

"And now?"

"You mind giving it a rest? Who's the dad here?

"What have I been saying? Money I can get. You they don't make anymore." Rising with her stack of flyers and heading out the door after a glare back at him.

Like Kate when she was riled—fierce logic rampant. Which triggered more feelings he tried to suppress by setting off in the opposite direction, flashing his sketches. But it was as Xochitl had intimated: One look, those showing even a hint of recognition, and the disengagement was total—shake of the head and *no sé.* Ten o'clock came, eleven. Finally twelve, with nothing to show except even more snappish moods when they reconvened.

"*God,* my feet are killing me," Shay said.

"Join the crowd."

"They're all lying."

"You want anything?" he asked as they slid into the booth.

"We can't afford it."

"Not that again."

"Okay, you tell me..."

"*Enchiladas con queso,* two forks," Ben said to the waiter who'd appeared, a different one from morning, this one not bothering to write it down. "One coffee, one *leche.*"

After the young man cast a look at her and left, Shay said, "It was like I had leprosy."

"Then it wasn't just me."

By way of response, she pulled from her stack of flyers a foot-printed and food-stained section of the English-speaking newspaper and laid it down.

"That looks appetizing," he said.

"It was under a table." Unfolding it for him as she spoke. "When I saw it was in English, I picked it up and thumbed through it."

Shay's milk and his coffee came. "Reminder of home?"

"Hardly," she said. "Check the bottom."

He did and caught a partitioned line of callouts, one in particular: SHIP DECLARED LOST. STORY, PAGE 11. Flipping inside and catching a small map with a star indicating the location. Under the same headline, the subhead: NO SURVIVORS IN REINA DISASTER.

Glancing up at her taking a gulp, then back, Ben read:

Guayaquil, Ecuador. *Like the Great Lakes ore-carrier* Edmund Fitzgerald, *the freighter* Reina de Aconcagua *is thought to have been the victim of a giant wave reported closing on her around midnight, March 24. Marta Fuentes, spokesperson for Galveston-based RouteStar Inc., owners of the North Africa-bound* Reina, *revealed the ship's last transmission indicates the wave likely rose under her stern to drive her down by the bow. "As a hammer would a nail," Fuentes stated.*

Compounding the tragedy is confusion over her last recorded position brought about by "storm-related transmission difficulties" and the recovery of neither survivors nor bodies. However, debris linked to Reina *was spotted on the Colombian island of Malpelo, which would indicate the ship, with its load of lumber and hemp, plus cotton acquired at Guayaquil, is resting in deep water off Colombia's west coast. The tropical-Pacific storm lashed French Polynesia and the coasts of Chile and Ecuador before dissipating into night showers throughout the gulf regions of Panama and southern Costa Rica earlier in the week.*

In her statement, Fuentes further noted that, "Though waves of this magnitude are rare, we can never underestimate the power of nature. We therefore reluctantly announce cessation of joint search efforts between RouteStar and the Colombian navy. Full survivor benefits will be going out with our deepest sympathies to those whose pain we can only imagine." Reported by Omar Barrera.

"Well?" Shay said, after he'd looked up. "One of the possibles, right? *Reina de Aconcagua?*"

"Not if you go by the dates." Ben pulled out the library printout, ran down the name, and showed her. "Scheduled to leave March twenty-fourth. Three days after we were hit."

"You're not struck by the coincidence?"

"Torrijos said *Reina* is a common name for ships, and the list confirms it. Even if that were our *Reina*, what was it doing so far north of where..."

Their food came, the waiter setting it down with another look at Shay before checking a table across the room.

"Where it sank?" he finished.

"Couldn't it have turned around?"

"You mean been lost as well as on fire."

She drank her milk.

"I'm not being critical, Shay, just realistic."

"Then *you* come up with something."

Two policemen passed by the restaurant, Ben letting out a breath when their attention stayed outside. "I thought we'd agreed. Snapping gets us nowhere."

"Fine." Jamming her fork into an enchilada and burning her mouth before dousing it. "*Perfect.*"

Ben pulled out a cracked ballpoint salvaged from the street; with it he drew a crude timeline in the article's margin. Calling the waiter over, he asked for change for a bill before sliding out of the booth.

"Where are you going?" Shay asked.

"Phone—I'm taking your advice."

"You going to tell me who you're calling, or do I just sit here like a lump?"

"Galveston," he answered, pointing to the part he'd circled: *Galveston-based RouteStar, Inc.* "And you're welcome to come along. Just hope Jeb hasn't changed his phone code."

* * *

After what seemed an interminable wait, Shay finally using the bathroom, Ben got past the recorded instructions to a female voice asking who he was holding for.

"Marta Fuentes."

"Ms. Fuentes is in a meeting," the woman responded. "Do you wish her voice mail?"

"Not if she wants the inside on a class-action suit before the press gets hold of it." Ben said.

Shay's eyes widened; there was a pause, kitchen sounds as the doors opened and closed, then, "One moment, I can transfer you now."

Giving Shay a wink as the line clicked and a female voice said, "Marta Fuentes. To whom am I speaking?"

"Benjamin Metcalf, Metcalf and Metcalf. Representing the *Reina de Aconcagua* families. I trust your associate informed you of the amount we're asking?"

"No, she did not."

"A hundred-eight, Ms. Fuentes. As in million."

Shay shook her head.

"Tell me, Mr. Metcalf," Marta Fuentes came back. "Why is this the first I'm hearing of it?"

"Because I thought you might appreciate the courtesy—time to assimilate, that sort of thing. If I was incorrect, don't hesitate to save me the time."

"I might have a moment to listen."

Ben felt a vein jump, let his eyebrows follow for Shay's benefit. "Ms. Fuentes, your ship was seen heading north off Costa Rica three days before your report indicates it sank off Colombia. Quite a discrepancy, I'm sure you'd agree."

"And that is the basis for this call?" Amused-sounding.

"Believe me, we are taking the matter very seriously."

"From a soup kitchen?"

"I happen to be hosting a media event. Shall I put my client on?" With the receiver partly covered and a look at Shay, whose eyes had widened again, he added, "Mrs. Villagomez, could you please—"

"That won't be necessary. Seen by whom?"

"A reliable source."

"*Quid pro quo*, Mr. Metcalf."

"Ms. Fuentes, your word that the sighting was in error might help steer us both from the shoals. On the other hand, the lack thereof might take us where no man has gone before, financially speaking."

"I'm not sure how much more explicit I can be."

"I have every confidence."

As if she were listening to someone, there was a muffled pause, then, "What about faxing you a copy of the report?" Briefer pause. "The detailed report."

Ben shuffled his flyers. "Already on my desk."

"That is impossible."

"Time wasted underestimating me could be better spent, Ms. Fuentes."

"Very well. What is it you want to know?"

"A satisfactory opening might be how a ship not yet scheduled to leave Guayaquil could be seen so far away three days prior."

Release of breath. "*Reina de Aconcagua* left port earlier than was listed, if that's what you're referring to," she said. "Surely you've checked it with the harbor authorities."

Like a pull-up jumper you weren't expecting, Ben rebounding with, "March twenty-first, of course." Figuring the worst she'd do was correct him.

But she didn't. Which meant he had at least a benchmark, thumbs-up at Shay as Ms. Fuentes said, "What wasn't in the report for obvious reasons was that *Reina* experienced engine trouble. A full day passed until we could secure the parts and helicopter them to the ship, two more to affect repairs." She let a moment go by. "Do you see what I mean about the impossibility of your sighting?"

Ben consulted his timeline, the article's map of Ecuador, Colombia, Panama, Costa Rica. "North Africa-bound," he said, avoiding her question. "That would mean east through the Canal."

"Correct. With a stop at Cartagena."

Colombia—Caribbean side. "Apart from the credibility of our witness, what engine trouble?"

"Shaft bearings, undetected in port. You have no idea the damage they can cause. Usually the time involved is far greater."

Ben's heart sank. "We'd have access to the repair records?"

"All but the ship's log, which went down with her."

"This debris you cited…"

"Company-issued PFDs," she said. "Life jackets—matched to the *Reina de Aconcagua* through purchase orders. Foodstuffs of a similar nature." Taking an audible sip of something. "Are we shedding some light here?"

Just then the waiter emerged with a full load and spotted Shay. Not far enough from the door, however, its backswing sending four heaped plates, glasses, and flatware to the tiles. By the time Ben was able to hear again, Ms. Fuentes was deadpan.

"And that would be the other shoe dropping?"

"Something like that."

"A note to end on, Mr. Metcalf—or whoever you are."

Nothing to lose at this point, Ben said, "I assure you that sound was nothing compared to the ship that hit our boat and drowned my wife."

"You'll forgive me for not making the connection to RouteStar."

Ben took a long breath. "Meaning if it turns out to be yours, Ms. Fuentes, God help you."

"Mrs. Villagomez…?"

"My fourth-grade teacher I had a crush on, Shay."

"I'm impressed."

"You should be," Ben said. "She was hot."

They were headed for the entrance when he saw the two policemen from earlier squinting into the restaurant's interior. Men, not boys as in Puntarenas. Starting in through the patio diners.

He grabbed Shay's elbow. "They can't have seen us yet. Side entrance."

"There is no side entrance."

"Kitchen, then. Come on."

She did, darted ahead, around the corner and into the waiter, sending him sprawling into the mess he was cleaning up. Ben pointed to himself and Shay, put a finger to his lips as the cops walked in the front.

"*Policía*," Shay said. "*Por favor. Please.*"

The waiter was glancing between her and Ben when she reached up, pulled his head down, and kissed him. For a second he just stood there. Then he pointed to the men's-room sign, checked inside and nodded, beckoned Ben over.

"No way," Shay said, following. "Teamwork, remember?" Over to one of two stalls each entered while the waiter closed the doors.

"Pull your feet up," Ben asided to her. "And snap the lock."

"What lock?" she said.

They heard a closet door opening; wheels, then, and the sound of water.

"What's he doing?" Shay whispered.

"I think he's still in shock. I know I am."

"Big deal—I've kissed boys before."

"Wrong answer."

"Will you shut up?"

Mop noises, water flooding in around the commodes—the mop being slapped into the rolling bucket, footsteps giving way to restaurant noise. Ben realized the waiter had left the men's room door open and thought *smart kid.* Then he heard them, official-sounding voices peppering questions: far too rapid for his say-again-*más-despacio* workplace Spanish, the waiter responding in the same fashion. He heard the scrape of shoes, Shay's little intake of breath, then nothing...almost feeling the cop's scanning eyes.

Finally there was a more deliberate exchange, more scrapes and a ten-minute wait punctuated by a male voice complaining loudly in English about not being able to use the toilet. Wet footfalls, then a rap on the doors, Ben noting the *Cuidado— Piso Mojado* sign at the entry.

"Okay now," the waiter said. "I say I think you here, but not sure. Leave before toilets back up."

"*Gracias*," Ben said, tapping his forehead to praise the kid's quick thinking.

The waiter cast expectant eyes on Shay, who smiled, glanced at Ben and echoed his thanks. Adding a shrug followed by, "*Es mi padre.*"

The kid looked resigned. "*Su hija es muy bonita,*" he addressed Ben. "You leave through *cochina*—kitchen." To Shay then: "You need, I here. *Buena suerte.*"

Kissing her hand before they took off.

"Don't even *think* it," she said to Ben moments later, three shades of flush as they wove their way through the blue flames and sizzling grills, cooks and condiments. Pushing out into hot light flaring off the whitewashed buildings.

They found another phone in an upscale hotel near the beach, Ben figuring Torrijos would concentrate on the low end based on his perception of their finances. This time both were able to fit inside the carved wood booth with glass panels in the doors.

"You have the article?" he asked Shay.

"Here," she said, pulling it out from the small of his back where he'd tucked it.

"Glad somebody's paying attention."

Minutes after Ben punched in the newspaper's San José phone number, a man picked up in Spanish.

"*Habla Englais?*" Ben asked, caught off guard.

"*Supuesto.*"

"Omar Barrera, please."

"Not in. Voice mail?"

"But he is in Costa Rica..."

"With him, one never knows."

Ben messaged with the booth phone number and enough reference to the article to tempt the man—he hoped—into calling back. Saying it was two-fifteen, that they'd be there every hour starting at three. Hanging up as Shay took a breath and looked at him.

"What."

"It just hit me. You were a *hundred* up last night?"

Ben shrugged. "For all the good it did."

"Going to tell me how you did it?"

"It's cheating, Shay. No better than that."

"So? You won."

"No I didn't," Ben said. "I stole to survive. Winning's when you compete for something."

"Come on. Just tell me."

"Why—so you can fleece poor Jen?"

"And who else have *you* fleeced?"

Payback time, read 'em and weep. "All told?" he said. "You're looking at him, kid." But from the shine in her eyes, she didn't get it. How could she?

"Fathers are supposed to teach their children. Especially adopted ones."

Ben yawned, suddenly drained. "Any law says we can't take it out by the pool?"

"*Dad, wake up.*"

She'd pulled the newspaper off his face and was shaking him. "It's almost three."

Ben dug in, this dream having been of the three of them collecting shells on a white-sand beach while *Angel Fire* rode at anchor. Wanting it to be real more than to wake up at all.

"Okay," he finally mumbled.

"Come *on.*"

Stiff and shaking out cobwebs, shells, and sand as he walked, he heard the phone ringing and hustled, finally reaching out to dial tone. Glaring at the receiver before thumping his hand against the booth.

"Great," Shay said. "The guy could be anywhere and we could be in jail in an hour."

Ben dialed the newspaper: *Come on, come on, come on* until he reached the same voice, asked was there a chance Omar Barrera had just phoned him from there.

"Lucky you," the voice said. There was a delay while he was put on hold, then an extension was picked up.

"Yeah?" Sounding like a long wet lunch.

"Omar Barrera?"

"Already told you—it's in the mail."

Ben explained it was about the *Reina de Aconcagua* article.

"The rust-bucket? What about her?" Drunk-sounding *and* suspicious.

"I have reason to doubt some of the conclusions."

"No shit. How you feel about a long walk off a short pier?"

Ben took a breath. "The report it came from—RouteStar supplied it?"

"You're implying I don't do my homework?"

"Mr. Barrera, at least let me get off the dime here." He took a moment to find the words, Shay mouthing *What's wrong?* before he came up with, "Are you a betting man?"

"What's that got to do with anything?"

"Coincidence, and how it sits with you. I have reason to believe this *Reina* might be the ship that sank our sailboat. Several hundred miles north of where it was supposed to have gone down."

"*It* meaning your sailboat..."

"*It* meaning *Reina*," Ben said, trying to hold on to his patience.

"Lighten up, that was a joke." Omar Barrera coughed, hawked his sinuses. "What you're saying is the tub didn't sink."

"If it did, not where the report indicates."

"Don't trust old RouteStar, huh?"

"Let's say the boundaries are strained."

"You have proof, of course."

Ben hesitated. "Not in so many words."

"But for reasons you've yet to tell me," Barrera said, "their ship is elsewhere."

"That is my strong feeling."

"Ah. Have a nice day. Mr...."

"Metcalf," Ben said. "And please don't hang up."

Pause, a rustle of paper followed by more shuffling. "The *tourista* the cops think blew up his wife?"

For a moment, Ben was unable to speak; finally he said, "Lost her to that ship, Mr. Barrera. Have you any idea how that feels? My daughter and I do."

"Look, I'm sorry. I also suggest you let the *policía* handle it. They're actually not bad."

Through hammer pulse, Ben racked his brain and got a hit: paper covers stone. He said, "If nothing else, does the name Matos mean anything to you?"

There was a very long pause—so long Ben thought the man might have hung up save for the soft click of a keyboard.

"Where did you say you were?" Omar Barrera asked abruptly.

34

Enrique tapped on Kate's door as she was applying a shoehorn she'd found to the plaster around the window bars. Only about a hundred years to go.

"Come in," she said, blowing residue off before tossing the shoehorn in among Serena Matos's things.

He entered in gray cotton pants, leatherweave shoes, a well-washed chambray shirt. She could see the fatigue and strain in his face, a deepening of the lines around his eyes.

"Tough day at the office?" she asked him.

"You could say that."

"And here it is, only afternoon." Before a little chill of cognizance swept over her. "Is it Anna?"

"No. Not Anna."

"Then what can I offer the returning hero?" Eyes casing the room to cover her transparency. "Bird calls? I've been working on my parrot sounds."

"I thought you'd like to take a walk."

"You're serious..."

"Have I your word you won't try anything?"

She just looked at him.

"No games," he said. "Yes or no?"

"Yes to whatever I have to do to get out of here."

He opened the door wider, and it was like stepping into an old hacienda film...*Captain from Castile* or one of the *Zorros*. Heavy furnishings, dark with age and spread with once-colorful cushions. Wood table and matching high-backed chairs through an archway, arch-shaped windows glowing with daylight-splashed greenery. Braided rugs on terra cotta floor tiles buffed nearly black. And, as she walked, faded tapestries and sepia photographs—harvest and fishing scenes, the participants hoisting giant banana bunches or trophy-sized catches.

For some reason New Year's Eve came to mind. Foaming glasses on silver trays, the insouciant blare of horns, flappered women and tuxedoed men, the charged sexuality of midnight. As though the new would forever hold its promise.

Nodding to Abuelita, who glanced up from crocheting, Kate got a look at her guard, a thickset man in a loose-fitting shirt and fatigue pants. She followed Enrique under a scrolled-iron chandelier to a stone porch and walkway that led under the big guanacaste.

And there were the banana trees, a surrounding green army. Stalks rising to support the pale foliage and hanging bunches— some ripe, some readying, others past prime and dark with insects. Dead leaves rattled among the seasonal growth. And yet they still spoke of a time when the revelers might have crept away to find pleasure among them.

"This way," Enrique said, gesturing to a worn path leading far out into a row.

Kate slowed her pace, discomfited at its vanishing point and aware the guard had taken up a position behind them. Out of earshot, but nonetheless there.

"Chávez won't bother you," Enrique said.

"Then why is Chávez following us?"

"For reasons I will attempt to explain."

Something in his eyes, a nonfabrication. "And if I prefer the house?"

"Then that is where you will stay."

Still unsure, she followed him: down one hillock and over the next, the trees like giant umbrellas, alternately cool and hot where some had fallen or been removed. Before the foliage closed around one such spot, the house long out of view, Kate glimpsed a road and her heart jumped. But was she north or south of possible help?

No way of telling.

"Here," Enrique said, stopping at a structure that had risen seemingly from nowhere. Square at the bottom, rounded above second-story height, its sides brushed with fronds looking particularly green. Stepping around a stack of crusted irrigation pipe, he opened the door and stood aside.

Road—keep oriented. Chávez hadn't shown himself in a while, but she knew he was out there.

"My hiding place when I was a boy," Enrique said as she entered to cool and musty, stained workbenches and tools, light slanting from offsetting windows and the upper stories. Watching her eyes follow the iron pipe running ceiling to floor, he added, "It's a well house. There's a holding tank upstairs. The system works by gravity—or used to."

"Abuelita was telling me about the plantation."

"She was from one of the original coffee families—she tell you that?" Leaning against one of the work benches.

"She told me she played chess."

"Like Rubenstein fooled around on the piano." He let a beat go by. "Costa Rican champion, plus competitive in archery. Nineteen twenty-seven, this was. The year my grandfather kidnapped her."

Here we go, Kate thought with a look at the door.

"Or she kidnapped *him,* it's hard to say. She was carrying my father by the time her family found out and disowned her." He smiled, and she was aware she'd not seen many from him.

"Veronica Alexandra Justina Castellanos y Obregón. *Abuelita,* out of respect. Means little grandmother."

"And your grandfather?"

"My grandfather was *pirata,*" he said casually.

Shit..."I see. Meaning what I think it does?"

"That depends."

"On something, I'm sure."

Enrique stepped to the window, rubbed a spot in the grime, and stood looking out. "The country's first money-laundering operation. Abuelita ran it. After a while they were making so much money, old Matteo quit pirating. Then the blight hit and he took up fishing. One day the phone rang, and she knew she'd lost him before a word was said."

"Forty-one years ago," Kate said. "She told me."

He widened the spot. "I don't think she and Serena spoke twice in the nine years we were married."

"What was she like, your wife?"

"Hot blooded, you could say. Everyone else did."

"What happened?"

One foot on the stairs, he said, "After I show you something. Topside."

She followed—second-story holding area for nozzles, hoses, and pipe fittings—third story to the covered tank, its sides taller than her reach by half. Beveled wood staves cinched with iron bands and caulked with tar, moss drooping with the seeps. Watery hollow sound coming back as Enrique rapped it.

"Not much left in there," he said.

"You take Serena up here, too?" Squeezed in and trying to avoid the cobwebs.

"One more," he said.

In for a penny...Up a nailed-on ladder and on the roof now, Kate squinted, let her eyes adjust. In the distance, the ocean danced with light. She felt a shortness of breath that ten days ago she and Ben and Shay were just setting out, and she had to focus hard on the few roofs she could make out. Red or green, galvanized or rusting to denote a utility structure. And the road: following the slope's contour, emerging at intervals from the bananas and a field of sugar cane directly across. Bright sun on the fronds touching the gently sloping eaves.

He pointed. "There."

Kate looked, saw nothing, then caught it: blue speck, cane side—roughly a quarter mile from where Abuelita's gate led to the gravel strip ending at the guanacaste.

"The parked car?"

"Not the car, as who's in it."

"And that would be..."

"Someone who works for the man who would kill you."

Her chill this time was lit with anger. "You said that before and I let it go. I won't this time."

"Whoever is in the car, behind it is a man named Valentin Torrijos. An official with the *Policía Nationale*."

"You expect me to believe a policeman wants me dead?"

"I guarantee you, this is a man to whom life means nothing when you stand in the way of his interests."

"And how am I doing that?"

"By knowing what you know," he said. "Being a link that leads to him."

"Trust you, in other words."

Enrique shaded his eyes, let them drift in the direction of the house. "Four months ago, my wife was murdered. Burned to death in a taxi with her lover."

"I'm sorry," Kate said.

"I'm not looking for sympathy—whatever we had in the beginning, only Matteo and Anna remained. Torrijos had her killed."

"I'm not sure I want to hear this."

"Valentin Torrijos was a partner of my father's when *he* took it up. They had a system: Torrijos would extort information, and my father would do the rest—seize the ship, loot the cargo, split the profits." Scanning the horizon as though seeing it play out. "Abuelita hated it, but by then my father was our sole support. With the stories he'd heard of *his* father, that was that."

"One man?"

"He had a crew he was good to."

"And you?"

Enrique broke off a dead frond and pitched it from the roof. "No, but I knew most of them. I was putting the pieces together when he sent me to merchant marine School in Virginia. I didn't care, all I wanted was to be at sea. Then he got hurt. He wouldn't have asked at all, but he'd waited to tell me and was close to losing the plantation."

A bird with a long tail cruised the trees and landed in one.

"One more run. I owed my father everything, so I did it—led the raid with him along. We were preparing to board when a force under a rival of his named Venegas opened up. He knew we had no chance. Our hands were in the air when Venegas had him cut to pieces."

"And you went to prison."

He raised his face to the wind. "Three years. Have you any idea how the mind works in confinement?"

Kate was silent.

"You imagine things—Abuelita on the street, Anna and Matteo without food...Anna, what she was going through. Six months ago, Torrijos got me released."

"I don't understand what this has to do with your wife."

"Torrijos showed me a letter he'd forced her to write implicating me if anything happened, photographs of what he'd done to her. The violent *pirata* avenging his wife's infidelities. Unless I cooperated in another hijack, I'd never see my family again."

He swiped at perspiration, the back of his shirt already damp. Kate waited as he bit at a nail, spat it out. "Not only that, Venegas would be on board."

"The ship that hit us..."

Nod. "Venegas rigged the cargo to burn if he lost. Believe me, it was not by choice."

Unbelievable—Ben and Shay lost over *that.* God*damn*it. "You realize what you've told me?"

"I wanted you to know why I've kept you here. To appreciate what will happen if Torrijos learns you're alive."

Kate scanned the car again through the green. "Why would he have someone watching?"

"He knows of your rescue. I told him you'd died of pneumonia. Obviously he has doubts."

"And I shouldn't have?"

"More is at stake than just you," Enrique said. "If he learns I lied to him, I might as well hand him my family."

Like a broken record, *his* problems in light of her own. "So why *did* you save me?"

"The truth?" he said, releasing his gaze again to the horizon. "Because I saw the way you looked at me that morning in Puntarenas."

Like a punch in the gut, fighting for air. Fronds dipped to the roof and rose. "And from that, you gathered—"

"I told you. I did not plan this."

"*But it happened, and you're responsible. And now you expect me to—*"

"What I expect and ask of you is patience. One way or another, this will be over and Torrijos out of my life—a few more days. If what I have in mind works, you'll be rid of us, if that is your choice."

"If that is my choice..."

"You must see how fond Anna and Matteo are of you."

Kate could barely form the words. "You hold your children up to me as bargaining chips?"

"I hold up nothing. No one ordered them to feel this way about you."

"Damnit, I am not Abuelita."

"Does that lessen what has grown between them and you? Should they not care and have hope? Should *I* not?"

Eyes filming in frustration or the wind or some other fucking thing, Kate could only shake her head, thinking, *I am not hearing this. I am not*...Finally, "Why should I believe what you're saying about any of it?"

"I repeat," he said. "The choice is yours."

Damnit, no...total bullshit. "You were in prison," she willed herself to say. "Talk to me of choices when *my* bars are gone."

35

They'd given up, Enrique having dropped back into the space beside the tank, when Kate decided what she'd been thinking might work if the banana tree on the left was as sturdy as it looked.

Despite the wind, it looked solid.

"I have to get back," Enrique said from the dimness inside.

Thirty feet, Kate told herself. *You can do this.*

"Give me your hand."

Now or never...Butch and Sundance...

In three steps, she was off the roof, feet first into where trunk met foliage. But what appeared solid was now bending with her weight—down, down until it snapped, air and the fronds she was gripping, sky and the other fronds in a kaleidoscope of blue-green.

Luckily, the earth around the well house was soft. Still, the impact knocked the wind from her. She was conscious of Enrique calling her name, the thud of his feet on the wooden stairs. Then she was up—scraped, abraded, and gasping, but intact.

Sun...west...go...NOW. For though she couldn't yet see him, she could hear Chávez beating through the foliage.

"KATE...STOP..."

But she was into a row now, regaining her wind, while the foliage slapping at her would impede the two men as well, she hoped. Not daring to slow for a backward glance, she ran, praying she'd made the right choice and wasn't heading deeper into the plantation. Here the ground firmed and she was able to pick up her pace—cutting across rows so as not to get outflanked, Enrique yelling behind her, Chávez answering on her right.

Their angling meant time expended, and she could make it in her condition, couldn't she? *Breath, breath, breath,*

breath...measured intakes and exhales, a long way from her pre-trip running shape.

The car. Just make it to the car.

Fronds stung and dust blurred her vision; she could feel her sweat in the cuts on her face and hands, her bare arms. At one point, a broken stem ripped into her blouse below one armpit. But it was dead and smooth and she was able to spin away, conscious that her pursuit was audibly closer. The heat and humidity were weights on someone laid up as long as she had been. Ragged, burning wheezes until one grouping nearly knocked her off her feet. Yet as the fronds parted, she caught a glimpse of the road.

Keep angling or bolt?

Bolt—time enough to use the hard-packed surface to gain separation. If only the cop behind the wheel were alert....

Aching for her Nikes, she suddenly was out and stumbling through the frontage ditch. And there was the car, thank God, where she'd hoped. She'd made up about a quarter of the distance when first Enrique then the flanking Chávez burst out onto the road.

"KATE..."

Breathe, she told herself. Limping after having twisted her ankle crossing the ditch, the nearer Chávez starting to make up ground.

Then the blessed sound of an engine, the blue car that now swam in her vision, Chávez not fifty feet behind as it shot from the sugar cane, ripping up roadway, sliding to a stop beside her. The door opening and a man wearing sunglasses leaning across the seat, pistol in his left hand and shouting "*Consiga en—get in.*"

She was pulling the door shut when the car leaped forward. She saw Chávez with his own pistol not yet leveled, hesitating as he made eye contact with her. Then the man in the tinted sunglasses was firing and Chávez was down.

They were accelerating at Enrique, feet spread and his own gun extended, when the driver cut loose again, Kate hearing someone yell "*NOOOOO,*" as much sound as her lungs could muster. But spiderwebs were appearing in the windshield now and glass in her hair, and trying to reprise it later all she recalled was the driver whiplashing off the seat, the wind in her eyes, and the ditch coming fast.

Something jolted the car and Kate awake to rapid-fire Spanish. Touching her forehead where a swelling already had begun, she realized she'd been out only moments. Especially when Enrique's face appeared at the window, and he yanked open the door, and she saw the car was still in the ditch.

"Can you walk?" he asked curtly.

Kate nodded.

"Then come with me."

Drained of anything resembling fight, she followed—around to where a pale-looking Chávez stood by the open trunk. Looking up from it as she approached.

"Are you all right?" Kate asked him.

Chávez nodded. "Okay."

"If you call a bullet through the arm okay," Enrique said with heat.

"I'm sorry."

"Is *okay*..." Chávez smiling at her. Pulling up his shirtsleeve to show her the crude bandage around his biceps, a seep of blood showing.

"Please...let me look at it."

He pulled away.

"If you want to look at something," Enrique said, "look inside the trunk.

Kate did and brought a hand to her mouth: blown-out lens in the driver's sunglasses, blood pooling on the trunk liner under his head.

"*My God.* Is he dead?"

By way of answer, Enrique flipped open a leather badge holder to reveal a *Policía Nationale* shield and an ID card.

"Fulgencio Rosado," he said. "Ex-Noriega, all-Torrijos. A man who lived for his work, according to a woman I know who now is blind. Check beside him."

Kate did and saw a gas-powered chain saw, a red square container marked *Gasolina*. Plastic handcuffs, pliers, a ball-peen hammer.

"No head, no hands or feet, no identity—after he'd spent time getting acquainted. Are you processing this?"

"I don't know what to say."

"Then listen for a change," he said. "Help us push the car out of the ditch."

It took three tries, grunting and shoving, the blue car wedged tight, Chávez nursing power to the buried wheels. Finally the extra weight in the trunk paid off, the dead fronds and branches laid down, tires catching in the soft earth and riding over the lip.

Running with sweat and dirt, Kate bent over panting as Chávez leaned out for instructions in Spanish.

"Not that it will do much good," she was able to decipher. "His man not checking in will be enough for Torrijos." A pause. "The car at least looks personal. Use it to find them, if you can. Enough is enough." Enrique glancing in Kate's direction.

Chávez said, "What about you?"

"With luck we'll have until dark. I'll hold *Machacha* for you."

"Not if there's trouble. And If I'm not there by midnight."

"*Vaya con Dios, amigo.*"

"*Y usted.*"

He watched Chávez weave through a curve as Kate touched her forehead and winced.

"*Machacha* is your boat?" she said into the rise of dust.

Enrique turned. "So you do know Spanish. Abuelita was right."

"We have clients in Mexico I deal with."

"And has it been useful to you here?" Dripping with sarcasm.

Brushing off dirt, Kate drew herself up, answered him in Spanish. "I didn't ask for this, and I didn't mean for Chávez to get hurt."

"Which changes exactly nothing."

"I was wrong. At least I admit it." Kicking a rock into the ditch. Then, "Is Chávez really all right."

"*Un hombre correoso.*"

"Find *them*, you said. Find who?"

He raised a hand in dismissal as the sugar cane bowed in a pulse of wind.

"Like it or not, I'm here," Kate said. "And if what you said is true, Torrijos isn't going away either."

"That is enough talk." Enrique's eyes took in the rising sweep of green, the sun on it and Abuelita's roof as he approached the gate. "We're finished here."

36

Ben reached out and touched Shay's arm. "Not yet," he said. She dropped back into her seat. "But he's been there a half hour. He's getting ready to leave."

"I see him. Keep your voice down."

Omar Barrera checked his watch, tossed off his second *tacita de café* ordered when he first entered the coffee place across the avenue. Rising, he threw down money: a thin man in loose-fitting pants and a white shirt, what looked to be prematurely gray hair.

Ben checked his own watch: five-thirty, sun still searing the avenue outside the market where they'd been nursing watermelon slices, then shave ice at a window bench.

"We're going to miss him."

"No, we're not," he said, dumping what was left of his ice. "We're just making sure he didn't bring company."

Omar Barrera stepped out into the hot afternoon. Looking annoyed, he wiped his long forehead with a handkerchief, stuffed it back in his pants with the notepad pulled out inside the café, and began to walk.

"Okay," Ben said. "This side and three car lengths back. I'll watch him, you watch for cops. And keep the cone, it's a nice touch."

"No more spy movies for you, Dad."

"Hey, I'm not as in with the local *policía* as you are."

Though the market had been warm, the heat outside was intense. Fanning himself with a manila envelope he'd also brought, Omar Barrera crossed an intersection and continued up the next block. For a moment they lost him as a bus slid by and hung there. But then it forged ahead in a huff of diesel fumes.

"Anybody following?" Ben asked. "Any out-of-place cars?"

"No, and I just had a thought. What if that isn't him?"

"It's him."

"How do you know?" she said.

"He described himself. He was the only one in the shop. Where do you get this stuff?"

"*Gotcha.*" Showing him orange lips and teeth.

"Good, Shay. And there he goes."

For maddening seconds, a rush of traffic prevented crossing. Then it thinned and they were able to spot Barrera's gray hair disappearing up a side street. One block...halfway up another. The reporter had unlocked an older white Mazda and was getting into it when Ben slid in beside him, Shay into the back.

"Mr. Barrera?"

"Scare the crap out of me, why don't you?" he said in the cigarette voice from the phone.

"Drive, please," Ben said. "Someplace we can talk."

He turned the ignition key. "You think I'm so flush with time I can waste it on you?"

"Sorry, but we had to be sure."

"'We' meaning your daughter, I assume."

Ben introduced Shay, and to keep it going as they wove out of Puerto Caldera, eyes working the rearview, he asked about the reporter's background.

"Cuban by birth, American by way of Miami. Came here four years ago on leave from the *Herald* and never left. For reasons you may hear in my voice."

"I don't—"

"Little health problem—where I was when you called. Not many know about it at work."

"Are you okay?" Shay asked.

"Reasonably." He pulled off the road and into a shaded turnout with picnic tables overlooking the ocean. "Health care's cheap if you trust doctors, which I don't. See anybody back there?"

"Not so far."

"My story in a nutshell."

They chose a table scattered with blossoms, breeze wafting their scent and ruffling Shay's hair. From their side of the table, she and Ben could angle glances back on the port, the town, the cruise and container ships hawsered to the docks. Barrera drew out a plastic bag and from it a fat joint, Shay's eyes going momentarily wide.

Winking at her, he said, "Helps with the side effects. You mind?"

"*I* don't." Glancing at Ben.

"I owe you an apology," Ben said as he lit it with a chrome lighter and the aroma spread. "From the call you sounded—"

"Drunk, I know—not that I haven't put away my share." Offering Ben a hit and taking out a micro recorder when it was refused. "You want to start at the beginning?"

They did—the trip, the collision, Valentin Torrijos—Shay filling in details where Ben was prone to go bottom line, Barrera listening and jotting as he drew down the joint. Ben had just described Xochitl's note when Barrera opened the manila envelope, slid a file across the table.

"You haven't seen that," he said.

Ben opened to sheets of fax paper, the uneven fine print in Spanish, inset photos showing a bearded man with longish hair. The man was holding a set of numbers under his chin; beneath the photos, letters spelled out *Enrique Rudolfo Matteo Matos y Gallego.*

Ben let out a breath but said nothing.

"You see mine, I see yours," Barrera said.

Unfolding a flyer, Ben handed it to him, Barrera comparing the two and nodding.

"You do this?"

"Shay did."

"*We* did it," Shay broke in. "I never saw him."

"It's good—the eyes in particular," Barrera said. "I'm not surprised at the reaction you got."

"How come?"

"You read Spanish?" Barrera asked her.

"Not much. A little from school."

He coughed, a series that deepened into rumble. "Actually, this one's clean compared to his old man and grandfather. Murder, extortion, piracy—compounded by lack of witnesses when the time came. Family's closely held around here. Those who even know it exists."

Ben said, "For God's sake, why?"

"Loyalty, fear, self-preservation. This is not a group you mess with. As for the shipping companies, they largely disavow the subject, though piracy's rampant, especially in places like the Far East and the Philippines. See, these guys know what's on the ships before they ever leave—might as well paint bulls-eyes on 'em. But admitting it exists not only drives away business, it jacks up insurance rates. Cheaper to absorb the losses."

"That apply to RouteStar?"

"Much as any. But RouteStar's no virgin, either. Their legal department's the size of Delaware."

Ben rubbed the back of his neck. "Any ideas here?"

"Yeah, find the ship. And if you're wondering about governments, most can't agree on the definition of piracy, let alone where their own waters stop and start. Hell, some even piece off the action."

A truck downshifted on the grade as Ben and Shay exchanged glances and Barrera rolled another joint.

"What about on a lesser scale?" Ben asked.

"Thinking Torrijos?"

"For want of a name."

"Always possible, but I'd tend to doubt it. From what I know, he's well connected and highly regarded." He lit up, inhaled, let it out. "Still, that's an ambitious target, in more ways than one."

Already half-imagining a buzz, Ben said, "*Reina*, you mean."

"Somebody would buy her, true, if only for scrap. But cargo's the game here—lumber and copper. Loaded at Guayaquil where she let off crew and took aboard a security force. And what's that tell you?"

"They were expecting trouble?"

"Get that man a cigar. And it gets juicier: Most of the lumber came from the Philippines—about the time a shitload, pardon my French, of ground-to-air missiles was stolen from Subic Bay. WASP IIs...very hush-hush. Shall I go on?"

"We're getting off the subject," Ben said after Omar Barrera had snapped off the recorder and rambled on about the WASPs being a likely reason for the security force. Incidental, so far as Ben was concerned, even if it were true—the man starting to sound the way he had on the phone. Touch of conspiracy nut thrown in.

"Can we just focus on Matos?" he added.

"You go around, you come around," Barrera said off an exhale. "Sure I can't offer you guys some?"

"*Daaaad...???*" A little smirk along with it.

"Some more, you mean—thanks, but no thanks," Ben said.

"Your call." He consulted his notes. "Enrique Matos: Born 1961, two years college, ran his own fishing boat before being admitted to merchant marine school in the states. No police record prior to 1996."

"And then?"

Barrera squinted at the sheet, the light having faded with the onset of dusk. "Arrested during a raid off Panama...father dead in the ensuing engagement...sentenced to ten years for piracy, of which he served three. Released last November." He began coughing again, Ben and Shay not knowing whether to slap him on the back or leave him alone. Finally he hawked into the weeds and wiped his mouth with a handkerchief.

"Sorry. Where was I?"

"Released last November," Shay spoke up.

"Just in time to murder his wife, it appears." Advancing to the second sheet. "Serena Caridad Matos, age thirty-seven. Mother of two—Matteo and Anna—both by Matos. Found with Ramiro Eduardo Cortes, incinerated in a taxi. Seen *semi flagrante* with Cortes earlier in a bar."

It gets worse and worse, Ben thought, accompanied by another: "Then why wasn't Matos arrested for it."

"Because suspicions don't cut it, even here," Barrera said. "Other than motive, investigators found no link beyond the circumstantial. Serena liked a good time and didn't much care with whom, but Matos had an alibi."

"What alibi?"

"He was out on a charter."

"But he could have ordered it."

"You asking or telling me?"

Ben tested the knot of muscles in his sore shoulder, eased up on it. After the shadow they'd been chasing, it seemed absurd to know so much about the man. Let alone think that Kate,

through some miracle, might have fallen into his hands. That as
the best they could hope for.

Incinerated in a taxi outside Puntarenas...

"Long as we're there," Barrera said, "let's say that Matos
finds the charterboat business lacking. He needs money to keep
the family digs going."

Ben looked at him. "Wait a minute. You know where Matos
lives?"

"The grandparents established a plantation or something not
far from here in the twenties." He waved the sheet. "Matos
gave it as an address when he was convicted. I was able to
locate at least the road."

"And we're sitting here?"

Barrera lit a cigarette this time, coughed at the inhale. "Let's
get real: If you're right and Matos *is* back in the family biz, it's
doubtful he's waiting for somebody to drop by and ask him.
Particularly about a ship listed as sunk off Colombia the day
you say you saw him."

"But he wouldn't know Dad survived to identify him. How
would he?"

"What about the TV thing, Shay?"

Barrera said, "If you're talking about the bulletin I saw, it
only mentioned your being wanted in connection with your
wife's death. None of the particulars."

"Then why wouldn't it be business as usual? Dinner with the
kids and old folks?"

"The grandmother," Barrera corrected him. "Gramps has
been dead for eons."

Ash fell from his cigarette, the sky having deepened into pink
and indigo. The breeze still moved the branches, but it had
cooled, and passing cars showed headlights. Below them, the
cruise ships looked grand lit up: ladies of the evening with
everything finally in place.

"When in doubt, hypothesize," the reporter said suddenly.
"Something pieced together we can shoot at."

"What happened and why," Shay said.

"Better put. May I?"

Ben raised a go-ahead palm.

Barrera coughed, this time steadied. "Say *Reina* isn't swamped by a wave, but is hit on her way to the Canal. This time Matos wins the marble and makes for home, where they can hide her and sell off the cargo. So why the fire?"

"An accident?" Shay.

"During the takeover," Ben added.

Barrera said, "Try intentionally set."

"Thought you said it was about cargo?"

"If I can't have it, neither can you. Happens in wartime. Different kind of war, is all."

Bingo—something Kate said off Bahia Drake—Morgan's plunder of Panama City: *What the Spaniards didn't burn first to keep out of his hands.* "The WASPs," Ben said.

"Plus, if they did set charges, the lumber would have cooperated big-time."

Shay brushed at a blossom. "But with the ship on fire, where do they go? Wouldn't they burn, too, or drown if it sinks?"

"Not if they were dead already," Barrera said with a look at Ben. "Last guy pushes the button on his way out."

"Why not just give up?" Ben asked. "Seems the more sensible alternative."

"It does unless we're talking rebels with a cause. Colombians are always in the market: FARC—Revolutionary Armed Forces. Shining Path in Peru, but they're pretty much done. Some Islamic types I could name."

"Move on," Ben said. "Say they're across the gulf before RouteStar knows they're gone. Wouldn't somebody have seen the fire?"

Barrera exhaled smoke upward. "Maybe. But, as you said, it was raining, and they'd probably have tried to smother it by keeping it bottled up."

"Not when I saw it, it wasn't."

"Key point. And one more: Matos on the foredeck. Why wasn't he on the bridge?"

It was almost dark now, color gone from the sky. Intermittent flashes on a horizon drawing clouds.

"Anybody...?"

"He was looking for something," Shay volunteered. "A place to fight the fire."

"There was no fighting that thing," Ben said. "And I didn't see anyone else, just him."

"Two points. They'd have been short of manpower to fight one. And Shannon's right: Matos would have been looking for a place to douse it and save what they could—to his mind, the copper."

"You're saying he didn't know about the WASPs?"

"Only that it's possible, assuming they were aboard. One thing's clear: Matos was out there for a reason. Which seems, if I may, to keep her off the beach. Over and done if that happens."

Ben noted the buzz was gone from his tone, perhaps a method there after all. "So how does he put out the fire?"

"The big question—by sinking her. Opening the cocks or blowing holes or whatever. Much farther, the whole enchilada's toast. So he's out hoping to spot land, maybe his instruments dead due to storm or the fire, and what does he see? You. And how much margin has he, even if he could avert?"

A ship's horn floated up, its lit shape easing from the dock. Barrera took a last drag before crushing out the smoke.

"I rest my case."

Ben said, "But wouldn't that mean—"

"Exactly. She's in salvageable water not far from your boat. And what would any Matos do under those circumstances? Right again—haul ass to bring it up and turn it into coin."

As if to punctuate, Barrera dropped his palm to the table, Shay and Ben jumping about a foot. Ben was about to snap back something, but Barrera already was thumbing his lighter, scanning the file sheets in its glow before heading for the car. Then he was back with what he'd gone for, a scuffed attaché out of which he drew a bound document.

"Going to let us in on it?" Ben asked.

"Something hit. Humor me." Asking Shay to hold the lighter, Barrera began flipping through what Ben had caught a glimpse of—an English title page: *RouteStar—Conclusions Regarding the Loss of the Ship Reina de Aconcagua.*

"Hunter S. Thompson and yours truly," he finally said. "Check it out."

"Who?"

"Later, Shay," Ben said, as they followed Barrera's finger to a list of the lost, down to *Rigoberto Refugio Venegas*. Then to the file sheets on Matos, a notation Barrera translated:

"Head of the detail intercepting the criminal force, accounting for the death of Rudolfo Matteo Matos, was *Rigoberto Refugio Venegas*."

Wind blew more blossoms down.

"The guy who did his old man," he said to their looks, the flame catching the triumph in his face. "Anybody still looking for a reason Enrique Matos was aboard your ship that night?"

37

Headlights off, the Caprice rolled to a stop by the closed gate, blocking it. Before opening his door, the man riding shotgun spoke into a cell phone in quiet Spanish to the panel van parked a half-mile back. Telling its occupants to stand by, he thumbed in another number and relayed the same message to the Land Cruiser off-roaded a quarter-mile up. The shotgunner then pocketed the cell phone, nodded to the driver and the man seated in back as both turned to him for last instructions.

"Beltran on point," Valentin Torrijos said after a reprise of earlier thoughts. "Armando on pump ten paces back with me. And hear this: Enrique Matos I want alive—repeat, alive. Everyone else is green light. *Comprende?*"

Nods.

"Then let's get it done."

The three stepped out of the Caprice, clicked their doors shut. Armando released the trunk and handed Beltran his weapon and three clips, one of which Beltran fed into his assault rifle. As he was pocketing the other two, Torrijos added, "Check the house, wait for us inside the gate." He and Armando watched Beltran slip up and over the walls extending out on either side.

Torrijos lit a cigarillo, stood smoking it as Armando slipped shells into his shotgun. They had perhaps a half hour before the waxing moon would appear over the hills to the east. Breeze hinted at the day's heat and dust, though it would storm tonight if the sunset were any indication...sometime after midnight, the air clean and earth-fragrant. Not like the rains that before long would turn this and most dirt roads into swamp snakes, broken by torrents even the four-bys had to respect.

He took a last drag, ground out the smoke. Securing his vest, he reached into the trunk and handed over the other, Armando struggling to get into it. Far off, a dog barked, followed by a faint yell, then silence.

Armando swiped a mosquito out of the air. "Does Beltran make it?" he asked.

"Let's wait and see, shall we—keep our options open? And on another subject, keep shoving in the *tamals*, you'll have to wear that vest on your arm." Chambering a round into his semi-automatic and setting the safety.

"I'm trying to lose weight."

"Your wife know that?"

Armando let it go, but as they strode toward the wall, he said, "I want this Matos, *Patrón*. Rosado was us."

"He was also careless," Torrijos said. "Matos and the woman are here and we finish it tonight or he's headed south." He slipped the pistol into its nylon hip holster. "One way or another it ends. I've seen to that."

"And the husband and daughter?"

"Very soon."

He was following Armando over the wall when Beltran materialized, saying, "There's light on downstairs, but it looks like candles."

"You see anyone?"

"Just the *vieja* in her chair."

"No one else?"

"Not that I could see, but the upstairs is dark."

"Hear anything?" Armando asked.

"Record player."

"All right," Torrijos said. "Plan A."

Beltran assumed the point, Torrijos and Armando flanking. Through the banana trees, their shifting foliage, Torrijos glanced up and saw first stars, no moon as yet, last glow of sunset from the direction of the ocean. *Where are you Rique?* he thought. *Even your father knew when it was done.* Ahead as they rounded a curve, he made out faint light, curving tile where it met thick walls, a stone veranda—not a bad spread from the years-ago time he'd been out there to serve warrant on Rudolfo Matos. Which had led to their arrangement—Torrijos a *rurale* on the make, Rudolfo more than intent on filling *his* old man's shoes.

Naturally, he'd not been welcomed back after what flared between Rudolfo and his mother over what he'd done to get served by the *policía*. No son of hers, and all that. Aside from standards applied to her son and obviously not her old man, she'd been feisty as the devil, righteous pissed at Rudolfo. Yet she had to be well over eighty by now, and no fire burned without consuming itself.

Enrique was another story—no difference between him and Rudolfo, so far as Torrijos could see. Cordite and salt water. Still, he was one man—distanced from his people and all but defenseless compared to what Torrijos had in place or would muster.

Soon, he thought: homes around the Caribbean and a Swiss account to go with the others. College in the states for his youngest—no need to get *her* married off to hulker cops like Armando—plus the luxury of tapping into those who owed him. Good to look forward to after a lifetime of lining up his shots only to have someone else hole them.

Not this time.

This side of the guanacaste, he saw Beltran pause to wave them forward, and once there, he heard it—thin and scratchy over a rustle of wind. *Bessame Mucho,* or some such tango music, hardly his thing. Torrijos felt prickles, shook them off, made a silent gesture for Beltran to position himself at the rear, wait until he was called or heard shots. He gave the man a minute or so to get there, then signaled Armando in from the left while he closed from the right.

The big front door was locked, so they eased around to French doors overlooking the veranda. Locked, as well. Torrijos set the bezel on his watch for ten minutes, during which time they saw no one in the house, no movement. Candle glow flickered from a wide entry that stepped up into another large room, the music eerily repeating itself, filtering out to where they waited.

Torrijos gestured to one of the lounges and Armando picked it up as if it weighed nothing and hurled it through the glass-wood doors. Inside almost before the sound had died away, weapons extensions of their eyes. No one waiting in ambush, no gunfire. Just a room that seemed airless after being outside, that damned music coming from up the steps. Torrijos felt the prickles again; waving Armando there, he cased the room a moment longer, then crunched over shatterings after the big man.

Up the steps and into 1927.

Candlelight gleamed off a silver-and-white dress of a style Torrijos recalled his own mother wearing when she'd left him and his brothers to step out with the man who'd taken his cop-father's place. The woman sitting there wore a pearl choker, another looping double-strand almost to her waist, a platinum tiara of a kind he'd only seen in photographs—like the two flanking a half-filled glass of what looked to be port. One was of a girl of perhaps fifteen holding a raised longbow and standing next to a target with arrows in the inner ring. The other showed a classically Latin man holding the same girl in a tango pose—he in the lunge, she bent backward and gazing at him across a shaft of light. In the corner, an old-fashioned record player clicked its needle arm back onto the spinning, black-and-gold labeled 78.

Torrijos forced his eyes from those regarding him—the arresting face and wrinkled braceleted wrists—upward to the darkened balcony. Realizing that if Enrique had been there they'd be dead now, he gestured Armando to it, the big man taking the stairs two at a time until he disappeared into the far room.

"I knew you'd come back," the woman said.

Twenty years, her voice as firm as he remembered.

"And *why*."

Torrijos lowered his gun, his gaze from the balcony. "No time, *abuela*. Where are they?"

"Safe from you. And time will be your gift to them." Bringing out an old bull-barrel target pistol from under her knitting yarn. "Put your gun on the floor."

"You know I can't do that." Wondering what, if anything, she knew about bulletproof vests.

As though responding to his thought, the woman raised the pistol to his eyes. "You not only will do it," she said, "you'll tell your *mozo* to come here and do the same. You'll then answer my questions."

From her glint, Torrijos thought she actually might fire, so he set down his pistol. "Come down here," he said toward the bedroom. Armando had reached the foot of the stairs, when he added, "And lose the pumpgun."

Setting it on the braided rug, the big man stood back up as the arm on the phonograph recycled.

"It's over," Torrijos said to her. "Give Armando the gun."

The eyes flashed. "You must think very little of him."

"Take her pistol and bring it to me, Armando."

He started forward—slowly, his hand out, eyes on hers. "You must have been some dancer. Cugat, isn't it? We played his records when I was a boy."

"You think your people would be proud of you now?"

"No one wants to hurt you, *abuela*."

"I know very well who you wish to hurt."

"Now why would you say that?" Smiling now. "You remind me of my own grandmother."

"Shame on you, using her that way. For this *depravado* who feeds on generations."

"*Vea aquí*," Armando said. "Time to stop playing games and—"

There was a sharp pop. Armando grunted, clutched his arm and stood rubbing it, fingers reddening as the smear bled through. Everything froze: Torrijos expecting another pull of the trigger, Armando like a bear on a chain, the old woman leveling her gun, the music swelling with trumpets.

Armando moved forward, the blood leaving her face telling him he could take the pistol. "You did the right thing," he said.

"I've seen too much dying to add to it," she said tiredly. "And if you give it to *him*, he'll use it on you."

"We don't kill grandmothers, do we, *Patrón*?" Handing Torrijos the bull-barrel .22 as Beltran burst in. Sweeping the room left-right-left with his AR-15.

"You're not needed here," Torrijos snapped. "Wait at the gate."

With a glance at the woman, Beltran left.

"Go with him," she told Armando. Not looking at him, but out the window where the wind had risen to a gust, creaks from the guanacaste audible over the scratchy music. "Now—while you still can."

Armando was smiling, turning to make light, when Torrijos shot him with the bull-barrel. And when Torrijos had finished the rest with his own gun, leaving it pressed into Armando's dead hand before approaching Beltran smoking a cigarette—the man not even asking what had happened, why Armando wasn't with him—he simply handed over the cell phone and said, "Plan B. Tell your people."

38

The wind kicked up dust, both behind the Mazda and in front.

"Is that the moon?" Shay asked, pointing to a milky spot, hill height in clouds that seemed to have formed from nothing.

"That would be the moon, yes," Omar Barrera answered.

"Then what's that?"

"Where?" Ben said, rousing from thoughts of Enrique Matos, the lethargy of a drive on top of little sleep, Kate's scream echoing off his slim reference points: black night, the figure on the bow, impact, chaos, a glimpse of stern. Precious little to add to Barrera's theories.

"Behind those trees," Shay said from the back. "There..."

Ben dipped, followed her point to a low orange smear—the lights of a runway through rain. Only there was no runway and no rain. Just its hint on the wind, in the lightning resembling distant field artillery.

"That what I think it is?" he asked Barrera.

"You're reading my mind."

Ben felt him push the car harder through a straight stretch as Shay put in, "Never mind me or anything."

"Grass fire, or something like it," Barrera said. "Up where we're headed. And if it's like that from here..."

Twenty minutes of rising road and forced curves later, the fire had defined itself. Flames licked a treed horizon, dust-brown smoke boiling toward a half-moon playing in-and-out with the clouds. Oncoming traffic was now a factor—pickups filled with kids and animals, bicyclists hugging the fringe, the odd cart. Not jammed up as yet, but getting there. Barrera eased over to let a water truck pass, then braked for a flashing light on the car blocking their lane.

"*What are you doing?*" Shay said as he got out.

"Get down. Stay down."

Not being able to see over the windows, Ben concentrated on what he could perceive: wheels popping gravel or pounding through ruts, dopplered shouts and straining engines, kids yelling as they passed, traversing reflections. Trying to reassure Shay they were safer there than outside and hoping it was true. Then Barrera was back, slamming his door and starting the car. Swinging around the flashing light and up the road.

"Okay," he said in a bit. "You can get up now."

"How did you...?"

He flashed a laminated card, leaned to stuff it in a hip pocket. "Power of the press, remember?"

Past the checkpoint, they encountered only sporadic traffic. Then they rounded a curve on a full-on inferno: fire advancing through a line of exploding banana trees, what looked to be a slim structure blazing like an oil well. Up beyond a ruined gate where most of the fire trucks and emergency vehicles stood, flames poured from the windows of a thick-walled, two-story Spanish-style, its burning rooms clearly visible from the road. Beside the house a huge tree shot sparks high into the night.

For a while they took it in, then Shay said, "Imagine being in there."

"Unreal," Ben said.

"I'll see what I can find out," Barrera said, pulling over.

With the windows cracked, they could feel the heat coming in waves. They watched Barrera, backlit and approaching those who seemed in charge—first one then another as the men were called away to consult or answer phones. Several more trucks discharged men and equipment; a van left the drive and before it could straighten, Barrera was leaning in and saying something to the driver.

Then he was back at their window.

"It's Matos's, all right. Lightning, they think, fanned by the wind."

"Any sign of him?" Ben asked.

"No, but they managed to pull out two bodies before the house went up. I told them you were an investigator who needed a look."

"A cop? Jesus, won't they—"

"They're young and want to get the hell out of here, so if you're coming, do it now."

"I want to see," Shay said as Ben opened the door.

"I'll tell you about it."

"No, you won't. You say you will, but you won't."

"Now or never," Barrera said.

"Sorry, pal—trust me on this one."

Outside, the heat felt like sunburn, crackle and the smell of charred bananas twice as intense. Beyond them, a group of men aimed water at the burn closest the road. Others tamped mini-fires that had jumped to threaten a field of sugar cane. Ash was collecting on the car and in Barrera's hair; between gusts, Ben could see the gray-white particles drifting down and thought of Pompeii.

Barrera slapped the van's flank, waited while a medic opened the rear. "Make it good," he lowered his voice as they stepped inside. But the ruse wasn't necessary, the medic left for a cigarette.

The first bag contained the body of an old woman, curiously made up. Her eyes were closed and except for the bloom across her chest, she seemed more at rest than dead. The other held a man shot three times in the face, small holes that had tracked his features, nearly obliterating them.

Nearly...

Ben felt the van imploding; swallowing, he backed out before Barrera could comment. Barrera watched the medic slam the doors and roar off, then came over to where Ben was distracting himself with the fire.

"You all right?"

"First time for anything like that. Give me a minute."

"Had to be the grandmother, it's her place. The guy's who I wondered about. You seen him before?"

Feeling the lack of food and sleep, stink in every pore—as if his life were on fire and had been for days—Ben nodded. "One of the guys Torrijos had put me on the plane."

"Well, now...Any idea how he got there?"

"Not even a guess."

"The kid said it looked like they'd shot each other. That sound right to you?"

"How would I know?"

Barrera thought a moment, then reached into his pocket and held out the Mazda keys. "Here," he said.

"What are you—"

"This, too." Pulling out his billfold and extracting most of the notes. "Five hundred American. Should be enough to get you down and back. Maybe even a case of Imperial."

"Down where?" All Ben could think of to say.

"Now what were we talking about? Begins with *Reina?*"

"In the car?"

"Charterboat would be my recommendation."

Ben glanced across at Shay's face ghosting the window: pale, questioning, wide-eyed. "What about you?" he said.

"Two things. I'm a reporter, and I'm fundamentally a coward."

"Which means what?"

"This is what I do. The car belongs to my partner's brother. Trunk the keys and leave it on the Puntarenas waterfront and I'll find it later, or he will. I'll hitch a ride with one of these guys." He coughed, spit in the ditch. "The money's an investment, just remember where it came from. Be a helluva story to go out on. "

"Out..."

Barrera smiled as if at some inner joke. "The virus is like that," he said, waving at ash. "Figured you didn't need your girl hearing it."

"I'm sorry," Ben said, sounding wholly inadequate to himself. Like most everything the past few days.

"Just make me look smart." Slipping a business card with a phone number written on the back into Ben's pocket before lifting his eyes to the flames. "Damn, that is some fire—like souls released from the earth. You ever think of things that way?"

"More and more," Ben said. Gripping the keys and the money and hurrying toward the Mazda.

* * *

Stopping first at a roadside hole-in-the-wall advertising *pollo*-something-or-other, Ben and Shay crept into Punterenas just after ten.

"Home, sweet home," he said as they cruised the residential neighborhoods, the mostly quiet commercial streets. Steering clear of the bars and tourist hangouts where there might be *policía*.

"We can't just drive around all night."

"Still upset with me, huh?"

By way of answer, she looked straight ahead. After several blocks, she cleared her throat. "We're a team—that what you told Mom before you ran around on her?"

"Cheap shot, Shannon Kay."

"Maybe I'm not mature enough to understand the term."

Ben took a breath; tapped out and excluded, she felt the way he would have at that age, every slight magnified. And despite the crack, it went with his territory.

"People like us who died violently, Shay—believe me, I wish I hadn't see them. Close your eyes, and they're right there. Like my father when I insisted on having them open the lid."

"How do I get through to you? I'm not a child."

"Then you understand a judgment call. What you do when you love someone—not because it's popular."

The street lights swept her face, patterns like ghosts in transit. After several blocks of silence she said, "What kind of person would shoot an old woman?"

"Barrera said the medics thought they'd killed each other."

"And you don't believe that?"

"I'm not sure what I believe," he said.

"How about a cop, maybe a bad one?" Glancing at a knot of kids her age passing something around. "Like in the movies."

Ben considered it as they reached the end of the spit, dark water extending beyond the sand. "How about somebody else in the room?" he said. "Matos, for instance. Cop draws on grandson, grandma shoots cop, cop shoots grandma." He turned the Mazda around and started back. "Kind of a Ma Barker thing."

"Like she was protecting him."

"Yeah. More or less."

They drove until Ben spotted an unlit house with a sign in front; circling the block, he came up on it, headlights off. Confirming one of the words on the sign as *Renta*—a rental— he backed in as far as he could under a side tree and killed the engine.

"What if somebody comes?" Shay asked.

"We leave. Meantime we keep our eyes on the neighbors."

Shay peered out at the houses. "What about Torrijos?" she said at length.

"As a possibility? Even if he is dirty, why would he take the risk?"

"Because he wants to find Matos, and grandma knows where he's gone?"

Ben scrunched down and yawned. "You're saying Torrijos shoots his own man, then grandma to make it seem as if they killed each other?"

"I don't know, does it matter? It's Matos we want, isn't it— where we're going tomorrow?"

"That's the plan, all right."

Watching her rub her eyes, he felt a bump of pride: already a long way from the kid who'd left Newport. Fourteen going on thirty-eight. He said, "Why don't you grab some sleep? No point both of us yawning our heads off."

"What about you?"

"First watch, remember?"

"Promise you'll wake me?"

"Scout's honor, Shay."

There was a pause. "*You* were a Boy Scout?"

"For a time. Until we had a falling out."

"What falling out?"

"Slight problem of interpretation. My scoutmaster didn't think making beer qualified for a merit badge in Personal Health. I always thought it was because my batch blew up in his garage. See, it was kind of a surprise."

"What did you put in it?"

"I shudder to think."

His head was against the door, settled in, when he thought to add, "You know, what you said might work if everything was coming to a head between them."

"Daaaad...I was almost asleep."

"Try this: Torrijos and his guy come to the house to nail Matos. But he's gone and you're right about grandma—she won't say where." Using the flat of his hand to massage first one eye, then the other. "Might explain why she had a gun."

Shay blinked open. "That's what *you* said."

"Whatever—buy him time to get away."

"From Torrijos? How would he know about Matos in the first place?"

"He's a cop."

"But in with him..."

Ben shrugged, trying to connect dots that wouldn't form, let alone line up. "Bad, like you said—they're falling out or something."

"You and the Boy Scouts..."

"Hey, inspiration's where you find it."

Shay yawned. "Can we talk about this in the morning when it might make sense to me, too?"

"Sorry." Hating what he'd just noticed and had to say next. "Don't look now, but we've got company. The woman out on her porch—heading back inside?"

"No way."

"Way. Buckle up."

Ben started the car and rolled, lights off until they were into the next block. He'd turned into a dead end, saw a jog that led out to the waterfront, everything quiet, maybe even late enough to go by the charters to see if the one he had in mind was docked. So that by the time he'd picked up on the darkened barricade with the two cops in the open lane plus the unmarked now blocking their retreat, Shay had already let out a scream.

39

It was over...finished. They'd given it their best shot, and now, finally, they could get some sleep.

Kate would understand.

Ben was almost relieved, Shay looking stunned after a momentary outburst when she'd screamed at him to plow through the policemen walking toward them. Break through and escape.

"Sorry, hon," he told her. "Not the way to do it."

"*We can still run.*"

"Where? Better we sort out everything we've learned and hope somebody will listen. They can't all be in Torrijos's pocket." Despite having said it, he felt no great optimism, just a weariness the size of *Angel Fire,* the thought only adding to his sense of failure.

He and Shay got out of the car as instructed: slow and deliberate, Shay's eyes shining and her face taut. The *policía* shouting orders were young—at second look, the ones Shay had charmed earlier in the week. But they were having none of it this time, not even looking at her. Directing their frustration at Ben via the sharpness of their commands, their shoves, finally the heavy flash wielded by the shorter of the two. Driving Ben to his knees while Shay screamed at them to stop, please stop.

From Ben's perspective it was like starring in the Rodney King video after having been on the viewing end ad nauseam: trying to fend off the lightning exploding in his back and forearms, protecting his neck and head—puking, finally, on the gritty surface. Which explained why they ran out of steam.

With the driver from the blocking unit, they dragged him to his feet, bent him over the Mazda's hood. They were preparing to put on restraints, Shay struggling against the cop holding her wrists, Ben calling to her to let it go, stop resisting, when he became aware of engine whine. Which in seconds had become, from Ben's angle—all of them turning toward it now—a pair of hi-beams hurtling at the barricade.

Just before impact, as in a stunt sequence, the driver spun the wheel, jammed on the brakes, crashed the barricade in a hard one eighty. The car slammed the Mazda's front end with its rear, the force knocking the Mazda into the cop holding Shay, her out of his grasp, and Ben to the ground. The two young cops were remembering their pistols when automatic rifle fire peppered the unmarked unit until the three cops broke and ran, cars that had backed up behind the scene now fighting for their own traction.

"*You come*," a voice said from what looked to be a blue Toyota.

"Who are you?" Ben shouted back, hurting and nearly mute from the crash and the gunfire.

"*Ahora—Now.*"

Ben heard the snick of a clip rammed home.

Some fucking choice.

"Dad, come *on*."

The driver hit the gas pedal, surged forward, braked and hollered something Ben didn't get. Grabbing Shay's hand, Ben limped them through the smoke floating in the Mazda's remaining headlight, steam from its shattered radiator, the spent cartridges. He'd torn open a back door and shoved Shay inside, fallen in after her, when acceleration drove them against the seat and off *Paseo le Las Touristas* in a squeal of burning rubber.

A dozen blocks, no pursuit showing, the driver slowed and turned his headlights back on. Into commercial districts, then, neighborhoods, denser commercial, the street lamps throwing enough glow for Ben to get a look at the man behind the wheel.

Late forties was his guess, a shine that became tracks running down from damp hair. Solid in the chest, regular features marked by stubble, dark-stained bandanna around his left bicep where the sleeve was pulled up. Even though they were well past the incident, his breath was coming in gasps. Grunting with the effort, he reached down to tap what looked like a scanner unit, and a tiny light came up, a crackle of static. Another block and the driver swerved to avoid an obstacle that wasn't there, and from the stain Ben could see on his shirt, he realized the man must have been hurt in the crash.

"You okay?" he asked him.

"*Si.* Okay."

Despite the windows rolled down and what appeared to be bullet holes in the windshield, the interior smelled of sweat. Sweat and something else...

"*Que es su nombre?*" Ben ventured.

No answer.

"*A dónde vamanos?*" Adding, "Where are you taking us," in case he'd blown the meaning.

Silence. Then, "*To safe.*"

"That's good news, at least."

Shay said, "Why is he slowing and speeding up like that?"

"I don't know, Shay."

"He's driving funny. Did he get shot back there?"

"I don't remember them shooting. Do you?"

She shook her head. "Dad, I have to go to the bathroom."

"Not a good time, hon. We need to get off the spit."

"That food...I wouldn't have asked if I could hold it."

"*Mi niña,*" he said to the driver. "*El baño?*"

The driver grunted something, drifted through an intersection.

"*Por favor,*" Shay spoke up. "*Hello...*"

They'd nearly run the length of Punterenas—beach and water right, less density left—when the driver slowed at a store with gas pumps in front that not only was closed for the night, but had been for some time. A mimosa tree nearly covered its entry and shallow-eaved roof with leaves and dead blossoms. Before he'd killed the headlights and rolled to a stop, Shay was out the door, saying she'd find *something.*

"*Usted?*" the driver asked Ben as she disappeared around the side. More like a gasp.

"*Porque no?*" Ben said, thinking *Might as well—who knew when again.* Glad for the darkness and the soft night air, he used the far side of the tree, was coming back when he heard the creak of hinges and Shay appeared around the other side.

"*Ohmigod*, it was horrible. I almost didn't make it." Almost to the car when she stopped. "Is he drunk or something?"

The driver had slumped against the car door, head on his chest.

"He breathing?"

"Yeah, but it doesn't sound good."

Ben touched him to no response, shook him gently; finally he leaned in to tilt him upright. But the man only tilted further, and Ben had to react to keep him from falling onto the assault rifle. Plus, the wetness that came back on his hands wasn't sweat. Even in the dark, Ben could tell it was blood.

The man groaned, tried to sit forward, almost made it before falling back. The scanner under the dash crackled something in Spanish, crackled again, and stilled.

"What do we do? We have to get out of here."

"I know, Shay. Give me a second."

"They'll *be* here in a second. Can't you drive us?"

Ben thought. "I could, into another roadblock. This guy knew where he was going—we don't. Besides, we're just assuming he meant us no harm."

"What are you saying?"

"That we don't know."

"But he got us out. Why would he have done that?"

"Permanently might have been the idea."

"This is totally wacked."

Ben was conscious of how loud the crickets were, the caress of wind: like a night on his own patio, smoke bending off his barbeque before a rain. How different that life was and wondering if they'd ever see it again.

"Dad, they're coming. Can we do *something? Please?*"

A night bird screeched and flapped away.

"Come on," he finally said.

"Where?"

"Back to the wharf. Find some place to hole up until morning when we can hire a charter."

"With the cops back there?"

"They think we're in a blue car tearing down some road they're sealing off."

"Until they find *him*."

"It's a chance we'll have to take. And he needs finding."

They'd rounded the corner, Ben trying to keep pace despite his hurts, when he thought he heard familiar car rev. But a gust of wind took it and at the moment he had more important things to worry about. Like when the remaining ibuprofen he'd forced down after taking a leak were going to kick in.

It was dark under the wharf, damp from the tide that had left plastic and glass containers beached and strung with gulfweed. Footfalls sounded on the planking above, laughter from lovers walking it off, the intermittent rush of cars on the *paseo*. Finally, even those gave way to the creak of lines and rigging. Out where the wharf bent right, Ben glimpsed the boat he'd had in mind, and they settled in to wait until it showed signs of life.

The earlier the better.

"You awake, Dad?" Crinkling under newspaper scrounged from a refuse can as he shifted on the carton they'd flattened and dragged over.

"Yeah."

"Still hurting?"

"I'll live. Are you warm enough?"

A beat passed; wavelets splashed down where the tide was mustering another charge up the sand.

"Dad, I tried to make them stop."

"I know, Shay. There was nothing you could do."

Up on the *paseo*, a bus ground to a halt in a hiss of brakes then ground off again.

"Can I tell you something else? Until they started beating you, I was halfway glad they'd caught up with us. Just so we'd be going home."

Ben reached out and touched her hand, gave it a squeeze.

She said, "Do you think Mom would understand?"

"If anybody would, she would. And she'd have to forgive us both for feeling that way."

"Guess we're not such hot stuff after all, huh?" Swallowing hard and looking away.

"She'd be so proud of you, Shay. I'm proud. And another thing. If this doesn't work out tomorrow, it's over. None of it's going to change what happened. Not the important part."

"I'm sorry, Dad."

"Me, too."

"With the cards and everything? You were amazing."

A siren whipped through town; Ben took a breath, grimaced down to an elbow, stiff and getting stiffer. "Other side of the coin, Shay—desperate. You want to know something? Before I met your mom, that *was* me. And that's the polite version." Brushing away her tears. "Whatever we did—whatever we are now—it's because of her."

"You think so?"

"Bank on it."

She sniffled again. The lapping increased as a swell rode in on the wharf, then subsided, and the wind hummed through the cracks. Ben could hear the sound of raindrops on the planking.

"Blackmail," he said.

"What...?"

"Try this: What if Matos is blackmailing Torrijos or vice versa?"

"I don't—"

"One has something on the other to make him do something, and *that* led to the thing at the house?"

In the dim light, he could see her eyes fixed on him.

Much as to convince himself, he said, "What if this whole thing is coming to a head because of it, and we were just in the way—when we were hit and since then. It might explain—"

"Dad?" she said pulling up the fold of newspaper. "I'm going to sleep now."

PART FOUR

Matos

40

He watched the glow swell and ebb, smoke billow and trail against the moon's diffused light. Ever since Matteo spotted it up the eastern hillside and asked about it, Enrique had stood on *Machacha's* bridge and watched, lowering the binoculars only as night deepened. Not that he'd seen much through them. Mainly they were a cover, something to do with his eyes...a device to confirm to Matteo and Anna that something near their house—most likely the sugar cane across the road—had caught fire but was coming under control, nothing to worry about. Short answers he could cope with without choking on them.

Joining him after getting the kids settled, Kate said, "Matteo knows."

Enrique raised the binoculars to a new flare-up, most likely the fuel tanks. Like watching your life burn and being able to do nothing—not and assure your children of any kind of future. All he had left now.

"And how does Matteo know?"

"From your responses. From not allowing him to look through the glasses."

"And you believe I should have." Lowering them again.

"Of course not. I'm just—"

He held up his hand.

"Tell me," she said despite it. "Does Torrijos know to come here?"

"Not from me, he doesn't." Raising them again and wishing he hadn't, the house roofless and crying out to him about the hell inside it.

"Which could mean any time now."

Still not looking at her, Enrique nodded.

"Shouldn't we leave?"

"Not until the hour I told Chávez. Or we're forced to."

"With your kids in the boat?"

He could feel her regarding him. "With whom I've asked you to stay, if you'll recall."

"Abuelita's dead, isn't she?" Kate said above a whisper.

"Abuelita refused to leave. Do you think she'd have let him do that if she were alive?"

Kate fell silent looking at it.

He said, "She used to tell me Old Matteo won her with poetry. One in particular: *I'll come to thee by moonlight, though hell should bar the way...*"

"*The Highwayman,*" Kate said to his fade.

"You know it?"

She nodded. "Strong stuff when you're that age. Defiant as I was." Eyes following the smoke as it oranged the moon. "*Though hell should bar the way.*"

"What's done is done," Enrique said. "Or almost."

She turned toward the hatch. Up on the pilings, the warehouse venting fan creaked. Burn competed with the smell of mud flat and salt-bleached wood, and the sky around the moon resembled a battle-torn regimental flag.

Kate was headed below when she turned, as Enrique did, at the sound of a car. Laboring to downshift, fishtailing and barging over the ruts, headlights bouncing crazily through the lattice of vines and branches. Sliding to a stop beyond where they could see it as the driver stalled out.

Dust caught up and drifted through the beams, but the driver made no move to turn them off. By then, however, Enrique was starting *Machacha's* engines, killing the lights in the main cabin. Telling Kate to run them out in the event of shots, he threw all but the stern lines into the boat, tried to catch sight of Chávez on the dock. But the moon was veiled now, and from where they were moored, he could make out only backlit warehouse.

Enrique took the steps to the deck three at a time, made his way to the corner of the building. The blue Toyota appeared to have been rear-ended. Steam rose from the sprung hood and the engine ticked loudly. Beyond that, there was no sound or movement. Crouching to let his other senses come into play before committing himself to open space, he edged closer, pistol in hand. Finally he made out Chávez slumped against the wheel.

He resnugged the gun, reached in the open window, turned off the headlights and ignition.

Chávez raised his head.

"*Lost them,*" he said. "*My fault.*"

Enrique lifted out the man's legs, and as he did saw the extent of the blood loss. Under the biceps wound where the bullet had dug into his ribcage, Chávez's shirt was crusted almost black.

"Can you stand?"

"*Supuesto.*"

"Anyone follow you here?"

Chávez shook his head, nearly pitching forward before Enrique dipped under his opposite arm for the long stagger back to *Machacha.* Halfway there, he said, "Fucking goddamn Superman. Why didn't you get this patched up?"

"Didn't know how close Torrijos was."

"Damn you," Enrique said under his breath.

Chávez coughed a grin. "Passed out. Her people gone when I wake up."

"And you have no idea where?"

"Too late. *Policía.* Figured you'd want to know."

They were at the steps now, Enrique's arm numb from Chávez's bulk. Though he couldn't see, he knew Kate and likely Matteo and Anna were looking up at them.

He said, "We have to get you aboard. Then to a doctor."

"*No doctor.*"

"You heard me, *Grande.* Come on."

"Not this time." Chávez let himself sag, more weight than Enrique could bear, and together they slumped to the deck. Then Kate was there, helping brace Chávez against a piling, the moon poking through a rip in the clouds.

"My God," she said. "His side..."

"Go back aboard."

"He needs help."

"Tell him that."

Chávez coughed blood that Kate dabbed with her shirttail. Trying to hold her in focus, he said, "Your people...they okay." His eyes drifted to the hillside. "*Pinche cabrón,*" he said, taking it in. "*Hijo de puta, Torrijos.*"

"Come on," Enrique said. "There's nothing—"

"Get me the *Quince*."

"Better I call you a doctor—"

"*In the car...*"

Knowing he was right and hating it, Enrique thumped across the planking, retrieved the AR-15 from the Toyota's front seat. Then he was back and ejecting the spent clip, shoving in the fresh one and racking the bolt. Guiding Chávez's hand to the grip.

"*Bueno.*" Fumbling to lever off the safety.

Enrique did it for him, then rose slowly. "Don't worry," he said. "I'll take care of all of it."

"Just like your old man." Chávez cracked a bloody grin. "Now, go."

Enrique squared up, led a grim-lipped Kate down the steps without a look back. That came as he eased *Machacha* beyond the pilings, lightning visible beyond the mangroved lagoon and the air smelling like approaching rain, Chávez's unmoving shape a benign growth on the shadows.

"It's because of me," Kate said.

"Don't talk nonsense."

"Bullshit, it's what you're thinking."

Enrique ran *Machacha* by the last of the mangroves, out into open ocean, where he throttled up, the sound and vibration, as they always did, going straight through him.

"Say something, at least."

"It's not your fault, it's mine," he said. Angle out, then a course south; even in the dark, familiar as the back of his hand. "There. You happier now?"

"*My people...*What did he mean?" Kate asked as water burst at the bow. Arms folded, hair swept by the wind, face in a determined set.

"There's a jacket below that should fit you."

"Don't tell me," she said. "Serena's."

"Rain's coming. You see that lightning?"

"*Answer me. What did he mean?*"

"Keep your voice down or you'll wake them."

"Then they'll be awake, won't they?"

Touching his shoulder, where the Virgin lived, Enrique asked for patience, focused on the horizon, where the flashes resembled a naval battle in progress. *Machacha* dipped through a bigger swell, a whipcrack of cooler air.

"Get the jackets," he said. "*Por favor*," to her glare.

She went below, leaving him to black ocean and starless sky, the shore lights falling away. Which gave him a chance to collect his thoughts to no great advantage. Certainly no insight. Where to begin...

"They still asleep?" he asked when she reappeared. Zipping the hooded slicker he'd bought Serena early on, when it had meant something. Serena hanging onto him, head thrown back and laughing as spray pelted them and sizzled past their ears. The sweet juice before the poisonous fruit.

"What did Chávez mean?"

Enrique shook off Serena's laughter, found himself blurting, "Your husband and daughter survived the collision." As though expelling something not right since the beginning.

For a moment she just stared, searching his eyes in the glow of the instrument panel. Then she raised a hand to his arm.

"Ben and Shannon...alive?"

He nodded.

"*Oh my God.*" As if the sun had rebounded and was bathing her face in those long, slanting gold rays.

"Fishermen found them," he said. "They were airlifted to a hospital. As of a few hours ago, they were all right. That's what Chávez was trying to tell you."

"That's where he went?"

"That's where he was."

"They were close and you knew it?"

Enrique obliqued a swell, slowing to ease the impact before accelerating again. "Torrijos told me—not until then. I didn't know how close until someone let me know she'd seen them. That they were looking for me."

"Looking for you...I don't—"

"To kill me, lead your government to me, something. Your husband saw me that night on the bow. He has a sketch. Somehow he knows the name." Enrique wiped at spray. "He's

221

also avoided Torrijos better than anyone would have predicted. Or Torrijos would have us believe."

"What does that mean?"

"I know what Torrijos is capable of, remember?"

For a moment she said nothing, then, "How could you keep this from me?"

"I told you, to keep you alive." Realizing how tired he was, that it had only just begun. "Your husband and daughter got away from him. After he attempted to frame your husband. Do you not comprehend the danger in that?"

"Ben, framed?" Clutching at the slicker as another gust of wind flattened it against her. "Why?"

"To discredit his story. Get him out of the country to protect Torrijos's investment."

"You."

"Hardly. It's the ship he wants."

"*Then why in hell doesn't he just go get it?*"

"*Because he doesn't know where I sank it.*"

Kate took a breath. "Can't he find it?"

"And be seen looking? Admit he even knows of it? Besides, that takes time and time is money he's counting on. Just as I'm counting on it."

"My God. What's in it that's worth all that?"

Enrique looked at her, then off into blackness. "American missiles," he said. "Stolen. Worth a ransom to people south of here."

"And you knew that?"

"Not until I dove the wreck."

Her eyes moved not at all. "Which is where we're going..."

"To finish it, yes."

Lightning flared in the southwest, thunder rolling after it. *Machacha* powered through a crest.

Kate said, "This is insane. We have to go back and find them."

"Listen to me. It's going to be very close. All along, Torrijos suspected I had you—that's why he had Rosado out there. That's why he's had the regular police looking. And if they found your husband and daughter first, he'd deal with that, an accident like Serena's. Same as he'd planned for you. There's no going back for him either."

"You're saying it may already be too late."

Nothing he could add to it, so he didn't—just slipped into the rain shell she'd brought up with Serena's.

"And you don't think I could have made up my own mind about this?"

"Could you?" Enrique asked. "And be truly objective?" First raindrops angling in to splat the flybridge.

Kate raised her hood. "There's more to it, isn't there? Something you aren't telling me."

"It's going to get rougher, if you want to go below."

"Damnit, you said it yourself. They're in *danger*."

"So are those two inside," he said. "Or did you miss what happened back there?"

"*I can't lose my family twice.*"

"And I told you from the beginning this has been about Matteo and Anna, giving *them* a chance. You think I'd abandon them now?"

Kate stood back from him. "I know why you won't go back. You *hope* he kills them, don't you?"

"*Madre*, will you listen to yourself?"

"So that is it."

He gripped the wheel. "Do you have any idea what it's like from here? Of course, I dreamed it: you and me, Anna and Matteo. They need you—I need you. Is that so terrible? You're right, I'd do almost anything. But not since you ran." Shooting a glance at the receding land, the barest flicker in the distance. "Not since *that*."

"All I know is, if anything happens to Shannon and Ben because of this, I'll kill you myself—no matter how long it takes. *Comprende*?"

"*Comprendo*," Enrique said after she'd left the flybridge and he'd raised and snugged the awning so tight the rain sounded like drumbeats when it finally cut loose and ran in torrents on the deck.

***

The squall had passed and stars were beginning to show before she came back and, without speaking, held out a fist. Dropped something small and square, cold and hard into the hand he extended.

"Matteo found this. He was trying to figure out what it was," she said as he held it to the light to confirm what he knew by feel. "I meant to give it to you before."

Enrique said nothing.

"What is it, do you know?"

"A tracking device. Rosado must have slipped it aboard."

She drew her arms in around her. "Which means they know."

"It would seem the case."

"Well…?"

"Well what?"

"You *are* going to throw it overboard." Looking intently at him.

"No."

"No? They'll find us with it. You can't want that."

Glancing at the stars, at their wake silvering with the reemergent moon, the lightning flashing now over land, he said, "This is a small country, Kate Metcalf. Whatever happens is a matter of time. Better I set the terms, be waiting instead of running." He dropped the device into his pocket. "Better for Torrijos to believe he has us."

41

Ben awoke board-stiff from the cops' blows and a night on sand, the stuff seemingly everywhere, even his pockets. Water dreams lingered, brought on by the ocean's surge, Kate's whisper in place of the waves: *Why, Ben...Why, Ben...Why, Ben...*

Vowing to take it out on Enrique Matos, every damn bit of it, he sat up slowly and painfully, confirmed that nothing was broken, just sore as hell. Last night's rain beginning to steam off the wharf, rise off the exposed and tide-packed flats.

The only thing he wasn't, was cold—something in that, at least. He raised his watch, focused on vertical hands. Not even daring to check for bruises, he touched the arm poking out from under the newspapers.

Shay rolled over, opened her eyes.

"Time is it?" she yawned.

"Six." Smiling at her.

"Do *I* look that bad?"

"You're too young to look this bad." Swiping sand off his wrinkled tropical shirt and chinos.

She sat up, brushed her hands together, shook them. "Sticky," she said, then considered him more closely. "How do you feel after last night?"

"Comin' up roses."

"Seriously."

"Words fail." On his feet and sizing things up. With the tide in this far, what would have been a wade last night to the lower deck where the charters where moored would now involve a swim.

Add soaked to everything else.

"Forget about it," Shay said from behind him. "Even if you weren't thinking it."

Ben regarded the greenish scud, crabs working a dead perch, the rainbow strings of fuel among other floaters, and said, "You win. It means walking topside, though."

"I'll go first, use the restroom, then tap that I'm moving on to the charter dock. Then you." Slapping sand off. "Okay?"

Ben mulled it, not liking the exposure, but aware it had merit.

"Hello," she said. "At least it's something."

"You realize you're beginning to scare me?"

"Tell me you weren't thinking it."

"Just trying not to hold you back."

He was listening to the waves and feeling the heat creep upward, glimpsing the charter dock through the pilings, wondering how *that* was going to play out, the inherent risk, when he heard a tapping above him and, "*DAAAAD.*"

"Sorry, lost in thought." Starting after her footprints. Hearing as he did, "*I don't believe it.*"

The pier at that hour was empty save for a vendor prepping for the day, scattered fishermen drinking coffee or hunched in folding chairs. Relatively clear at water level, the air still bore bus fumes and things frying, the hum of Puntarenas waking slowly. After using the facility, Ben toyed with seeing what food the vendor might be selling, finally passing on it as pushing his luck. Trying to ignore his stomach as he walked the length of the pier to where the charters were moored.

To his dismay, the boats had left.

All but one.

"About time," Shay said. "Here—I couldn't stand it." Handing him a half-eaten container of *gallo pinto* and a plastic spoon. "And it looks like it's *that* or nothing." Wrinkling her nose at the remaining boat when he'd finished and dumped the empty. "The others have left already."

"I wonder why?" Ben said. Despite last night's rain, the boat seeming even dirtier than the last time he'd seen it. He stepped aboard, banged on the hatch.

"*HEY IN THERE.*"

"What, you know the guy?"

"An old friend. Just wait."

He banged a second time and a third, until a familiar face, puffed with sleep and hangover, slid back the hatch and peered out. Blinking as Shay, recognizing him from the bar, let out a breath.

"Surprise," Ben said, holding up the wad of Barrera's bills. "Guess who wants to make you rich."

The man named Delura raised a hand to bloodshot eyes. "*Shit*," he said, regarding them with a dawning awareness.

"Ain't it the truth," Ben said, waving Shay aboard.

After Delura had gone ashore to use the head while Ben started coffee on about the grungiest maker he'd ever seen, Shay shaking her head at the result, they cast off, eased past the wharf, and headed out, trailing a flock of circling screeching gulls.

"Coffee's extra, you know," Delura said. Eyeing an incoming craft as Ben ventured to taste some and found it not too bad.

He threw a bill on the instrument panel. "Cover it?"

A grunt, followed by, "Where you want to go?"

"South," Ben said. "Bahia de Coronado."

Silence.

"You know it?"

Delura threw him a look. "What do you think? Big bay— better than thirty miles wide."

Ben let a beat go by while he thought. "You know the mooring buoys?"

"I look like the yacht club type to you?"

Ben checked the navigation station, found a recognizable corner under a pile of debris, pulled until the chart came free.

"Watch it there. Break anything, you bought it."

"Right...here," Ben said, pointing. "North of this mark."

"Make that twenty-five miles," Delura said, angling a glance. "What you want down there? Something to do with the face you showed me?"

"Tell you when we get there."

"Nothing but snakes, crocs, and mud—everybody eating everybody else," he said. "That really your daughter? Doesn't look much like you."

Ben raised a hand to Shay, who was poised to say something. "Your two cents come with the coffee, or is that extra, too?"

"Just trying to make conversation."

"We'll settle for the coffee."

They were well out to sea now, the land a hazed shape on their left, the gulls long since on to more promising fare. Ben noted from the unmarred handle in Delura's scabbard that he'd replaced the scaling knife with a new one.

"This thing go any faster?" he asked.

"You want fast or sure? Or maybe we just go back and forget it. All those other boats waiting to take you out."

Ben let it go. "You have diving gear aboard?"

"Some. Old, but I use it."

Ben nodded, not sure if they'd need it or not, the magnitude of what they were attempting rolling up from the chart. Twenty-five miles: *Shit* was right. He glanced at Shay, drifting off from the closeness and vibration, and caught himself drifting, too. Trying to keep in mind that all they needed was a sighting—divers or men working a crane, Enrique Matos working his wreck. Half-dreaming that the engines had slowed, but too tired by then to be certain.

They'd get there...in time...

Ben snorted awake, his first concern after a glance at Shay how long he'd been out. *Couldn't be that long.* Except his watch was at least an hour past last check, the engines were idling, and Delura was not behind the wheel.

Nor was he in the cabin at all.

Ben sat up stiffly as the hatch opened in a flare of sun and Valentin Torrijos was followed inside by Delura and someone else. This man was younger: muscled legs and wrists, cargo shorts and olive tee, shoulder holster with clips attached. In addition to the semi-automatic in his right hand, he carried a black duffel bag. Torrijos's hip holster revealed a polished wood handle; his right hand held what appeared to be a laptop case.

Shay lifted her head and looked around as Ben glimpsed a Scarab-craft veering toward shore. Then Torrijos was running a knuckle along his lips, saying, "What luck...not only a boat going our way, but companions." Smiling at them.

Delura's trip ashore...just long enough for a phone tip.

Son of a bitch.

Delura looked at Ben, fondled his knife. "How you like that, *pendéjo*? Where's the big talk now?"

Torrijos snapped his fingers and, as Delura throttled up, the younger man searched first Ben then a wide-eyed Shay. Winking at Ben as he did, a flick of tongue across even teeth.

Ben saw tunnel red and moved; the gun came up quicker. He was aware of pain in a tight white circle on his forehead, "*Daaaad*" from Shay, "*Not in here, not in here*" from Delura.

Not now, he found himself thinking. Not in front of—

"Mr. Metcalf? My associate, Mr. Beltran," Torrijos said calmly. "We don't want to say good-bye to Mr. Metcalf or his daughter just yet, do we? Not while they're of value."

For seconds no one spoke. Then Beltran backed Ben up a step, lowered the gun, and grinned wider. "Lucky for you," he said, swinging a wink at Shay, who stood frozen.

Ben pulled her to him, said into her ear, "It's all right, I'm all right. Everything's okay." Sitting her on the banquette, Delura clearing his throat.

"You don't mind my asking, where were you?" he said to Torrijos. "I was beginning to wonder."

Torrijos swung his eyes off Ben. "I hate boats. The more I'm not on them, the better I like it. Anything else?" As Beltran snickered, winked again at Shay, Torrijos gathered up the chart and spread it across the instrument panel.

"Where are we? Show me on this."

Delura glanced at land, took a hand off the wheel, pointed to a bulge before the coast resumed its southeast direction. "Here," he said, scratching the web tattoo.

"And how far to here?"

"Three-and-a-half hours, four to be safe."

"To be safe..."

"If the wind stays put," Delura said. "Which it should."

"And if not?"

"Pick a time."

Torrijos looked at Beltran, who'd opened the laptop and was monitoring something on it. Though he barely looked up, Beltran's head moved in a nod. Torrijos pulled out a cell phone and went out on deck. Steadying himself with a shroud, he punched in a sequence and, after moments looking out to sea, began talking. Ben could see him moving to maximize reception and had the odd thought it might be one of Kate's old customers providing the service.

Kate...

He saw Torrijos check his watch and nod, pocket the phone, wipe the shroud hand on a handkerchief.

Reentering the wheelhouse, Torrijos said to Delura, "You ever think about cleaning this pig? How do you live like this?"

Delura shrugged, kept his eyes on the horizon. "There's coffee if you want, or guaro. Bunks forward, you want to sleep." Obvious deference in the reply. "Which reminds me," he added as if it were the farthest thing from his mind—a topic, like the weather. "I was wondering when I'd see my money?"

He was turning to add eye contact to the question, Beltran coming to his feet, when Torrijos said over a knuckle, "What would you say to doubling it?"

"So you know where we stand," Torrijos said to Ben and Shay, "you're alive because I say so. The slightest provocation and she dies first. Is that clear?"

Silence, then, "Why are you doing this?"

Shay, flushed from the heat and sitting on her hands.

They were in the forward cabin, little more than a chain locker—offsetting bunks, no ports, single light fixture. There since Torrijos ordered Delura to empty it and lock them in before returning with the laptop device an hour later.

"Why does one do anything, Ms. Metcalf? And would you prefer a gag?"

"That won't be necessary," Ben said to her as much as Torrijos. "We understand."

"Good. Now I'd like you to see something?" Swinging the unit around to them. "Does this look familiar?"

Ben studied the contour, placed it from the chart in miniature: coastline, slight bulge under the more prominent knob where they'd nearly lost *Angel Fire*. The sweep of bay where they had lost her.

"Bahia de Coronado," he said.

"And the flashing dot up that little indent?"

Neither spoke.

Torrijos ran a hand over thinning hair. "A guess," he said, attempting a smile. "I insist."

"Something you're after," Shay volunteered.

"Promising, but unspecific."

"Some*one*," Ben said, remembering the lush canopy, the steaming, sound-filled jungle. What they'd seen coiled around something on a mudbank half a lifetime ago. "Enrique Matos."

"I did underestimate you, didn't I?"

Ben said nothing as the half-smile regrouped, Torrijos saying, "And might you guess why?"

"Something he knows and you don't. Something you want that he has."

"Which would be?"

"*Reina de Aconcagua.*"

The smile vanished. "Don't stop on my account."

With Shay trump in any game between them, Ben let the man have it—or most of it. Shay's sketch and the flyers, the library, their interpolation of the ship registrations and departures, the call to RouteStar. No mention of Omar Barrera or the missiles.

"Interesting tale," Torrijos said. "If one is to believe a known liar and a cheat."

"That's not true," Shay said.

"You know that he was cheating on your mother?"

"Yes." Quietly.

"Torrijos, I swear—"

"Then you must be aware of the man whose death he caused."

Despite the heat, Ben felt a cold bubble as if from a shipwreck at great depth. Decompressing geometrically as it rose.

"Dad? What is he talking about?"

"She's waiting, Mr. Metcalf," Torrijos said, the smile back in place. "Tell her. As her grandfather told me."

"Tell me what?"

"Now. Or I will."

"Shay, before I met your mother, I shaved points against my college basketball team. I did it for money."

"Like the cards here..."

Nice attempt to defuse, hon. Just not this time.

"Not like that, no. The man who gave me a chance to play the game ate and breathed it—slept in his office, the whole deal. Norv Schander. Thirty years coaching and one chance to go out on top."

Unaffected by time or memory: Norv's face when Ben copped to the fix. NCAA and the media swooping down, then the administration. Photos of Norv's garage, the rope hanging from a crossbeam, the only man who remotely resembled a father in his life. Norv's funeral from the deep fringe, Ben willing to take whatever his teammates dished out, but not his friend's widow's eyes.

"I took care of that for him. Brought the whole thing down."

"Your coach killed himself?"

"Because of me, Shay. Bottom line."

She met his eyes, looked away. "Did Mom know?"

Ben nodded, the cabin feeling as if it had filled with green water. Shay was about to say something but stopped, raised a hand to her hair, dropped it with the realization they'd cut it off.

Torrijos said, "Shows you that smart money isn't always so smart, Ms. Metcalf."

"And does that apply to you?" she said.

"Never mind, Shay. It's not worth it."

"Good advice. Take it."

"You're better than he is," she kept on. "That's what you're saying?"

"I expect you'll find out soon enough." Clicking shut the tracking unit. "And regarding Enrique Matos, you might even see your mother with him. That is, if he hasn't killed her."

For a moment his words hung there. Then Ben was off the bunk, Torrijos aiming his pistol at Shay until he sat back down.

"Damn you, if you're—"

"Your wife survived the wreck, did I fail to mention that? You can only hope she survives Enrique Matos."

Ben felt lightning prickle his scalp, sting his eyes as Shay covered her mouth and made a small, tight sound.

"Oh, he tried to tell me she died after he fished her out and took her home to who knows what," Torrijos went on. "But I've had a man watching the house."

Part of Ben thinking he'd been dead-on about the mistrust between thieves, the other thinking Shay was about to burst from her skin along with him, he managed to say, *"And...?"*

"Matos murdered him and fed him to the sharks. Is that answer enough?"

They were still in the cabin—Ben trying for caution, no luck, Shay's adrenaline sync'd to his own—when they felt the engine revolutions drop, the boat lose way.

"Can you hear anything?" he asked her.

She cocked her head, in a moment shook it. Without a porthole, they could only guess why the boat had slowed, was now proceeding at that speed. Shay thought she made out surf breaking, but after that much engine throb their ears rang and she couldn't be sure. At any rate the boat was taking swells. River mouth, Ben figured from the way they were pitching. Tidal race.

The boat slowed further; there was movement outside the cabin, a key in the lock. Then the door opened and Beltran's face appeared under a field cap, black smeared under his eyes. Torrijos in similar issue with the sleeves rolled up.

"Wish us luck," he said.

"Take me along," Ben said. "I can help."

"Daaaad..."

"Leave it, Shay. It makes sense."

"Don't listen to him," she said.

Torrijos smiled. "You helping me, Mr. Metcalf?" He was about to close the door when something stopped him.

A thought, Ben hoped. "Matos has my wife. You don't think I want him?"

The knuckle rose to Torrijos's chin and stayed there.

"Three beats two every time," Ben added. "One more gun. What about it?"

"Gun...?"

"My father was a cop."

"Oh, yes. Shot himself or something." Hesitating now, the thought obviously germinating.

"Got shot," Ben said, fighting the urge to wrap his hands around the man's throat despite the consequences. "What do you say?"

"No way are you leaving me," Shay said.

"Wherever and however, Torrijos. What you have in mind is your business."

"NO WAY..."

"We need to move, *Patrón*," Beltran said from behind him.

Ben could make out grenades dangling from the vest he'd donned. Belt and pistol holster, strapped-on AK-47, cut-down pumpgun. CNN direct from a jungle hotspot: rebels humping it across creeks and up hillside trails. Automatic rifle and mortar fire. Stunned-looking villagers fronting still-smoking homes and fields. Bodies laid out in media-friendly rows.

"*Momento*," Torrijos said, still looking at Ben. "I'm getting an idea here."

42

Kate awoke to voices—urgent-sounding, near-unintelligible. Abuelita's name the exception.

She set her feet on the worn floor, checked the kids on their cots, none of them having slept well aboard *Machacha* before heading upriver, Enrique not at all. Even after the storm, the swells had run high nearly all the way to a coast she'd recognized when dawn became sun cresting the mountains, gilding the jungle and the water. Not far from where she'd nearly died, Kate had thought, as Enrique'd slid the boat toward a barely visible inlet that widened as they entered, the jungle reaching out as though in welcome. Earth and rising heat replacing the cooler sea air.

Monkeys had screeched, flung themselves among the branches at their passing. Crocodiles—iguanas farther up the banks—moved not at all. And still only the children took note, Enrique on the flybridge steering in silence, Kate feeling something that only the sight of Ben and Shay could dispel.

She'd been dreaming about them in the camp where they were now—little more than a rain-silvered shack on stilts. *Machacha* tying up at what looked to be a dock dating back to Morgan days, Kate thinking they'd never truly ceased, just evolved. As had the participants, the man on the flybridge a case in point.

Yet he was not like that.

Just *not*.

She knew it.

Or was that wishful thinking, no less than her thoughts of Ben and Shay? Hard to tell anymore—waking up in a sagging fish camp, for instance, thoughts of those you'd lost and might never see again fading beyond your power to will them into permanence.

235

Kate found her sandals and slipped them on. Leaving the children behind the sheeted-off sleeping area, she heard Abuelita's name again and tracked the source: Enrique and an older man, stocky with a weathered face and sun-shot eyes. Someone she'd seen briefly and whose name—Pineda—she'd heard in passing from one of the others. Men who blended in like iguanas when they wished.

As she let herself out onto the screened porch, they turned and, as if by reflex, quieted. Enrique nodded to Pineda, who in Spanish told her, "If I had known you spoke the language, I'd have kept you for myself." Khaki shirt he wore buttoned to midway, religious medal on a chain showing under it. The hint of a smile.

It took a moment, but she caught on.

"You're the one who found me?"

Pineda nodded.

"*Mil gracias para mi vida.*"

"*De nada.*"

"What he means is *con gusto,*" Enrique said.

His silence broken, she asked him, "What is this place?"

"Refuge. My father knew of it from his father. Beyond that..." He shrugged.

"Who are they?"

Pineda followed her gaze to three men securing a pile of something with a tarpaulin. Again he looked at Enrique, who nodded.

"My people," Pineda said. "The last of them, anyway."

"Cargo from the ship that hit us?"

"*Reina de Aconcagua,*" Enrique spoke up. "Copper ingots, blackened but saleable."

"Rique, is this wise?" His look echoing it.

"Figure the cost and tell me—was any of it?" Fishing in his pocket for the tracking device. "No matter, this is where it ends."

Pineda examined it, set it on the rail. "When?" he asked.

"Soon, I expect. I phoned the contact last night. The best they could do with such notice was four o'clock today."

"Been a long time coming. I'll see to it."

Kate checked her own watch, somehow still running.

Two forty: an hour-twenty to go.

"Contact with whom?"

Enrique met her gaze, shook his head this time.

"I see," she said. "Anna and Matteo."

"Your safety and theirs. Here for a while longer, later aboard *Machacha*. If you don't mind, that is."

"No," Kate said, thinking of Shay. "Of course not."

There was a palpable easing of his expression, the muscles in his shoulders. Reaching to brush a mosquito from her cheek, thumbing the bite or a smudge or something—whatever it was, she couldn't see—he said, "The other day...you're not responsible. Chávez knew it and so do I. This was set in motion a long time ago."

Like a blow taking her breath as he went on.

"When this is over, I'll find your husband and daughter and bring them in. That I swear to you." Using the backs of his fingers to relocate a wisp of her hair, send a feeling through her as if she'd lightly touched warm water.

Kate cleared her throat. "After you've killed Torrijos..."

His eyes stayed on hers.

"Or he kills you. Nothing if he kills you."

He said, "I've tried to explain. Knowing Torrijos is coming gives us an edge."

"You couldn't just leave?"

"Ask yourself the question. Could you?"

Images came: Abuelita in the photographs in the big house. Abuelita raising him. Not only him, but his father and Anna and Matteo. The big house on fire. Her in it.

"*Though hell should bar the way*," she said.

"As it would be with your people. I take it back—as it is now."

"Can't you at least talk to him?"

He stood and faced the jungle, the work going on below. "I'm sorry, Kate Metcalf. Sorry for what I put you through."

Something shrieked high in the trees.

From someplace farther off, Pineda cleared his throat.

Kate drew a breath, stood, and without looking back eased the door shut behind her, thinking, *Damn all of it to hell.*

43

The island was a curled fetus, the indentation toward which they now inched the right side of a narrowing arm of river. Assuming it *was* an island, Ben observed from the wheelhouse: best guess about a mile around, no more than a half-mile wide where they'd made out the blue sportfisherman tucked into an overhang.

"*Machacha*," Beltran raised his binoculars to read off the stern. At which point, Torrijos ordered Delura back to where the river widened, then to circle and come in at the camp he'd made out through the trees beyond *Machacha*. From where anyone watching would least expect them.

They'd rounded the island, were coming in from the east, when Delura slipped it into neutral, let the boat drift in the brown water.

"Around that bend," he said.

Chained through a support rail, one in each handcuff, Ben and Shay were able not only to view the sportfisherman's bow, but this time the rusted roof of a raised structure a quarter mile off. A blood-colored postage stamp among the green.

"Well?" Torrijos, without lowering Delura's field glasses.

"Gotta be trails in there," Beltran answered. "You just have to know where to find them."

At Torrijos's nod, Delura eased the boat back upriver, past a rotting dugout canoe, Ben thinking of Bogart emerging covered with leeches, their *African Queen* banter bringing with it an almost tangible longing for Kate. He watched Delura secure the boat to a pair of mangrove trees, then join Torrijos and Beltran on deck.

"What are they going to do with us?" Shay asked.

Hoping to lip-read the conversation—but forget that—Ben said, "If I had to guess? Take us along as some kind of ace in the hole."

"Will they hurt us?"

"Are you kidding?" More convincingly than he felt. He watched Torrijos take out his cell phone and ease toward the stern. "Bargaining chips, you take care of."

"Meaning us."

"Right."

"Dad?"

"Yeah?"

"Your coach who died. It wasn't your fault."

"Actions have consequences, Shay. You're looking at proof."

"You can tell me that all day, but it's not who you are. Remember me saying I knew you didn't play cards? I was wrong, but it didn't matter because you're still who you are inside. *You* told *me* that, Dad, remember? On the boat."

Ben could say nothing, the thought hitting like the proverbial bolt that whereas a father might be one thing or another— witness his own and Kate's—Dad was earned. Like a merit badge, it was the sum total of what you put into it. No free rides, no quits, no random. Intentional. And if you did fall, you got back up and took it on, full court and that much smarter. That of all the things she could have called him at this stage— his name, *Hey*, or just nothing—*Dad* was her choice.

Dad. Right there the whole time.

"I mean it," she said.

"That's why it's about the best thing anyone's ever said to me."

"Dad?"

"I love you, too, in case you wondered."

"I might have said some things earlier that—"

Beltran and Delura's reentry cut her off.

Beltran held the shotgun he'd brought aboard. As Delura unsheathed his knife and stood by grinning, Beltran set it down, fumbled in the duffel, and came out with black electrical tape he wrapped around the barrel. He looped the roll several times around Shay's neck, then the barrel again, the rage rising in Ben like a roller-coaster coming off near-vertical.

"Daaaad...?"

"I know, Shay. Play along. It's for effect."

Beltran racked a round into the chamber, set the safety, handed the pistol grip to Delura, who took it as if it were a cone of shave ice on a blistering day.

"Dad, I'm scared."

Ben's vision was a photograph on fire, the edges blackened and curling. Knowing who it was meant to control, he said, "That's why he's doing it, Shay, to frighten you. Because he's no man at all. Just a second-rate coward."

As though cued by Ben's words, Beltran pivoted, drove a fist into his middle. Doubled over and gasping, the blow reverberating in last night's cop shots, Ben blinked up to see Delura showing a spread of teeth, Beltran saying, "Would you want his finger on that trigger? I sure wouldn't."

"*Dad, are you all right?*"

Ben nodded.

"Course he is, *chica*," Beltran said. "Making sure nothing happens to this old boy, right?" Slapping Delura on his non-gun arm.

Torrijos poked his head inside, the heat and humidity as though someone had yanked open the door to a sauna. "Time to move," he said.

They went: single file through jungle smelling like mold with a flame under it. Ben leading Shay, Delura behind her with the pumpgun so that Ben, even if the cuff that bound them at the wrists vanished, could do nothing.

Behind Delura, Beltran and Torrijos were faint squishes, the sounds of branches. The plan, they'd explained debarking, was to head inland, come in from dead behind the camp.

"*Move*," Delura said at one point, giving Ben a shove.

"Go easy with that thing."

"Dad, I can't go any faster."

"Try, Shay."

"How you like it now, shit-for-brains? Piss *me* off and see what happens."

Ben pictured his thumbs in the man's eyes, popping them out as he screamed. "She's trying. And he wants us alive, remember?"

240

"Why they got me walking point," Delura said in a stale float of guaro. "Not afraid of the dirty work."

Ben said, "You really think they're going to let you live after this?" Reaching out to hold a branch for Shay, his other hand supporting her the best he could. "Who takes an ambush? You see *them* up here?"

"*Gringo pendejo.* Shut your hole."

"And what are you—a native?" Ben said.

"My nationality ran out with my vet checks. All she wrote."

"And you think that puts you into a loop like this? Use your head, Delura."

"*Bastante.*"

"Help us, you walk away," Ben said. "My guarantee."

"Shitcan it, I said."

"Better to be on the side with a future."

"I know what side I'm on."

"You may, but do they?" Ben said, helping Shay over an uprooted strangler fig.

They were in a particularly dense patch now: vines and branches, dripping foliage, spiders from belladonna size to those of spread hands, mosquitoes rising in clouds from standing water.

Suddenly Delura recoiled at a web, cursed, furiously brushed something off him, stamping around with his boots. Farther on, he said, "Ever see a kid nailed by one of those things? Swell all up and die? I have."

"He doesn't mean it, Shay," Ben said to her look.

Delura grinned. "Belladonnas and ants. Lord have mercy."

In the struggle to hold a line, time became one foot in front of another, direction little more than the rays that found their way in. Caked in mud and fatigue, Shay's feet were becoming increasingly difficult to extricate. Her face was a cautionary shade of red when Ben, in the lead, stumbled into unexpected sunlight.

A raised area roughly the size of a soccer field.

"*Back*," Delura ordered. "*Get down.*"

They dropped. Moments later, Torrijos, also flushed, and Beltran emerged alongside to peer briefly through the green.

"What now?" Delura asked.

"*Rest,*" Shay panted. "*Please.*"

Ben found his handkerchief, wiped dirt and sweat, bug squash from her face, gave her a smile she did her best to return. Behind them the jungle, stilled at their passing, resumed its cacophony.

"Not much more," he told her. "You can do this."

"Anybody see you?" Torrijos asked Delura.

"Nobody *to* see." Switching the shotgun to wipe his grip hand on his pants. "Whoever's here must be at the camp."

Torrijos checked his watch. "Almost four. Let's go."

"They'll have guards posted."

"So what?"

"No point looking for trouble."

"Not your worry."

Beltran cocked his head. "You hear anything?"

They listened.

Listened...

Ben heard it then: helicopter, the high whine of a light-duty executive model. Which became a red-and-white gumdrop with a stabilizer tail and *RouteStar* painted in blue skimming the far trees.

Shay looked at it settling in the clearing, then at Ben, back to the logo. "Dad? That's—"

"I see it."

"I don't understand. RouteStar knows about this?"

"Looks that way, doesn't it?" Ben said, thinking the oldest trick in the book. Obvious when you put the signs together: RouteStar's pat story and parsing, Barrera's comments about their having a legal department the size of Delaware.

RouteStar's no virgin.

Like hiring an arsonist to torch your house, turn a lagging asset into a more productive one. Or maybe you just needed the cash. Mentally he kicked himself for having missed something as obvious as insurance scam. Dar wouldn't have.

"More like set it up," he said.

Without warning Delura backhanded him.

Ben shook it off, tasted blood. "That'll impress them," he said. "Might even buy you thirty seconds."

Delura was cocked for another when Beltran caught his arm as he might a child's and thrust it down. Looking through the field glasses again, Torrijos smiled.

"Well, now," he said as a woman with a briefcase got out of the helicopter, bent low under the rotors, and was met by three men emerging from the jungle. "Looks like Enrique had it figured out after all."

Enrique...
Like a charge of electricity through Ben.
And there he was—had to be—the way he walked and gestured. Command, for want of a word. Light blue shirt under a black body vest, fatigue pants, utility cap, Ben thinking hard *not* to see him on deck, squinting at the horizon. Any ship, any era. Courses set, orders issued, fates determined.
What have you done with my wife?
To her, damn you?
Where is she?
He felt Beltran tense, looked to see him staring at Matos as a hunter would prey. Obviously wanting him as Ben did.
Fuck him.
Ben forced focus on the others: guards—sweeping the jungle with their eyes and AR-15s as the woman followed Matos back the way he'd come. Ben was wondering if it was Ms. Fuentes—she of the ice-calm indignation—when Beltran ordered them to stand by after an out-of-earshot exchange with Torrijos.
Squeezing her hand, Ben said, "Whatever happens, Shay, we'd never have made it this far without..." The rest catching in his throat as she stared at the helicopter.
"Will we see Mom?"
Ben swallowed. "If she's here, we will. You bet."
"You two don't shut up, I bury you right here."
Like a spark igniting latent fumes. "Stuff it, Delura. You think they can hear us over the rotors?"
"Maybe I do it just for fun."
"You're an asswipe loser dickhead," Shay said in a voice Ben had never heard from her, "I'm not afraid of you." Looking at

Beltran and Torrijos as though seeing them for the first time. "I'm not afraid of any of you."

Scrambling to her feet, she nearly pulled Delura up by virtue of his grip. "And this hurts." Trying to remove first the handcuff, then the tape, only to stick to it. "You all can go to hell. I want my mom."

Torrijos joined Beltran in a laugh. "All your women treat you like that, or just the young ones?"

Ben pulled her to him; with his free hand, he stroked her hair, felt her forehead. "It's okay, okay...a little farther." And to Torrijos, "She's burning up."

"Rain'll be here soon. Wash it all away."

"I have to go," Shay said. "That's my mom out there."

No losing it now, Ben told himself. *Improvise*.

"That's the woman we talked to on the phone, Shay. You'll see Mom. Just hang in." Wiping her face, blowing on it.

"She's here, I can feel her."

"Me, too." Ben turned to Torrijos, lowered his voice to just over the whine. "For the love of God, take the shotgun off her," he said. "She's no threat."

"I'll be the judge of that."

"You want a promise I won't do anything? You got it."

"Not you I'm worried about."

Delura scratched his stubble. "I can use the knife, if you want. Quieter that way."

"Everybody just shut up," Torrijos snapped as Beltran touched his arm and pointed to the clearing.

This time, the woman held a bar of something obviously heavy, while Enrique Matos held the briefcase. She said a last something to him and moved away, slipped and went to one knee, brushed mud from it, then passed the bar to the pilot, who'd opened the door for her. As it was closing, the rotors hit liftoff rpm, the men on the ground backing from the wash. At tree height, the helicopter swung east and dipped off upriver, its whine fading with the seconds.

"They're getting away," Shay observed.

In a beat, she began singing something Ben half-recognized from home: toneless notes in a meaningless cadence. Peggy Lee in *Pete Kelly's Blues*. Torn by her need and his to stay in the game, he willed his eyes to where Matos—flanked by the men with the rifles—stood watching the helicopter vanish.

Almost as if he were expecting them.

Marking that off as absurd, Ben watched Torrijos lower the glasses and gesture to Beltran, who racked the bolt on his AK-47.

"You know what to do?" he asked Delura.

"Oh yeah." Wiping the shotgun hand again.

Torrijos punched a number into his cell phone, spoke briefly after checking his watch, Ben thinking the turned-away mumble sounded like English. But before he could add to the thought, Torrijos and Beltran had stepped into the clearing and Delura was yanking him and Shay to their feet.

44

Kate was restless and so were the children. Cooped up all day, they'd played games from the boat—chess and Parcheesi, some naval thing Kate in her preoccupation was unable to follow. They'd counted parrots and monkeys, assigned them names to keep it going: Lupe, Chico, and Paco for Anna; Pele and Diego after Matteo's soccer idols. Mothers and babies and loud ones and shy ones and hyper ones.

Fords and Chevys on trips when Shay was younger.

Wondering if she'd ever see her again, picturing various stages to dispel the unspeakable, Kate let her eyes drift to the gathering clouds, late for afternoon showers.

Where is she?

God, I will not lose her again.

Kate sensed them looking at her and tried smiling, but it was no use. She felt her eyes filling, then Matteo at one shoulder, Anna the other. Neither knowing what to say—Anna close to losing it herself—but knowing. Wanting to be with her, to take it away.

Moved, she smiled, touched their faces.

"You two are something else, you know that?"

"Just don't cry," Matteo said. "Papa will find your little girl."

"Is she as big as me?" Anna asked, brightening.

Kate was on the verge of telling them Shay was not so little anymore, that in a few weeks she'd be fifteen—*fifteen*—when she heard the helicopter.

45

"Rique—good to see you." Torrijos said when he and Beltran were close enough, Pineda's two men spread out to cover them. Beltran's mottled features flirting with a last-laugh smile, Enrique thinking he doubtless was an ex-cop rescued off the shitpile or saved from prison, a Torrijos specialty. His man aboard *Reina*—everything falling into place from that knowledge.

"Why am I not surprised?" he said to Beltran.

"Who knows? Because you're so fucking smart?"

"I see you're a little dryer than last time."

Beltran ran his finger along the trigger guard, though he kept the weapon down. Nodding at the two guards, Torrijos said, "Spanish or English, Rique?"

Enrique eased the .40 out from behind his back, thumbed off the safety. "As if the option were yours."

"My concern was for them, what they don't know might not hurt them, but it's up to you. We're still partners."

"We were never partners. We were never anything."

"English, then. And why have I the impression you were anticipating us?"

Enrique tossed him the homing device. "My son found it. Our lookout made you where he wouldn't have thought twice about a fishing boat. Right now, you're in Pineda's scope."

"That old fool? And I was set to be worried."

"Better an act of contrition," Enrique said. "Or smarter company. Right, Beltran?"

"Fuck you."

"Cut the crap," Torrijos said. "Where's my ship?"

"So near and yet so far."

Torrijos let his eyes counter as Enrique went on. "What's left of the cargo—that we discussed, anyway—is under the trees. One of your real partners just left with a sample, a woman named Fuentes? Amazing, what comes from the threat of exposure."

"A page from my book."

"She seemed anxious to recoup some of their expenses while the market held."

Torrijos laughed. "You think I set this up for copper—for what's in the briefcase? Rique..." The laugh falling away as if greased. "You know what I want, or on the off chance you don't, give me the coordinates and I'll have Beltran bring up the missiles."

He shook his head. "Is there anyone in this you haven't double-crossed?"

"Myself. So far."

"You don't think I left them in the hold, do you?"

"One chance to come out of this, Rique. Where are they?"

"No place you'll find them. And I'd recommend against sudden moves."

Reaching up to mop his forehead, Torrijos thought better of it. "You think I care who you are? I'll burn your children alive, I swear to God. Your son first, while you watch."

"Before I signal Pineda, why Abuelita? Why her? She did *nothing* to you."

"Or for me when it mattered."

Reply escaped him. Colors swam.

"Betray me, kill one of mine," Torrijos went on, "I leave no one standing. Old women, children—ask Carthage how that worked. I mean, how would it look if I did?" He smiled. "It's finished, all right. Just not the way you figured."

Enrique raised a hand to signal Pineda, pictured the man taking aim—Beltran first, so he could deal with Torrijos himself. The feeling of *that.* "You'll tell me why, of course."

"Because you have the woman," Torrijos said. "Alive, as we both know. Because of what you're capable of and what you're not." He glanced at his watch. "Because the high-bidders will be crossing the border about now. And knowing the softheaded way you think, because of this..."

Looking back at where he and Beltran had emerged.

Enrique saw the foliage part and two people he knew, even though he'd not seen the girl, stumble into the clearing, shoved by someone he definitely did not. As they drew closer, as the breath caught in his throat and he raised his palm toward Pineda's position to call it off, he saw they were handcuffed together. That it was indeed a shotgun in the stubbled man's hand.

From far away he heard Torrijos say, "Oh and, Rique, you'll get a kick out of this. Guess who outbid the FARC?"

46

Face-to-face with Enrique Matos.

What Ben had dreamed of.

Now all he could do was stare at the man as Delura fidgeted beside Shay, regripped and shuffled his feet while Beltran and the guards eyed each other.

To Ben, strictly peripheral.

At slightly under his own six-one, Matos was not as tall as the flyer's description. Other than that, he and Shay had captured him: even features, dark hair under the utility cap, suntan over light brown, those eyes he'd never forget. Caged now, as though trying to find a way out.

Torrijos said, "Lose the weapons, Rique. Tell them now."

Matos stood silent.

"I said—"

"Where is she?" Ben interrupted. "Where's my wife?"

Nothing, the eyes still on Torrijos.

"*Goddamnit, where is she?*"

They swung his way, the lines around them deepening. "Your wife is safe, Mr. Metcalf."

"Prove it," Ben said after he'd taken a breath to steady himself. "Let us see her."

Matos glanced at Shay, glassy-eyed and defocused. He said, "Your daughter should not be out in this heat. She's not well."

"*My daughter should not be here at all.*"

Torrijos said, "If you don't drop your weapons at the count of five, she won't be. One..."

"Do it," Ben said.

"Two..."

"*Please.*"

The guards glanced at Matos, who said, "The irony, Mr. Metcalf? If I didn't love your wife, you'd be dead by now."

"Three..."

"I don't—"

"Four..."

Matos nodded and laid down his pistol, followed by the guards and their ARs.

"Step back, that's better," Torrijos said. Nodding to Beltran, who gestured for the two guards to take off.

As they did, he shot each. Short, loud bursts from the AK.

Shay screamed, tangling her right hand with Ben's left and the electrical tape as she tried to cover her ears.

"Now—where were we?" Torrijos asked.

Pulling Shay in tight enough to see into the shotgun's bore, Delura's face in close-up, Ben heard, "Oh yes, I'd almost forgotten," and looked over in time to catch Torrijos relieving Matos of the RouteStar briefcase.

"This what you signed on for?" Ben said to Delura.

"Shut up."

"Still think he won't kill you, too?"

Delura backed up, the shotgun coming to level as he did. "I won't say it again."

Ben caught movement, saw Matos extending his cap to Shay; he reached out and put it on her. He was touching her cheek to cool it when Beltran drove the AK-47 into Matos's back and, as he went down, laid into him with his boots. The sound of melons splitting.

Torrijos held up a hand. "*Enough*, let the man answer. The missiles, Rique—where are they?"

Missiles. Ben tipped an imaginary hat to Omar Barrera. And now what? Matos's face was a mask; Torrijos nodded and Beltran landed more kicks, Matos curling into a ball.

"*Where...?*"

"You're killing him," Ben said.

"Oh, not nearly, Mr. Metcalf. And you should see what our Colombian friends can do." He took a folding knife from his pocket, one-handed it open. "Much as we'd all enjoy that, time is a factor."

Stepping past Ben, he grabbed a fistful of Shay's hair.

Ben was conscious of her gasp and frozen cry, everything else fast-forward blur, the blade suddenly at *his* throat. Of feeling it's bite when Matos groaned something.

For a moment they were an obscene *Laocoon and the Serpents*—Torrijos and Delura, Ben and Shay, Beltran and Matos. Then, over the roaring in Ben's ears and the new throp of rotors—military helicopters from their deep rising sound, multiples—he heard, "Take me to the missiles? Enrique, what a generous and timely offer."

47

They found an old Chinese Checkers board, enough marbles to start a game. But as it progressed, Kate was conscious of every movement outside, each whispered command. It took everything in her to focus, Matteo nudging her, Anna giggling each time she botched a move.

Which discouraged them not at all. As if by helping her try to beat them, they were doubling their own fun. And though their patter brought Kate momentarily back, it was where she'd been that was the problem—out there with Ben and Shay, wherever they were. Would be until Enrique could bring them in, her thoughts of him as well—finally admitting it to herself. So that when she heard the sound of gunfire and the scream, Kate was at the window.

Just as quickly, Matteo was beside her, Anna wide-eyed and frozen in mid move, a fawn at the roar of a jaguar. Kate grabbed Matteo, spun him around. "I need you to be brave," she said in Spanish so there'd be no mistaking it. "I need you to take care of your sister for me. Will you do that?"

"Why? For how long?" *Matteo* was wide-eyed now. "Where are you going?"

"That was my daughter who screamed. Can you understand why I have to go?"

Nod.

"Not long. You'll stay inside?"

"Yes."

Anna said, "Will you bring her back with you?"

"Of course I will," Kate said, halfway out the door. "She's much better at games, you'll see."

God, God, God—down the wood steps, the porch seeming to shake the whole structure. Weaving her way through tree trunks and packed-mud trail toward the cleared area she'd seen earlier, and from where this new helicopter sound was coming, more

253

than one. She was almost to daylight when an arm reached out and grabbed hers.

Pineda packed a rifle and scope, cartridge belts, a look like death.

"Out there is no place for you," he said. "*Estan muerto.*"

Kate felt something tear loose. "Who's dead. *Answer me.*"

"Two of my people."

Three men with guns ran by, their neck chains and medals bouncing. Kate broke from Pineda, but she'd telegraphed the move and he grabbed her again.

"If Enrique is bad hurt, I fire no matter what his order," he said.

"What do you mean?"

"*Es muy malo.*"

"My daughter's out there, isn't she?"

Pineda just looked at her.

"Get out of my way."

He said, "You take this, get close if you can." He reached into a pocket, came out with a revolver he put into hers like an accessory she'd forgotten.

"I don't—"

"They may not search you."

"So what?"

"Be smart or be lucky," she thought he said to her. But by then she was past the trees and into the open, where two bodies lay sprawled. Enrique was on all fours being kicked by another man, and two black helicopters were clearing the far river, their sound rolling through her like thunder overhead. Or the pounding in her chest when she saw Ben and Shay, *God-oh-God* alive and standing.

48

Es muy malo.

Running toward Shay and Ben, Kate grasped Pineda's meaning. She was conscious of the revolver slapping her thigh. Of the cold fury willing her to pull the trigger—keep pulling it until she'd blown the son of a bitch with the shotgun away from her daughter. What Enrique had been unwilling to risk when he ordered Pineda not to shoot.

As she ran, the helicopters pulled up and hovered; trees whipped in their wash, dust billowed. They appeared to be sizing up the situation while Torrijos and the man with the automatic rifle and the grenade vest waved them in.

Run...

Shay was first to spot her: the silent *Ohmigod, Moooom,* followed by Ben's *Kaaaaate* and her own blurring vision. She saw the shotgun man do a double take and yell something, Torrijos swivel, the other man sling his automatic rifle and move toward her, a pistol in his hand. She saw Ben's arms reach out, Shay's face all but dissolve, felt *that* cut through her as the shotgun man looked back and forth with uncertainty. *Who the hell is that?*

She saw Enrique raise his face to her, the pain and dirt and sweat and blood there, his headshake *NOOOOO.* She saw Ben's initial exultation give way to *GO BAAAACK....*

But there was no going back.

Like a gust striking her, Kate felt the shock of her husband and daughter as she raced past them to Enrique. She glimpsed the grenade man and Torrijos brought up short, their gapes turn to hoots as she helped him first to one knee, then to his feet. Embraced and maneuvered him to shield the now-laughing shotgun man as well. She tried not glancing at Ben and Shay, but it was beyond her, a haunting and poignant news photo. Relatives being informed the loved one they'd waited for was indeed lost. So that in the instant after pressing the revolver into Enrique's hands, seeing his eyes register, Kate wasn't sure of what she'd done. Only that she was where she belonged.

49

Ben was fixed on the helicopters—combat Hueys, that unmistakable shape, rocket and cannon pods plus an M60 on each side—when he felt Shay stiffen. Heard her scream: *Ohmigod, Moooom.* Felt the electricity as he turned and saw her.

Kathryn Alice Hallenbeck Metcalf.

Running toward them.

"KAAAAAATE," he heard himself yell, felt everything recede into nothing. Afraid to move, afraid to breathe, that she'd somehow vanish if he did, he stood as did Shay—stock still, Kate beginning to mirage as his eyes and throat peppered. He was aware of blinking to clear his vision. Of wanting to hold her, feel her, fill himself with her.

Almost to them now: olive shorts, sandals, a camp shirt that billowed over something white as she ran, Ben thinking she'd never looked so beautiful. When he was able to think beyond the mere fact of her to the danger.

"BAAACK," he yelled. *"GO BAAACK."*

Not back, however—directly to Enrique Matos on his hands and knees. Ben could tell he'd spotted Kate, because the man was yelling something similar to his warning over the helicopter noise.

Ben felt as if a main had ruptured, or he'd just spun into a semi's path as he and Shay watched her help him to his feet, pull out a handkerchief. And with it, something that in Ben's inability to tear his eyes from her looked like the handle of a revolver.

No way...

"Nice piece of tail," Beltran yelled over the rotors. "She gonna do him right there, or what?"

As in slow motion, Ben saw Torrijos laugh, the helicopters dip forward, Matos whisper something in Kate's ear. He saw

257

the man's eyes connect with his own, flit to Delura, back to Ben.

Can you do something? they asked. *Something now?*

Ben willed himself to shift up past the hurt, to think as Kate must have: dead maybe if she did, dead for sure if she didn't—nothing that had stopped her. That kind of thinking. Twisting slightly, he stuck his free hand into his pocket, came out with a pinch of sand from their night on the beach. The only thing that came up sevens when he rolled them.

"*Delura...*"

"What?" Sweat running down the man's face as he eyed the choppers.

Ben flicked the pinch at Delura's gun hand. Dropping his eyes, he shouted, "*Belladonna, don't move*"—as much terror as he could put into it. Praying that with the spiders they'd seen, jittery as the man was, his spiderweb tattoo, what could happen might.

Unaware, Shay screamed; for an instant, Delura's hand fled the gun to shake loose what was on it. And even though his left replaced it on the pump, Ben's right now had the grip and trigger guard. He'd managed to twist it off Shay's neck when Delura abandoned the struggle for an underhand grip on his knife.

Dodging the initial thrust, Ben arced the barrel the final six inches and pulled the trigger.

Nothing—*shit*—safety: Delura'd had it on the whole time. He was fending off a second thrust when he heard a pop, saw Delura's head snap as though hooked, his body jerk sideways. Then Matos swinging the revolver back to its original target, Beltran firing before he could: three semi-auto rounds to Matos's wide one. He saw Matos spun down, Beltran looking toward *him* now and smiling. Then Beltran was flung backward as though on a string as something with serious grain behind it caught him in the chest.

Jungle, Ben thought, because Torrijos had flattened and was now facing it, pistol aimed at him and Shay. He saw Kate come to one knee with the revolver, trigger rounds that distracted Torrijos long enough for Ben to find the safety, yell at Shay what was coming, and fire.

He was thinking birdshot—positional fire—from the dust and the spread, a miss in front, and had jacked in another round when Torrijos suddenly rolled from the cloud. Firing blind, face blood-pocked, his screams were all but lost in the roar of the approaching gunships.

50

Debris swirled, the helicopters standing off, hesitant. In his rush toward Torrijos after the man's pistol had locked open, Ben could see the pilots talking on their intercoms. Deliberating. And something else that flashed: a face—unhelmeted and looking down at him.

From the hospital.

Alan Killfoile.

No time, the handcuff keys—move, Shay largely dead weight on two feet.

Trying to ignore the horror that was Torrijos's face, Ben rolled him, searched his pockets, and came up with them. He'd released Shay to Kate who had knelt beside him, was about to fling the cuffs off his own bleeding wrist, when a hand caught his arm.

Matos took the handcuffs. Backpocketed them.

"I thought you'd been..." Shot, Ben was about to say, when he noticed the red: right armhole where the vest came together.

Matos grabbed Torrijos's arm. "Help me get him up," he said. "Might work as a shield."

Much as to press the point, the forward Huey laid down a zipper of warning fire, *Tiro abajo de sus armas y entrega. Ahora hágalo o encenderemos* on its loudspeaker. At that, the side door slid back and a camouflaged soldier put a foot out on the skid.

"*What did they say?*"

"Surrender or they fire for real. Help me."

As they were lifting Torrijos to his feet, Kate said into Ben's ear, "Shay—what's wrong with her?"

"Fever, heat, I don't know. We thought you were dead."

"Same—I love you." Running Shay toward the jungle as Ben and Matos each grabbed an arm and hustled Torrijos after them.

260

"An American's in one of them," Ben shouted to him as they ran. "Consulate guy from San José."

Matos nodded acknowledgment as another burst came closer, the gunship seconds from touching down. Then flashes answered from the jungle, sparks bouncing off the engine housing. Immediately the chopper rose, circled out of range, brought its pods to bear as the other helicopter steadied up. Forty yards...thirty...twenty...Torrijos bearing some of the weight now as both helicopters fired at once.

Orange lit the jungle.

And still the flashes came.

Close enough to count the shots.

Two more rockets, a tree falling, explosions closing on the tin roof Ben now saw topped a weathered house on stilts. He saw Kate and Shay make it and disappear, cover almost there for *them*, another rocket find the house, the whole thing disintegrate. He felt Enrique Matos jerk to a stop, scream something, then literally pitch Torrijos into the forest as yet another rocket hissed above them.

"*Matteo...Anna,*" he heard Matos yell to the man shouldering a sniper rig and helping him to the base of a tree. Graying hair and a coarse-featured round face.

"*Machacha,*" Ben heard.

The sportfisherman.

Matos closed his eyes; touching his right shoulder, he took a deep breath and opened them to the canopy. The gunships were closing now, the twenties kicking in tracer rounds, the jungle beginning to shred around them. Ben heard shouts, looked to see two men hustling Kate and Shay down a strip of packed earth toward the river.

Follow or stay.

Pick one and lose.

Or gain them time.

Turning back, he saw blood and more blood—Torrijos feeling around with red hands, his eyes swollen shut; Matos opening a military-olive container to extract something that looked like a bazooka. Another tree toppled, splinters dart-flying, all ducking, wood smell like pungent breath. Rising with the help of the older man, Matos hoisted the thing to his shoulder, braced it against the trunk, and pushed some buttons. He met Ben's eyes briefly and nodded, flipped up a guard, warned him to hold his ears.

There was a bright hiss as the warhead detached, lasered in to strike the lead Huey, dissolving it in fire. As they watched, the carcass pinwheeled into the remains of the house and exploded.

For a moment the second chopper hung there. Then it sheered off and was gone. Ben could hear its thump from beyond the far trees and the river.

"Waiting to see what we have left," Matos said, his face pinched as the older man unVelcro'd his vest and tossed it aside, began ripping out first-aid pads from envelopes in a kit. Adhering them with tape and a bunched shirt to the wound. "Won't take them long to figure out we only brought up the one. My idea, not Pineda's here."

"Be gone by then," Pineda said. "*Resto fácil.*"

Matos coughed, coughed again; Ben could hear it venting in the hole he'd seen. He exchanged glances with Pineda, who'd begun wrapping Torrijos's head above his mouth in wide-rolled gauze.

"Bad sound, Rique," Torrijos managed.

Matos caught a breath. "Just so you know? They work."

"Tell me where the rest are and live."

"You'll see. So to speak."

Torrijos spat, or something approximating it, held still as Pineda finished up, the wrap already spotting through. "I look forward to hearing you die."

"The fishing boat," Matos said to Pineda. "*Comprende?*"

Pineda nodded.

"Half a mile upriver, under the trees," Ben put in, Pineda already up and running.

Torrijos said, "You think you're safe from these people, Rique? Before dark you'll be begging them to end it."

Matos ignored it. To Ben, he said, "You did well. That it turned this way is as it is."

"Out there," Ben said. "Thank you for what you did."

"We'll see to what end." He coughed, coughed again. Though his eyes were bright and focused, his color was draining. "Pineda knows how I want this to go. Kate knows the background. Are you with me?"

Kate...

"I am—yes."

Shallow breaths, as though he were building to it. Then: "Torrijos had my father killed. They were partners. He arranged it with a man named Venegas."

Paperwork around a picnic table at sunset—Omar Barrera again. "RouteStar's security chief," Ben said.

Nod. "*Pirata,* that's why they hired him—one to catch one. You see, nobody quits Torrijos. And so, one last raid, me along to get my father through it. Four years ago this was."

Breaths.

"Six months ago, Venegas gets wind of the missiles. Next trip to the Philippines, using his crew and some locals, he infiltrates the base and steals them, stows them until things cool down. He's done business with Torrijos before, so he arranges with him to job them off." Another cough, a nudge of Torrijos with his boot. "Right so far?"

"You're a fool, Rique. As your children will find out."

Matos shifted, grimaced. "The same Torrijos who has just struck a deal with RouteStar. Hijack *Reina* in exchange for *her* cargo, slip her back for scrap after the insurance company pays up. But there's a problem: no reliable help. Thanks to him my father's dead and I'm in prison. Plus he knows I'd never risk going back." Breath. "Unless it was the only way to *stay* out."

He closed his eyes against a crest of pain.

"So Torrijos arranges my release, murders my wife to make it look as if I did it, then gives me a choice. Two weeks work or a life back in. Unthinkable. Meantime, he infiltrates Beltran to make sure I find out zero from Venegas.

"It's one big setup. We concentrate on the cargo while Torrijos shops the missiles. High bidder becomes the Colombian government when your friend in the Consulate twists arms, the U.S. slipping in money to buy back its own armament. Guerrillas lose, army wins—after I take a bullet, of course. Beltran, too, when it's over. Everyone off the board but Torrijos."

"They're almost here, Rique."

Matos spat. "Meanwhile, Venegas rigs the ship to burn if he's double-crossed. As planned, Beltran takes care of Venegas. But that leaves no one to deactivate the charges. When I throw Beltran off *Reina*, Torrijos loses everything—eyes, ears, control. Nor can he risk searching for a ship alleged to have gone down two countries south."

Red soaked the makeshift dressing. "And now there's an even bigger problem. Pineda finds the missiles and calls me. One domino becomes another. You're still with me?"

"So far," Ben said, knowing what was at stake in his getting it. "How did you learn this?"

"People I knew or had access to. Hunches like Beltran that proved out. RouteStar, once I got who stood to gain, and they understood what I'd reveal if they didn't open up." Coughs, a string of them. "Turned out they already suspected Venegas of an inside operation—much came from that. Your man in the helicopter completes the money circle."

He paused for breath. Sounds were returning to the jungle—screeches and calls, flutterings. Movement in the slide toward twilight. Ben said, "You know about your grandmother..."

Matos looked at Torrijos, then at him. "Do you?"

"I was there. They were able to get her out before—"

Matos gripped his arm.

"Shot," Ben said. "Made to look as if she'd shot the cop who was also dead. I'm sorry."

Long breath. "Did your daughter see her?"

Ben shook his head.

"Good—no child should see such things. Help me into my vest, please."

As Ben did, Matos wincing from the effort, he had a thought and asked about the briefcase.

"With luck, Pineda's people will recover it," Matos answered. "As for my children, that part of their history is finished."

Gunfire rattled, the helicopter rising at the clearing's far edge.

Torrijos said, "Time to pay for all that wisdom, Rique."

"True enough—*Valentin.*" Freeing the cuffs from his back pocket, he snapped one to his own left wrist, the other to Torrijos's right before the man could react.

"What are you—"

"Partners, remember?" Jerking Torrijos to his feet as he made it with Ben's help. "Nothing you wouldn't do for me."

Pineda was beside them, then, eyeing the cuffs as he caught his breath. "As ordered, Rique—*Machacha* and the other boat. Set to go."

"Time for your people, too, *amigo.*"

"They'll know when."

Suddenly he smiled. "*Mil gracias para todo.* About time a Matos said it, no?"

Pineda shook his head, blew an exhale. Mumbling to himself and thumbing his eyes, he began pulling blind Torrijos along, Ben there for Matos.

"My father's friend. Since my son's age I've known him."

Spent, Ben nodded.

Another tree fell.

Matos turned to him. "It's important that you understand something else, Mr. Metcalf. Your wife...what I said earlier. Nothing happened."

"No need," Ben said. "I know."

Hoping to hell he did.

51

Kate was bathing Shay's face with water, not liking her daughter's flushed look at all, her shivering in particular, when she heard the footsteps.

Matteo entered the cabin, followed by Anna.

Pineda a presence behind them.

"Thank God you're safe," Kate said, reaching out with her free hand. And to the retreating Pineda: "Why this boat and not *Machacha*?"

"Rique," he said simply. Then he was gone.

Kate set down the towel, embraced Anna and Matteo, who were looking at Shay.

"You found her," Matteo said.

"She found me."

"How old is she?" Anna asked.

"Fourteen, sweetheart—going on fifteen."

Going on fifteen...

"Does your daughter like to play chess?"

"What Shay loves more than anything is to draw."

Anna's eyes grew large. "Would she draw us?"

"She's not feeling well," Matteo said. "Anybody can see that."

"She has a fever—that's why she feels bad." Immediately wishing she could take it back, the distracted and condescending way it sounded.

"Anna gets them," Matteo said. "And I'm not six years old."

"Of course you aren't."

"I am," Anna spoke up.

A rocket landed near enough to rattle the cabinets. Closer by half than the last series, Kate thinking both kids looked as though they were holding it together, but barely. All too familiar a feeling. She was conscious of the idling diesels, that steady, luggy, clacky symphonic. Of wanting to get the hell out of there NOW. Of Anna moving closer.

Saying, "I'm scared."

"Not me," Matteo said.

"Good thing you're with us, then. We need you," Kate said, dipping the towel and squeezing out the excess. Applying it to Shay's face again.

"*Mooooom?*" As if from a dark well.

"I'm here, Shay." *We're here.* "With me are Matteo—"

"And Anna."

"My *sister*," Matteo said.

Touching Shay's hand, Anna said in a knowing tone, "Never mind him. He's a boy."

Kate left Matteo to bathe Shay's face, Anna holding her hand. She was on the foredeck, scanning the darkening jungle for Ben, Enrique, anyone—imagining the worst and fighting going in after them, regardless of consequence. Then a burst revealed moving silhouettes almost to *Machacha*, tied to a weathered landing overhung by trees. Runners of mud and beaten growth leading to the boat Kate was on.

"*BEN...?*"

Ben raised a hand but didn't leave the figure Kate recognized as Enrique, plus a seemingly faceless man being dragged along by Pineda.

What in hell...?

Pineda slid down the embankment and thumped onto the landing. Leaping aboard *Machacha,* he disappeared below, while the faceless man—Torrijos, she recognized now from the suspenders—cocked his head for sounds. His shirt was a spattered mantle, the gauze fronting wounds bled through.

She was about to yell "*What are you doing? We're here.*" But as though timed to a burst of gunfire, *Machacha*'s engines came to life, burbled and spat. Pineda emerged from the cabin, stowed something in the starboard locker. He then went to Enrique—who by this time had shrugged off Ben.

Fear rose in Kate like a wave. Crested and spilled as Enrique tried moving by himself and his legs nearly went.

52

The river bank was steeper than it looked.

Ben kept glancing over at Kate and wondering where and how Shay was—how *Kate* was—his lost footing twice nearly taking them down. Torrijos, showing surprising strength, was almost able to throw himself off the landing, Matos into the water with him. Valuable seconds wasted wrestling him back as the Huey closed, aiming its spotlight and raking suspected positions. Finally they heaved aboard *Machacha* and stood panting, Matos braced against a shroud.

"What now?" Ben asked over the engines.

"You leave," Matos said.

"And where will you be?"

"No more questions, Mr. Metcalf. Go see to your wife and daughter."

A winded Torrijos said, "Mistake. I can still cut a deal. For all of you."

Ben ignored him; from the corner of his eye, he could see Kate on the fishing boat—looking at him.

Which him flashed, a persistent mosquito.

"There must be a better way," he said.

"There won't be for three children unless you get aboard that thing and do what Pineda says."

Torrijos croaked a laugh. "It's coming apart, Rique—you know it and I know it. Turn me out and I'll do what I can."

"Look, if you'll just—"

"Last chance, Mr. Metcalf." Matos drawing his pistol and cocking it.

"I don't think so," Ben said.

"Get off my boat."

Torrijos said, "You have no stake in this now, Mr. Metcalf. Finder's fee plus a helicopter ride home, free and clear on my order. What do you say?"

Ben didn't even look at him. "Captain's law?" he said to Matos. "Is that it?"

"You know he plans to kill me," Torrijos said. "Do you want that on your conscience?"

"*Ben,*" he heard Kate yell. "*Come on.*"

Matos looked him deep in the eyes, lowered the pistol to his side. "There is no more time," he said. Homing in then on Kate as Pineda cast off the lines. "Thank you, but go."

Which is how Ben left it.

53

Enrique slid *Machacha* from under the trees, down the arm to where the main channel widened. Making sure his running lights were on, he stuck his head outside, felt the first drops of rain. He'd already keyed the cuff off his wrist, snapped his end to a railing out of Torrijos's reach of the wheel and throttle. He found a stash of water bottles, drank one and opened another, his thirst worsening, if that were possible.

Pace yourself...

"Rique, Rique," Torrijos was saying as he ran his cuff along the rail. "All they want is the missiles. We can split the money."

Engine sound, the hiss of wake.

"Well—say something."

Machacha's surge threw Torrijos back onto the seat where Matteo and Anna had played chess, the thought hurting Enrique worse than his wound. Ten more like it he'd take to hold them, breathe them in, tell them he loved them instead of having it twisted later by people he barely knew. Worse, their never hearing it at all.

But he could barely feel his left side now, and between chills, sweat poured from him. His vision was going, convincing him for a moment that the figure beside Valentin Torrijos was Rudolfo Matos instead of the double image he blinked back.

The helicopter had no such problems.

He'd spotted it hanging back as they cleared the river and headed up southwest—out of the tidal race and into the deeper water holding *Reina*. Toward Golfo Dulce, he hoped they'd think, his grandfather's ancestral home. Banking that Torrijos had been that thorough in his briefings.

Maxing the throttle, he felt *Machacha* live up to her name: forty-seven, forty-eight, forty-nine knots—faster than he'd had her before. He couldn't remember the ocean being this calm: no wind to speak of, the rain not yet a factor. Boat and sea. Stigmata of sunset through the clouds.

"They're coming, Rique. I can hear them."

Enrique took breaths as a spasm passed.

"*Momento*—you're leading them to the ship." A dawning in Torrijos's tone. "Float a marker and let them dive it, up and gone by morning. Tell me you're not."

Enrique checked outside, caught the chopper's lights: half mile and closing—four, maybe five miles from the river mouth. He prayed that by now Pineda had the fishing boat pointed north. That those in the helicopter weren't thinking to look behind them. Only at *Machacha* flying south.

"Plenty of money for your kids now," Torrijos went on. "I knew you were just putting on a show back there."

"Who else but you?" Enrique said.

Fifty knots, fifty-two—*Machacha* smooth as glass, as if somehow knowing. Enrique let the sound take him a moment, then bent for a lanyard and lashed the wheel to course, nearly fell as he was releasing Torrijos from his handcuff.

"You've always been my nephew," Torrijos said, rubbing his wrist. Moving his gauzed face from side to side. "You just lost your head for a while. Over that woman."

Enrique coughed, dropped to a knee with the pain.

"Mark the wreck, they lower the money," Torrijos added. "On our way to get us patched up. And to think I doubted you."

Enrique led him to the hatch, opened it to a wall of engine roar and rushing water.

"Damn thing moves," Torrijos shouted. "That rain or spray I feel?"

"Rain," Enrique said, reveling in its cleanliness, the drops coming harder. "And they need to see us together for this to work."

"Smart, I always told Rudolfo, that's Rique. And about your old man: He went crazy and threatened me. Me, who'd put food on his table. Half-brother or not, how would you have felt?"

Enrique bit back images of Rudolfo—of Old Matteo straying on Abuelita to create this mutant bastard version of an uncle.

"Damn right," Torrijos pressed. "Pay as you go. Blood or no blood."

Caught up now, the helicopter was keeping pace aft. Enrique could see instrument glow in the gunship's windscreen, its forward cant, the armament angled down at them. He could make out pilot and copilot and, through the nose glass, their feet on the controls. Imagining thumbs over fire control buttons, he led Torrijos to the handrail, saw *soldados* with lowering lines and, briefly, an American face among the charcoal-marked ones. Just as the spotlight illuminated *Machacha* and a metallic voice said in Spanish: "Slow your speed and stop. Prepare to be boarded."

Almost there. Almost to Reina.

Bathed in white, his strength nearly gone, ever farther from his children and from all of it, Enrique yelled to Torrijos, "Wave, wave." With an effort that defied his deadening reflexes, he opened the locker and braced the AR-15 Pineda had stowed there against a strut. He thanked the Virgin for Matteo and Anna, asked forgiveness for having killed, told Kate he loved her and had from the beginning, his father and Abuelita that he was coming, and pulled the trigger.

PART FIVE

Papagayo

54

Watching it through binoculars was surreal, a poorly lit and jumping video without sound. Helicopter catching up to the speeding boat, hovering for what seemed an eternity; flashes from the boat causing Kate's heart to stop; all hell raining down then. From the unlit stern, she watched the pieces fly off *Machacha*, flames become a silent explosion that threw her bow into the air like a broken toy.

Then nothing.

No one.

Kate forced herself to keep watching, Ben below with Shay, Matteo, and Anna. Still numb, she saw the helicopter circle toward *them*, was about to shout in to Pineda for more speed, damnit—*anything*—when she saw the trailing smoke. Backlit in the growing rend. A thread that became a dark leash pulling the helicopter back.

Over the land and then gone.

Colombians, Ben had said—special forces on a covert mission to lock in the WASPs, keep them from the opposition. Enrique doing the only thing possible to save the rest of them. Walking dead, if not close to it.

She lowered the glasses, took deep breaths, pictured him cruising past *Angel Fire* that morning. Looking down at her coming out of it at Abuelita's. His eyes after she'd run from him. Watching the plantation burn, telling her he didn't blame her. The flood came then, mixing with the warm drops she'd stepped out into. Just wanting to feel something pure and simple.

She was letting the tears flow, Shay and Ben in there as well, everything they'd been through, when she felt a hand, eyes boring into hers. And in the fading light, the image of someone far older than Matteo Matos.

"He's dead, isn't he? My father. Out there."

275

Like Enrique's it was not a voice or a face you lied to, so she didn't. When he asked for the binoculars, she handed them to him.

"I don't see anything," he said after scanning where she'd indicated.

"You won't, Matteo."

"They killed him, didn't they? That helicopter."

"He drew it away from us. He must have hit it with his own fire, because it left after that."

"You saw?"

Kate nodded.

"Why didn't you call me?"

"Because he watched his own father die. Because he loved you and he wanted it that way."

Matteo looked at her. "Are you going to leave us now? Are you going to leave Anna and me?"

That face: She reached out to brush rain from it, but it shied away. Toward the ocean and the slash in the clouds.

"Come inside, Matteo. We need you."

"No," he said. "I want to be out here. With him."

With nothing to do but go where she was needed, Kate went in and cooled Shay, sat talking with Ben in the cramped cabin until he began to nod off, listened to Ben and Shay and Anna sleep. So full of the music of it she could barely form thoughts. And later, when she'd awakened Ben, turned over the fever watch to him, she passed Pineda at the helm. Knowing the answer, she asked if he'd like a break, was going outside after he'd shrugged it off, when she turned, addressed him again in Spanish.

"What will happen to them?" Low, so her voice wouldn't carry.

Nothing came back. Assuming he hadn't heard, she drew closer—so that in the glow, she could see his fatigue. And something else as he offered her the rest of his pack of cigarettes.

"My wife and I," he said. "I promise Enrique."

Kate shook one out, put it in her mouth but didn't light it.

"My wife is not in good health," he added. "Still, we will try."

"You have children at home?"

Pineda shook his head. "One son dead, two in jail for *la coca*. My daughter *es puta*. You know the term?"

Kate nodded.

She was turning from him when he said, "*Su esposo* is a brave man. Like you are brave. But he is not the only one who loves you. For a fact, I know."

He cleared his throat.

"You thanked me for your life. But Enrique's the one—he sent me back to find you. He doesn't order, I don't go."

Kate looked at him until her eyes began to burn.

Kissed him on the cheek and left.

On deck, stars showed and the air was fresh, the rain driven south by the wind now flattening their smoke. Asleep on a coil of line under an awning, Matteo was unaware of the storm coat Kate put over him. Unaware of her presence as she smoked Pineda's hard cigarettes and stared at the lightning-lit horizon and the night.

55

With an assist from the cruise-ship doctor, Shay's fever broke the next day. To Ben's relief, the abridged version of what happened seemed enough for her, and she and Kate were catching up, Kate inquiring as to who'd done *that* to her hair, when Ben found a phone and dialed Omar Barrera.

This time the reporter was in his office—San José to Puerto Caldera by afternoon, their departure not until six.

Shop by day, cruise by night, he joked, hanging up.

Four o'clock now—Barrera looking around as he and Ben settled on deck chairs under an overhang near the fantail.

"Little different than last time," he said.

"RouteStar money," Ben answered. "With Torrijos missing, Pineda figured the airports were the quickest way to jail or worse. Even *with* Kate alive."

"Pineda..."

"Matos's man. His contacts are why we're aboard."

Barrera ran a hand through his gray hair and looked bemused. "Enrique Matos. Who'd have thought it?"

"How about a reporter whose money I intend to send him as soon as possible."

"I'll get reimbursed. Forget it."

"Not this time," Ben said.

"Don't like owing people, huh?"

"Something like that. And don't forget the Mazda."

"Just a front end the insurance is picking up. No big deal." Accepting their drinks from a steward, he lit up with a smile.

"How are you feeling?" Ben asked.

"This week, not too bad. Every now and then it lets me think I have a chance. How's your wife?"

"Good. She's with Shay." Loving the way it sounded.

"Impressive kid. Give her my best, will you?"

"I will. And Kate asked me to add her thanks to mine."

Pausing to light a cigarette, Barrera coughed out the smoke. "Reporters don't get thanked—they get stood up, shined on, and lied to. Speaking of which, are you ready?"

"Out here?"

"Can't beat the view." Winking as he said it.

Ben went through it: Torrijos's role, the squeeze he'd put on Matos; Barrera's being right about the WASPs and RouteStar; the Colombians and Killfoile. The reporter really perking up at the idea of the U.S. buying back its own armament. Payment funneled through a government with whom it had military ties.

"Any proof you can add?"

"Pineda said when they retrieved the briefcase, they found Beltran more or less alive."

"Damn—he'll talk?"

"I believe that was the option given." Ben handed him a folded slip of paper. "Pineda said to call this number if you're interested."

"If I'm interested..." After a drag on the smoke, he pulled out a fax and unfolded it. "Early wire service," he said. "You think what your man has to say might jibe with it?"

AMERICAN LOST DURING MANEUVERS, Ben read.

Bogotá—*Assistant to the American Consul Alan H. Killfoile is feared to have been the victim of a helicopter crash during an exercise involving U.S.-trained units of the Colombian army. The exercise was related to recent U.S.-Colombian efforts to sever ties between rebel forces of the FARC and the lucrative cocaine trade. The helicopter evidently encountered severe weather, crashing into a mountainside near the Panama—Costa Rica border. Recovery teams have...*

Ben handed it back, gulped rum and tonic.

"Keep it," Barrera said. "And what's behind that look?"

"I'm that readable?"

"Don't get in any poker games aboard."

"Matos," Ben said. "I was just thinking he got them all." He had a darker thought involving Kate and slapped it out of bounds. "So," he said after a beat. "You get what you came for?"

"Kidding me? More—though what gets run isn't altogether up to me. What about you and the authorities?"

"I thought we'd let them sort it out on our way home."

Barrera took a pull on his drink, head-followed a pair of oiled men in bathing briefs who regarded him with equal interest, and deadpanned, "You might consider getting yourself a chaperone."

"Got one, thanks," Ben said.

There was a pause, a spritz of bright music as the doors behind them opened and closed. Splashes and laughter from the pool.

"Home meaning Southern California?" Barrera asked.

"Last time I was there."

"Now *that* feeling I'm up on."

He was standing to go when Ben said, "You mind an off-the wall-question?"

"My middle name."

"Know anything about Costa Rican adoption law?"

Barrera coughed, coughed again. "The Matos kids..."

"It's a thought."

"*Buena suerte*, much as I know about it. Helps if you live here, but it's not impossible." Separating out several of his cards, he stuck them in Ben's shirt pocket. "Call me when you get to wherever, I'll have a name. And if this story flies the way I hope, maybe even an official apology." He shook Ben's hand, was appraising another steward on the way out, when he turned and raised a thumb.

"*To beating the odds,*" he shouted.

Ben was raising his glass as Barrera disappeared through the double doors.

Kate found him as they were getting underway. "Hey, sailor," she said, kissing his ear. "Ever make it with a strange woman in a faraway place."

"Not in a while, but I've heard it's like riding a bicycle."

"You're looped," Kate said, sniffing his empty glass. "How many of these have you had?"

"Two," Ben said. "Sad, isn't it?"

280

"Pathetic." And to a passing steward, "White rum and tonic. *Doble, por favor.*"

"I love it when you talk Spanish."

Kate winked. "All the boys do."

"Speaking of all the boys..." Nodding at two casting looks his way despite Kate.

"I'm jealous."

"Deal with it," he said. "How's Shay doing?"

"Got the games, the TV, the sketchpad. What more, right?"

"You should have seen her, Kate. She just tapped in and went with it. Talk about growing up under fire."

"So she said of you."

Ben had to smile.

"One of you had to," she said. "I never figured it would be both." She nuzzled him again, the steward concentrating on her drink as he brought it and left. Draining half, she let out a breath.

"Do we know how to get lost, or what?"

His smile faded. "Serious for a minute?"

"That might be tough, I'm pretty happy right now." Then, "All right...serious."

He took her hand, led her to a spot he'd scouted out, a railing on the highest deck. Nobody around, Ben speculating that after the cruise's initial leg sunset likely ranked somewhere after happy hour, early buffet, and electronic bingo. They watched the lights of Puerto Caldera. Sky turning orange and red, pink and blue. Late gulls wheeling with the ship.

"I talked to Barrera," he said. "He's going to refer us."

"Ben, I wish you could have spent time with them."

"From what I saw, I'm sure you're right."

"Already I miss them."

He took a breath and said it: "And Matos?"

Kate broke from him. "*That's* what's on your mind?"

"Maybe. At the risk of sounding like a fool."

She set down her glass. Leaned on the varnished rail and regarded the horizon.

"I'm talking about *them*, Kate. Making choices for the right reasons."

"Like choosing you..."

Touché, so he shut up.

"They're not reminders, Ben, they're children, what we'd help make of them. Are we clear on that? He was like nobody else, but the die was cast. Eight years ago, to be exact."

Wind popped the flags above the forward windbreak.

"Shay was right, you know," he said. "About me and Loren. All of it."

"Old news—Jeb hired somebody who took pictures." Her eyes filled with light. "I burned them, flushed the ash off me that day at the waterfall. Remember?"

"I remember. I'm also sorrier than you'll know."

Her eyes stayed on his. "Put up or shut up, sailor. Talk's cheap and the boat's leaving."

He kissed her, felt it come back, her arms encircle his neck. That little sigh that made him unravel.

"Now if you hadn't come for me..." Pulling back to look at him. "Something else on your mind?"

"Home," Ben said. "Barrera got me thinking."

"Come to any conclusions?"

"It's wherever you and Shay are."

"Which leads us...?"

Ben shrugged, casual con he knew she'd see through. "I don't know, Puget Sound? Office down the hall? Your own personal water-taxi driver?"

"Thought it out, have you?"

"Nothing you couldn't improve on. Idaho, if you want—hell, Tierra del Fuego. Newport just means Jeb. More bullshit."

"I see." Kate with the flash of a smile. "Anything else?"

Ben took in the darkening land, the water looking like wind-planed slate, the sky shading now toward grays and pinks. Afterglow. "Two things," he said, enveloping her so they could both look in that direction. "I love you, Kate. There's never been a moment I haven't."

"Say I believe you," she said into his pause, the ship's muted vibration. "What's the second thing?"

He closed his eyes and took in her fragrance, the night air, the soft-hard feel of her, both familiar and new.

"We'll think of something."

56
Golfo Dulce, Costa Rica, Two Months Later

The boy smiles at his sister playing in the sand, oblivious to the rising wind.

He is the man of the family now.

The one setting the example.

Soon she'll have to go back to the clinic and it weighs on her, he can tell, making her anxious and cranky. But he knows what to do: games to distract her, tide pools and little adventures, stories to read and act out. Though he draws the line at dolls, puppets are okay. Pirates, damsels in distress...the kind Abuelita used to make for them, her memory more distinct now than even his mother's, a woman of loud laughter and strong perfume who left them frequently.

The older ones—friends of his father who have taken them in—will follow, he knows. Because that is what grownups did. Like the papagayo, *they blew in and out of your life.*

Watching the sunset fade, the river of gold turning to lead, the boy thinks of what is to come, and the pain returns like a blow to the heart. Yet he forces it down into a place with a lock and a key he can turn. He has cried enough, looked out to sea enough.

His father would want him to be strong, even though he still hurts. He must think as a man would about their future—about what waits. Fearsome, like the blue-black shadow of a shark.

For surely what is at sea is what awaits him. Just as it did his father, his father's father, and before them, his own namesake.

Anything else would be like playing with dolls.

The wind is gusting now, whipping up the fringe-line of palm trees. It drives a stinging veil of sand against his legs and Anna running up the beach toward him.

PUBLISHER'S NOTE

Lost, Richard Barre's "lost" suspense novel, was completed during the period 1999-2000. When this extraordinary work was made available to us last year, we decided to leave the references to dates as written, preserving the integrity of the original. We hope it keeps you up as late turning pages as it did us.

ABOUT THE AUTHOR

Richard Barre was born in Los Angeles and raised in California. He is the author of seven novels, including *The Innocents* (winner of the Shamus Award for best first P.I. novel), *Bearing Secrets, The Ghosts of Morning, Blackheart Highway, Burning Moon, Echo Bay,* and *Lost.* Prior to writing crime fiction and short stories, he was a copywriter and creative director at his own advertising agency and wrote and edited travel publications. He lives in Santa Barbara with his wife, Susan, a very large cat, and innumerable space aliens posing as dogs.

OTHER TITLES FROM DOWN AND OUT BOOKS

See www.DownAndOutBooks.com for complete list

By J.L. Abramo
Catching Water in a Net
Clutching at Straws
Counting to Infinity
Gravesend
Chasing Charlie Chan
Circling the Runway (*)

By Trey R. Barker
2,000 Miles to Open Road
Road Gig: A Novella
Exit Blood

By Richard Barre
The Innocents
Bearing Secrets
Christmas Stories
The Ghosts of Morning
Blackheart Highway
Burning Moon
Echo Bay
Lost

By Rob Brunet
Stinking Rich

By Milton T. Burton
Texas Noir

By Reed Farrel Coleman
The Brooklyn Rules

By Tom Crowley
Vipers Tail
Murder in the Slaughterhouse

By Frank De Blase
Pine Box for a Pin-Up
Busted Valentines and Other Dark Delights
The Cougar's Kiss (*)

By Les Edgerton
The Genuine, Imitation, Plastic Kidnapping

By A.C. Frieden
Tranquility Denied
The Serpent's Game

By Jack Getze
Big Numbers
Big Money
Big Mojo

By Keith Gilman
Bad Habits

(*)—*Coming Soon*

OTHER TITLES FROM DOWN AND OUT BOOKS

See www.DownAndOutBooks.com for complete list

By Terry Holland
An Ice Cold Paradise
Chicago Shiver

By Darrel James, Linda O. Johnston
& Tammy Kaehler (editors)
Last Exit to Murder

By David Housewright
& Renée Valois
The Devil and the Diva

By David Housewright
Finders Keepers
Full House

By Jon Jordan
Interrogations

By Jon & Ruth Jordan (editors)
Murder and Mayhem in Muskego

By Bill Moody
Czechmate
The Man in Red Square
Solo Hand
The Death of a Tenor Man
The Sound of the Trumpet
Bird Lives!

By Gary Phillips
The Perpetrators
Scoundrels (Editor)
Treacherous

By Gary Phillips, Tony Chavira
& Manoel Maglhaes
Beat L.A. (Graphic Novel)

By Robert J. Randisi
Upon My Soul
Souls of the Dead
Envy the Dead (*)

By Lono Waiwaiole
Wiley's Lament
Wiley's Shuffle
Wiley's Refrain
Dark Paradise

By Vincent Zandri
Moonlight Weeps

(*)—Coming Soon

Made in the USA
Monee, IL
21 November 2023

47040923R00173